Coastal Lights Legacy – Book Three

REDEEMING LIGHT

Marilyn Turk

Marilyn Turk

ISBN-13: 978-1-947523-00-5
ISBN-10: 1-947523-00-7

DEDICATION

To my husband Chuck, who believes in my calling to write and supports me with unbelievable patience.

.

Chapter One

St. Augustine, Florida, May 1875

"Momma, there they are! There's the Indians!" Emily danced on her toes, her blonde ringlets bouncing as she pointed up the shell road leading into town.

Cora kept her hands firmly on Emily's shoulders as she cast an anxious glance down the street, her heart in her throat as she glimpsed a horse-drawn wagon rumbling along, a procession of other wagons following behind. Why had she allowed Emily to talk her into being here?

"I see 'em!" One of the boys who had climbed up on Constitution Monument to get above the throng of townspeople called out.

The crowd waiting on the town plaza craned their necks to get a view of the captive Indians arriving to be imprisoned at Fort Marion. When the wagon emerged from a canopy of moss-hung trees, Cora caught sight of tawny-skinned, bare-chested men with long raven hair sitting across from each other in the crowded wagon.

"There's Lieutenant Pratt." The man beside her nodded at the soldier riding a black stallion at the head of the procession. "He's in charge of the Indians."

Cora eyed the uniformed man who sat tall, emanating an air of accomplishment. From his demeanor, one would think he'd captured the Indians single-handedly. Balancing her parasol with one gloved hand, Cora kept her six-year-old daughter from getting too close to the wooden fence bordering the town square, thankful for the barrier between them and the prisoners.

Soldiers on horseback clip-clopped alongside each wagon. The jingle and clang of harnesses and chains filled the air as the wagons rolled by the town plaza.

"Look at them Injuns!" A boy in the crowd shouted. "Wonder how many scalps they took from white folks?"

Cora's stomach churned at the horror of such a thing as the Indian captives from the West passed by. She cringed at the hostile atmosphere of the crowd and the pitiful sight of the natives. She should have listened to her cousin Katie who advised her to stay away. She certainly wasn't the only curious person in town, but did anyone else feel as uncomfortable as she did by the scene?

Most of the Indians stared straight ahead, as if they could ignore their current situation or unfamiliar surroundings. But the citizens and visiting tourists tried their best to get the captives' attention as they shouted, pointed, and laughed, reminding the Indians that they'd arrived in an unfriendly place. Cora winced at the distasteful remarks.

"Momma, look at those strange necklaces they're wearing." Emily pointed at a wagon.

Cora had also noticed the choker necklaces with three of more rows of beads some of the Indians wore and wondered their significance.

"I heard they make 'em out of bones," a man nearby commented.

Bones? Cora shuddered.

"Indians are dirty, aren't they?" Emily lifted her face up to her mother, her sky-blue eyes questioning.

Cora eyed the dirty rivulets of sweat streaking the captives, but didn't comment as she grabbed Emily's hand. She needed to take her daughter away from this repulsive exhibition. But as she tried to push through the crowd, it pressed in on them, preventing their escape.

"I doubt they had an opportunity to bathe," Cora offered to her daughter.

"They're like animals," a male voice shouted. "Don't even know what baths are."

"Shoot. They probably wouldn't have clothes on if Lieutenant Pratt didn't make them," an equally rude person joked.

Others made similar derisive comments as they gestured toward the Indians. Cora wanted to cover Emily's ears, so she wouldn't hear such crude talk. She leaned and whispered to her daughter. "Emily, don't listen to those people. They are very ill-mannered."

She held Emily close to shield her from the unpleasant noise and didn't mind when others squeezed in front of them, blocking their view of the procession. She hoped Emily wouldn't have nightmares about what she'd seen and heard. All she could do was avert her eyes and try to find something else to focus on and perhaps distract Emily until they could get away from the plaza. She surveyed the crowd gathered to witness the event, assessing the social status of each person, and spotted a group of wealthy tourists in town for the winter, definitely northerners according to the heavy clothes they wore in the St. Augustine heat. Perhaps these women would be customers for her new millinery shop.

Tuning out the din around her, her attention was riveted to a matron dressed in the latest fashion. Although the woman's clothes were elegant, it was the hat that captured Cora's eyes. An exquisite assemblage of feathers and folded felt adorned the purple headpiece that matched the purple in the woman's silk walking suit. No doubt such an elegant creation had come from Paris, for she'd seen nothing as grand in America. Cora studied the small hat perched above the woman's coiled-high hair braid and tilted forward in the latest style, trying to remember its details so she could recreate something similar in her shop. Such a wealthy patron could increase Cora's business and provide income to purchase materials necessary to make such fine hats herself.

"Emily, look at the lady over there with the pretty hat!" She tapped her daughter on the back and gaining her attention, nodded in the direction of the woman. Cora lifted her hand and gently touched the two small quail feathers on her own hatband, making sure they were still in place. Her own hat, though tasteful, was simple in comparison.

Emily stood on her tiptoes and tried to peer through the crowd.

"I can't see. There's too many people."

Cora pressed through the crowd to get closer to the group,

pulling Emily with her.

"See? The pretty purple one that matches the lady's stylish suit."

"Oh, I see it! Can you make one like that, Momma?" Emily peered up at her.

"I'd love to try." Emily's pride in Cora's hats made her heart swell.

Beside the woman was a younger lady, perhaps a daughter. She was rather plain, with pale skin and honey-colored hair whose curly bangs peeked below her hat. She was equally as well-dressed in a two-tone brown walking suit although her plain hat lacked style. But Cora could help her with that. In her mind, she searched the inventory at the shop, thinking of ways to accent and improve the hat. If these ladies became her customers, then introduced Cora to their friends, why she'd be set. She'd be able to move out of Mrs. Gardner's boarding house and buy a comfortable place for her and Emily.

"Maybe they'll come to your shop."

"Maybe they will." Cora smiled to herself. She and Emily shared similar thoughts.

As the last wagon rumbled past, the townspeople fell in step behind to follow the procession to the fort where they could witness the captives being unloaded. Cora trailed behind the crowd, keeping her eyes fixed on the marvelous hat of the woman walking ahead of her. If only there was some way they could meet.

Emily tugged on Cora's sleeve, drawing her attention. "Momma, there's women in there! And children too!" Emily pointed ahead to the last wagon.

A wave of shock quivered through Cora at the sight. She hadn't expected the Indian prisoners to include women and children. But sure enough, two native women with long black braids were crowded in the vehicle as a couple of young children huddled about them. The women's eyes were cast down, no doubt trying to hide from the stares of the townspeople, but the wide-eyed children looked anxiously around them as they took in their surroundings.

"Emily, it's not polite to point." Cora leaned down to speak into her daughter's ears. Even if other people were rude, Cora didn't want anyone to think her child had bad manners. Cora adjusted the large pink grosgrain ribbon bow at the back of

Emily's straw bonnet, tearing her gaze from the sight of the native children and ignoring the pinch in her heart.

"I can't wait to tell the girls! They'll wish they'd been here too!"

Cora doubted that. Not only would Katie not come over from the island for the event, she wouldn't allow her daughters to see it either. She'd expressed pity for the Indians, worrying about their treatment en route from the West. But that was her cousin, always caring for others, even Indians. Besides, with five daughters to manage and a new lighthouse keeper's home under construction, Katie had little time for leisure.

The wagons drew to a halt in front of Fort Marion, and slowly, the Indians climbed out as best they could with shackled feet. How they managed to move with such heavy chains around their ankles was a wonder.

"Would you look at that?" A man nearby hooted. "One of the squaws is wearing shackles too. Wonder what she did?"

Cora scanned the assortment of men, women and children and saw the chained woman at the end of the line of men. Vulgar remarks flowed through the crowd, but Cora tried to tune them out. What on earth had that one woman done to be in leg irons like the men? A shiver crawled up her spine as newspaper stories about Indian raids out West flitted through her mind. She shook her head. No, she didn't care to know.

Cora glanced back to the tourists she'd been watching before, hoping they didn't catch her staring. Two well-dressed gentlemen stood beside the women, both quite handsome. The taller, serious-faced one with the top hat leaned down to speak to the older woman. He was younger than she, so perhaps he was her son.

The other man laughed and joked with those standing nearby. His clothing exhibited a taste of flamboyance, his fitted frock coat open to reveal a large gold watch chain across his brocade vest, much like his trimmed goatee and mustache that tipped up at the ends reflected a European air. A contrast to the rest of his attire, a straw hat barely contained waves of thick, coal-black locks that curled freely over his collar. The younger woman beside him blushed and giggled at his remarks, while the other man frowned and cast disapproving glances his way.

Cora wanted desperately to meet the people but couldn't think of a suitable way. She couldn't just waltz over to them and introduce herself, could she? Where were they staying—the Florida Hotel or the St. Augustine? Perhaps she could arrange for the manager to give them her card. Then again, some of the wealthy looked down on this practice as common.

Her pulse quickened as an idea took root. Why not just compliment the lady on her hat? Although a bold act, surely the woman would appreciate the admiration. Since Cora knew more about hat fashion than anyone else in St. Augustine, her remark would reveal her expertise. She sidled a bit closer to the group nudging Emily over with her. Meanwhile, the rest of the crowd kept their attention on the line of natives across the way.

"Momma, that little boy is looking at me!" Emily pointed at a young Indian boy whose gaze was fixed on her.

Cora jerked Emily behind her as a jolt of fear raced through her body. Her heart thumped at the thought of the boy staring at her precious daughter. Why was he looking at her? She glared at the young Indian to convey a warning to stay away from her child. The child's mother glanced at Cora, then pulled her son close, saying something to him. The boy's head drooped as he gave one last sad look at Cora before turning away. She breathed a sigh of relief, even though a pain pricked her heart.

"Who could blame him for looking at such a pretty little girl?"

A man's voice nearby startled Cora. She spun around to see the smiling face of the jovial gentleman she'd noticed beside the women tourists with good taste in hats. Cora straightened and gathered her composure.

"Sterling Cunningham." The man bowed slightly. "You do have a lovely daughter." He smiled broadly at Emily, took her little hand and kissed the back of it. Raising his eyes, he addressed Cora. "Of course, the girl takes after her lovely mother."

Cora's face warmed at the unexpected compliment. She gave a polite smile. "Thank you, Mr. Cunningham. My name is Cora Miller, and this is my daughter Emily."

"Well, hello Emily. It is a pleasure to meet you ... and your mother." Mr. Cunningham's wide grin revealed sparkling white teeth, a stark contrast to the dark mane that escaped when he tipped his hat.

Cora glanced at the group beside him. Judging by the frown on her face, the younger woman was not pleased with the attention Mr. Cunningham was giving to Cora and her daughter.

"Allow me to introduce my friends." Mr. Cunningham swept his hand toward the others. "This is Mrs. Priscilla Worthington and her daughter Judith."

Cora nodded and smiled at the women, then looked at the other man.

"Oh, and this chap is Daniel Worthington, Mrs. Worthington's son." Mr. Cunningham slapped the man on the shoulder. Mr. Worthington touched the brim of his hat and gave Cora an obligatory nod.

"You are visiting in town, I assume?" Cora addressed the older woman.

"Yes, we're here for the season. Do you live in St. Augustine?"

"I do. I just recently moved here from Philadelphia."

"Your husband's business?" The older woman eyed Cora up and down.

"No, ma'am. I'm a widow." Surely the woman noted her black mourning dress. "I moved here because my dear cousin invited me. Her husband is the new lighthouse keeper and moved here recently herself. She thought I'd like a change of scenery."

"I see." The older woman's tone reflected an air of dignity.

Cora considered Mrs. Worthington's hat. "I've been admiring your chapeau. It's one of the most wonderful I've ever seen! Did it come from Paris?"

A smile eased its way across the woman's face. "As a matter of fact, it did. It was designed to match my suit when I had some clothes made on our last trip to France. Your hat is lovely too."

"Thank you. I ..." A strong gust of wind blew off the bay, and Cora grabbed hold of her hat. Unfortunately, Mrs. Worthington didn't react as quickly, and her hat came loose from her hair.

"My hat!" The woman shrieked as the freed hat blew across the street wildly through the air toward the fort.

Cora gasped as the lovely hat settled on the ground right in front of one of the natives who was stumbling along, chained to a man in front and a man behind. Unable to stop, he stepped on the hat, crushing it to the ground.

Sterling Cunningham rushed across the street and retrieved the damaged headpiece.

"You idiot!" He leaned into the offending Indian's face. "You should've been shot out West!"

Cora sucked in a breath. She didn't know what horrified her more, the Indian crushing the hat or Mr. Cunningham's reaction.

A soldier moved forward and stepped between the two men, facing Mr. Cunningham. "Sir, if you'd please step back across the street, we'll do our best to get these prisoners into the fort. Sorry for your trouble."

Mr. Cunningham glared at the Indian, then strode back to his companions. Holding the hat at arm's length, he shook his head. "I suppose this one's of no use anymore. Filthy savage."

Mrs. Worthington studied the hat, her expression mournful. Daniel Worthington frowned at Mr. Cunningham. "Sterling, the Indian didn't intentionally ruin the hat. He couldn't very well help himself."

Mr. Cunningham shot Mr. Worthington an annoyed look, but Cora admitted to herself that he spoke the truth. It was a most unfortunate accident indeed. But her heart trembled with excitement as she saw her opportunity to rectify the situation.

Cora took a slight step forward. "I can make another one to replace it. Perhaps it won't be exactly the same, but I'll do my best."

"You can make a hat?" Mrs. Worthington's eyebrows lifted.

"Oh, yes. My shop, Miller's Fine Millinery, is on St. George Street. In fact, it's right around the corner from the St. Augustine . . . and the Florida Hotel, if you're staying in either of those."

"We're at the St. Augustine." Mrs. Worthington's gaze dropped to the ruined hat. "Do you really think you could replace it? It was one of my favorites."

"I'm certain I can create something you'll be happy with, even if it doesn't come from Paris."

The woman shrugged. "Well, it's worth a try. Perhaps if I'm happy with your work, you can make a hat for Judith too." She glanced at her daughter beside her.

"I'd love to." Cora restrained herself from dancing and twirling like Emily when she was excited. "Please come by the shop next week and we'll do a fitting."

"Do you make men's hats too? I might like a new chapeau as well." Sterling Cunningham grinned as he removed his hat and studied it.

"I'm afraid that's not my area of expertise, but there is a haberdashery in the next block." Which also carried plain, cheap ladies' hats, but nothing these refined people would like.

Mr. Cunningham laughed aloud, placing the hat back on his head. "I suppose I'll have to find another excuse to come visit your shop then."

Cora's face warmed at the twinkle in his eye. A sidelong glance at Judith chewing on her fingernail revealed a look of jealousy. Was there some type of commitment between them? Mr. Cunningham certainly didn't act as if there was. And shy, plain Judith didn't seem to be the kind of woman he'd be attracted to anyway. But was Cora? Why not? Wasn't it appropriate for her to enjoy the attention of a handsome man, especially a wealthy one? It had been a long time since she'd enjoyed a gentleman's notice.

Cora brushed aside the flirtation and focused on the business at hand, Mrs. Worthington. "Will I see you on Monday?"

"Yes. I'd like to see what you can do. I must say, I never expected to find a milliner here. This could turn out to be quite an advantage."

Indeed, it could. As the last prisoner entered the fort, Cora breathed a sigh of relief that she would no longer have to view the wretched Indians. And now that she had met these tourists, something good might come out of today's event after all.

Chapter Two

Daniel could barely stomach the sight of the Indians as they struggled to move. He could only imagine what they had gone through to get to St. Augustine. The paper said they'd traveled by train most of the trip, one thousand miles across the country to reach Florida. Had they ever ridden a train before? And riding in a freight car like an animal— how miserable that must have been.

Watching the prisoners shuffle about in heavy chains while curious onlookers gawked disgusted Daniel, and he hated being one of them. Many of the bystanders acted like fools looking at circus animals as they pointed and laughed. Only a few nuns standing in front of the Catholic Church appeared sympathetic. Perhaps they were the only people beside himself who thought of the natives as people and not animals.

Then that unfortunate incident with Mother's hat blowing off and landing in front of that Indian. Poor man couldn't avoid stepping on the hat. But Sterling's behavior was abominable. His gut wrenched as Sterling rebuked the helpless Indian. As usual, Sterling found a way to draw attention to himself and become the center of attention. What his sister saw in the man was beyond him. She wasn't alone in her attraction though. Sterling had no trouble attracting women.

And now he'd found another one to charm. Daniel had to admit the petite blonde woman was quite attractive, an older version of the pretty little girl beside her. So she was a milliner? She better be a good one, if she hoped to please his critical mother. Milliners and seamstresses from America and Europe could attest to her high expectations. Well, at least Mother would have something to occupy her time while they were in St. Augustine. And so, it seems, would Sterling.

Daniel frowned at the thought of Sterling trifling with Mrs. Miller, a widow with a child. Surely, she wouldn't be fooled by his shenanigans, as she appeared to be an intelligent woman. As he watched the last of the Indians head over the drawbridge into the fort, he wished he'd carried his sketchbook to capture the scene. Perhaps Lieutenant Pratt would allow him to sketch the prisoners. They might be uncomfortable around him, though, and rightly so. He doubted they trusted any white men. But he'd like to have the opportunity to show them he meant them no harm.

"Will you be joining us, Daniel?"

Daniel jerked his head toward his mother. "I'm sorry, I didn't hear what you were saying."

"Daydreaming again, old chap?" Sterling grinned. "Ah…the artist's mind."

Daniel frowned at Sterling. What would he know about an artist's mind? Or any worthwhile pursuits?

Mother spoke up. "We're headed back to the hotel, but on the way, Mrs. Miller is going to show us where her shop is located."

Daniel glanced at the milliner and was stunned by the blue-green eyes that stared up at him. Mrs. Miller gave her parasol a slight twist while she waited for his response. He ran his finger along the inside of his collar. The weather here could be quite warm for this time of year.

He cleared his throat. "That so? Well, then, let's proceed." He gestured for the others to go ahead. Sterling placed himself between Mrs. Miller and Judith, extending an arm to each lady, assuming his position as their escort while the little girl skipped ahead of them.

"Shall we make a grand entrance through the City Gates?" Sterling nodded over to the large coquina columns that the Spaniards had built centuries before to mark the city's boundaries. He proceeded toward the outdated landmarks, making a show of the event by sweeping his arms and describing them as if he were a tour guide. Daniel followed behind with his mother, studying the group in front. He couldn't help but notice Mrs. Miller's tiny waist accentuated by the small, bow-adorned bustle of her black dress. Did she say she was a widow? How long ago had it been since her husband died?

"She's pretty, isn't she?" Mother peered up at him as she walked alongside.

"Who?"

Mother's eyebrows knit together, and she pursed her lips. "Daniel Worthington. Don't you try to fool me. You know good and well to whom I'm referring." Mother nodded to the group ahead.

"Oh, you mean Mrs. Miller. Yes, I'd say she has a pleasant appearance."

"Sterling seems to think so."

Daniel lowered his head and voice to his mother. "And we all know how discriminating he is."

Mother slapped his arm with her gloved hand. "Daniel, sarcasm does not become you."

"Sorry, Mother. Sometimes Sterling's behavior is so boorish. Apparently, Mrs. Miller doesn't mind, though."

Mother faced him with a raised eyebrow. "Do I detect envy in that remark?"

Daniel faced his mother. "Absolutely not! I've no interest in Mrs. Miller or anyone else, for that matter." Especially in someone who found Sterling attractive.

The group made their way down St. George Street, its hard-packed sand partially shaded by overhanging balconies. A slight breeze ruffled orange blossoms on the trees that rose above high coquina walls bordering private yards.

"Ah." Mother lifted her head and took a deep breath. "That aroma is one of my favorite things about this town."

Daniel inhaled the sweet fragrance as well, appreciative of the scent he'd miss when he'd returned to Boston. A sense of dread weighed his shoulders at the thought. The last place he wanted to go was back home, where he'd be expected to work alongside his brother Henry in his father's law office. Daniel preferred staying in this southern hamlet with its leisurely pace. Or even return to Europe and resume his art studies. However, his family had summoned him back to the States, so here he was, escorting his mother and sister on their winter vacation until they all returned to their home in Boston.

His gaze followed the little girl in front of her mother. Her cheerful innocence belied any sadness she might have felt from her father's death. Had she known him well before he passed from this world to the next? His eyes traveled from the child to her lovely mother. Had her husband been an adequate provider? If so, why would she need to have a millinery shop, unless it was just a pastime? He turned away to take his thoughts off the woman. No need to trouble himself about her affairs.

The group in front paused, and Sterling called back over his shoulder. "Mrs. Miller's shop is up ahead."

No doubt the business was near others in the quaint commercial area. Passing the cobbler's shop and a gentlemen's furnishing store, they walked another two blocks.

"I love the clean appearance of these white buildings." Mother gestured toward the stone-looking structures. "What do they call this substance?"

"Coquina. It means 'little seashells' in Spanish. It's like a natural plaster found in this area. From what I understand, they used it to build the fort over a hundred and fifty years ago. Apparently, there was a quarry over on Anastasia Island where they found the substance. Pretty sturdy material, it withstood attacks by cannonballs."

They turned at the next corner and passed the drugstore before coming to a stop in front of a small storefront window.

"So, this is where you create your works of art." Sterling grinned as he studied the modest façade, looking up at the overhanging balcony. "And I suppose you live upstairs?"

Mrs. Miller blushed, either at the intimate question or the teasing. One never knew when to take Sterling seriously, since he was skilled at covering his bad manners with smiles and laughter. Daniel and Mother joined the others to peer through the glass of the little store where three hats were displayed, two on stands and one on a mannequin head.

"That's my favorite!" The little girl pointed to a straw bonnet festooned with flowers and ribbons.

"Emily loves the more colorful hats," Mrs. Miller said.

Mother gestured to a black felt hat boasting a couple of quail feathers. "That's a nice one. It's very tastefully done. Don't you think so, Judith?"

Daniel's sister edged closer to Sterling. "Do you like it, Sterling?"

"If you like plain hats, I suppose. I believe I'd prefer something more exotic, something with impressive jewels or a splendid plume! Perhaps a peacock feather. What do you think Mrs. Miller?"

Mrs. Miller studied Sterling before she replied as if giving consideration to his outlandish suggestion.

"Those are pleasant suggestions, but I don't have many real jewels, mostly glass stones in a few brooches and hatpins. I agree that peacock feathers are lovely, but usually too large for the latest fashion. However, I do have some lovely quail feathers."

"Nonsense! Such a feather would make an extraordinary chapeau! I think you should create one. Such a hat, dear Judith, would definitely become you."

Judith's pale skin turned scarlet, and something akin to pity crossed the features of Mrs. Miller's face. What did his sister see in Sterling?

"Sterling, I'm sure you're not serious," Mother said. "We know Judith wouldn't be comfortable in something so dramatic. However, perhaps Mrs. Miller could create just the right bonnet for her. Don't you think so, Mrs. Miller?"

Daniel bit his tongue, as usual, to keep from telling the family friend how ridiculous his suggestion was. Thank God for Mother's wisdom in countering Sterling's foolishness and coming to Judith's rescue.

"Oh yes, I can think of several styles that would complement Miss Worthington quite nicely." Mrs. Miller nodded and gave Judith and Mother a warm smile. "I'll gather some things together, so we can discuss my ideas when you come in on Monday."

Mrs. Miller's aplomb was admirable. She gave Daniel the impression she would not be deterred in her commitment to satisfy Mother's wishes. Such confidence in her work would serve her well.

"Wonderful." Mother fanned herself. "I'm ready to get back to the hotel now. It's getting quite warm, and I'd like to rest."

"Yes, let's get some libation!" Sterling was always ready to quench his thirst with strong drink, no matter the time of day. He turned to Mrs. Miller. "Won't you join us?"

To Daniel's relief, Mrs. Miller shook her head. "Thank you, but I'm afraid I've made plans to visit with my cousin's family this afternoon. Perhaps another time?"

"Absolutely! Then we're off." Sterling tipped his hat and strode away in the direction of the hotel.

Judith watched with a look of chagrin, as Sterling seemed to have forgotten her. Daniel stepped forward and took her arm, then tipped his hat to Mrs. Miller and her daughter before taking his mother's arm also.

"Good afternoon, Mrs. Miller. We'll see you again on Monday," Daniel said.

Mother nodded. "Yes, we will. I'm very much looking forward to what you can design for us."

As they left Mrs. Miller standing in front of her shop, Daniel was glad his mother and sister had found something to look forward to. A memory of the Indians' faces flashed through his mind, their forlorn expressions stamped on his heart. What did they have to look forward to?

Chapter Three

Cora tried to restrain herself from entering her shop and starting to work right away. It was the weekend, after all, and despite her eagerness, she could wait until Monday to begin gathering things for the women's hats. She ran through a mental list of her inventory—ribbons, feathers, hat forms, artificial flowers, buttons, thread, lace, netting. Just a quick look and she'd know what else she needed Monday morning. Would the Worthingtons be pleased? Cora fought a tremor of fear that threatened her confidence. Yes, yes, she could make quality hats equal to those the ladies already owned, and she'd prove it. She reached for the door, then stopped when Emily tugged on her sleeve.

"Momma, when are we going to Aunt Katie's?"

Looking into her daughter's bright eyes, Cora's heart melted. How could she be thinking about business and forget their plans?

"Right now, Emily. Let's go to the boat basin and find someone to take us over to the island." As they hurried down the block toward the plaza, she glanced at the clock outside the barber shop. "My goodness, I had no idea it was so late. Katie must wonder what happened to us!"

"Did you remember the honey?"

Cora gasped. She'd forgotten that her cousin asked her to bring some orange blossom honey.

"Oh dear. We'll go to the plaza market right now and get some." And pray the vendor that sold the product was still at the market. She grabbed Emily's hand and hurried along, passing the large St. Augustine Hotel on the corner. Would she encounter Mr. Cunningham or the Worthingtons on the way? She resisted the urge to glance up at the balconies to see if any of them were out enjoying the breeze off the bay. And in case they were, she didn't want them seeing her rushing along like a ninny.

She slowed her steps as she approached the open marketplace on the edge of the plaza nearest the waterfront being careful not to look at anyone besides the honey vendor. Wooden stalls displaying fruit and vegetables filled the small, open building. Cora always dreaded going to the market, not only because of the mixture of odors coming from the meat and fish displays, but many of the coarse, unrefined vendors made her feel uncomfortable by the way they looked at her. Even though she had to associate with them to purchase their wares, she'd keep her contact with them minimal. She made her way to the back corner of the market where a large woman sat on a wooden crate. At least this part of the market caught a breeze in the shade of the plaza trees. The woman gave a wide toothless smile as Cora approached.

"You needin' sum honey, ma'am?"

"Yes, please. I'll take a crock of it." Cora reached into her reticule, retrieved some coins and handed them to the seller.

The woman grunted as she leaned over to pick up a clay pot beside her, then handed it to Cora.

"Sure you can carry that? It's a mite heavy for someone little as you." A man's deep voice came from behind.

Cora didn't bother to look at the speaker, but whirled away from the vendor, holding the crock firmly in her hands. She whispered to Emily to stay close while she worked her way back out through the piles of wares in the small, congested marketplace. Wishing her hands were free to cover her nose with her handkerchief, Cora held her breath to block the body and animal odors in the confined space. Once out in the open air again, she took a deep breath, inhaling the salt air off the bay. At such times as these, she longed to have a male companion to protect her from unwelcome attraction. But there was no one protecting her anymore, not that Jacob had been much protection for some time before he died. He'd been far too weak to accompany her out on her errands.

The sound of laughter rang out through the open doors of the

St. Augustine Hotel, and Cora felt certain she recognized Sterling Cunningham's voice. She slowed her steps and glanced toward the hotel, expecting to see the charming, spirited man. From the looks of him, Sterling Cunningham could afford the finest taste in clothes, food, or whatever else he desired. She didn't know type of business he was in, but perhaps he was a lawyer like she'd overheard Mrs. Worthington say. Or maybe he'd inherited his wealth. Some people were just lucky and didn't have to work to provide for themselves or anyone else. Cora's life hadn't turned out that way, but she was as good as they were, and she'd prove it if she got the chance.

Emily hurried toward the water, pulling Cora along. When they reached the boat basin, she hailed one of the Minorcan boatmen. Residents of St. Augustine since the Spanish settled the area, the Minorcans were descendants from Greece and the Mediterranean and were the city's best fishermen and boaters.

"Can you take me over to the island?"

Wearing a large straw hat, the olive-skinned boatman nodded. "Fish Island or Anastasia?"

"Anastasia, please, near the lighthouse."

"Good, because the tide's too low to go to Fish right now."

The boatman reached for the crock, taking it from her and placing it securely in the bottom of the small sailboat before helping her and Emily step in. As wind filled the sail and the boat moved out of the harbor, Cora looked back at the shore, this time glancing up at the balconies of the hotel that overlooked the bay. Daniel Worthington sat on one of them.

She squinted to see what he was doing. He seemed to be writing or perhaps drawing. It must be the latter, as there appeared to be a sketchbook in his hands. As she watched, he lifted his head and looked toward the water. His gaze rested on her boat, making her heart flutter. What was he thinking? His expression didn't seem to change often, giving an impression of indifference. In fact, she was certain he'd barely noticed her, so she doubted he'd even recognize her out there.

As if to settle her doubt, he raised his hand in greeting. Cora glanced around to see if he was waving at anyone else and realized he was waving at her. A rush of heat coursed through her body, and she hoped he couldn't tell she was blushing. She moved her parasol to partially conceal her face but lifted a hand to return the gesture. Did he really smile or was that just her imagination? The increasing distance apart made it impossible to know for sure. Maybe she just hoped he did. Not that she needed his approval anyway, as long as she had his mother's. She turned away from town and fixed her gaze on the sandy shore of Anastasia Island, observing the two separate lighthouse towers as the boat approached.

Before they reached the beach, Cora noticed two of Katherine's daughters poking in the sand, no doubt trying to catch tiny crabs that skittered across before popping into a hole. As the boat struck the sandy bottom, the girls ran up to greet them.

"Emily! We've been waiting all day for you!" Eight-year-old Molly, always prone to exaggeration, hugged Emily as soon as her feet reached solid ground.

"We can't wait to hear all about the Indians!" Ruby, the eleven-year-old, grabbed Emily's hand and began to lead her away.

"Hello, girls." Cora called out to the retreating group of giggles. Was it so long ago that she was just like them?

"Oh, hello, Cousin Cora. Momma's waiting for you in the kitchen." Ruby shouted back over her shoulder before the girls disappeared up the path between dense palmetto.

Cora paid the boatman and told him not to wait because Katie's husband, Captain William Harn, would take her back to the city later. She closed the parasol and hung it from her wrist to free her hands, so she could tote the heavy crock of honey, enduring the bright sun for the walk up the sandy incline to the keeper's house. As she neared the area around the old square lighthouse built by the Spaniards centuries before, she eyed the cracks running along its coquina walls, relieved to know it wasn't used anymore. No longer safe with the encroaching water undermining the tower, it could topple over in a strong storm and with it, anyone unlucky enough to be inside. Thank goodness, its replacement stood half a mile away.

Cora glanced to her right at the new lighthouse which had only been in operation a few months, marveling at the contrast between it and the old one. Much taller, painted with black and white stripes spiraling around, the new lighthouse was commonly called the "barber pole" by St. Augustine residents. Rising high above the land, the tower added an unusual accent to the barrier island and was the highest building for miles around. Through the trees, Cora could see glimpses of the red brick keeper's house that was being built beside the lighthouse. Katie would be so happy in her new larger home instead of the ancient one where they currently lived.

A tittering chorus drew her attention to a circle of girls singing "Ring a Ring o Rosie." Cora smiled as she counted six children in the group with little Ida toddling around in the middle. How her cousin managed all those girls amazed Cora. Sometimes she thought Emily was enough to handle, but she'd always wanted more children. But here she was a widow at the age of thirty, her hope of a large family dying with Jacob. Her heart squeezed, knowing she might be too old to have more children if she ever did marry again.

The aroma of stewed chicken and dumplings greeted Cora as she staggered into the kitchen building, happy to set the heavy crock down on the wooden work table. Katie stopped stirring a large pot and wiping her hands on her apron, rushed over to hug her.

"I'm so glad to see you! I was afraid something had happened, and you weren't coming!"

Cora removed her hat and placed it on the windowsill before taking an apron from a peg on the wall.

"I'm sorry we're late." She scanned the array of pots and dishes spread around the room. "What can I do to help?"

"Everything's ready—just needs to be brought to the dining room. Thank you so much for bringing the honey. It'll be our dessert, a perfect addition to dinner. My girls love to drizzle it over their biscuits. Of course, William does too." Katie stepped to the outside door and called out. "Girls, wash up and come in. Ruby, you make sure Ida is clean."

Dinner was a noisy affair, with Katie's girls and Emily all sharing about the day, but before long, the noonday meal had ended. Cora helped Katie clean up, then Katie suggested they take a walk over to the new house to see its progress. She carried baby Ida as the other girls skipped ahead.

"So how long before you move in?" Cora asked.

"William says two more weeks. I'm so excited to have a brand-

20

new house!"

Passing a group of strangers as they approached the house, Cora's gaze followed the group headed toward a waiting sailboat. They weren't very well-dressed folks, and the three women had terrible tastes in hats. She had a mind to go after them and offer her services but squelched the impulse. "Who were those people?"

"Tourists. My goodness, they're here all the time wanting to see the lighthouse. Sometimes William has to make sure they don't get hurt climbing the stairs. Several women have tripped on their skirts, but thankfully, none fell. And some almost fainted from the climb or the height as well."

Cora shuddered, gazing up at the towering structure. "I would be in the latter category. That's too high for me." She glanced back over her shoulder at the departing tourists. "But don't you get tired of their intrusion?" She wouldn't appreciate strangers tromping around her home uninvited, especially those with poor tastes.

"No sense in letting ourselves get worked up about it. We're a government facility, and people think they have a right. But William has had to block the entrance to the old lighthouse because some of the tourists even want to climb it too, dangerous as it is." Katie patted Ida on the back as they walked. The baby couldn't take her big blue eyes off Cora. "I imagine they'll be coming to the door of our new house to look inside too."

"How rude! What poor manners some people have." Cora frowned, then let the baby's smile spread to her own face as it reached out to her.

"Oh, we get used to it."

Cora took the baby from her cousin as they stopped in front of the two-story brick house, its freshly-painted white railings accenting the double porches.

"This is my favorite feature of the house." Katie waved her arm toward the double porches. "I can just see us sitting out here enjoying the breeze off the water while drinking a cool glass of lemonade."

"When do you ever sit, dear cousin?" Ida tried to grab the ribbons from Cora's bonnet.

Katie laughed. "When I'm rocking the baby, of course. I intend to put some rocking chairs out here for that very purpose."

Her cousin was the happiest person she'd ever known. Katie

never complained about anything and never said a bad word about anyone. Cora studied the fine new brick dwelling. She'd be happy to live in such a nice house as well. "I know the girls must be very excited too."

"Oh, they are. Even though we'll share the house with an assistant keeper who'll take one side, it'll still be nice to have a new place that doesn't leak or smell like our present one."

They walked to the front porch and sat down on the steps. Cora placed Ida on the sandy ground and the toddler began to crawl around before trying to climb up the steps. The other children ran around the house, playing hide and seek.

"Please tell me about your morning." Katie redirected the baby's attention by sitting her back down and clapping her hands together in the pat-a-cake rhythm. "I know you went to see the poor Indian prisoners come to town. I do feel so sorry for them, being so far from their homes. They must have been terrified of all the strange sights."

Cora huffed. "Katie! How can you feel sorry for those uncivilized savages? You don't know what they did to the settlers out West!"

"No, I don't. It's a shame we couldn't live peaceably with each other." Katie shook her head.

"Well, maybe now we can, with them in prison."

"I wonder how they'll be treated there."

"As well as any prisoners, I'm sure." The picture of Mrs. Worthington's hat being stepped on by the Indian flashed through her mind, relieving her from thinking about the "poor savages." "Oh, I haven't told you—I met the most interesting people! And a new customer for my shop as well."

Katie's eyebrows lifted. "Oh? Do tell. How did you find this customer? Your shop wasn't open today, was it?"

Cora went on to tell about meeting the Worthingtons and the hat incident. "I can't wait to create something wonderful for the ladies."

"I'm so excited for you! I've been praying that your store will do well."

"Thank you, cousin. I have, too."

"You mentioned a couple of men—any of them eligible?"

Cora's face warmed, and she gave Katie a playful shove. "Still playing matchmaker, cousin? I haven't given those gentlemen a second thought." No thought she wanted to share.

"Were they handsome? What did they look like?" Katie's eyes brightened with curiosity.

"They're both nice-looking men but couldn't be any less alike." Cora removed a stick from Ida's mouth. "Sterling Cunningham is a fun-loving person, but Mr. Worthington is rather melancholy and distant. I don't think he cared for me." Cora tried not to sound disappointed about Mr. Worthington's lack of interest.

Katie pulled a small, worn rag doll from her pocket and handed it to Ida who promptly began chewing on its button eyes. "Why would you think that? Was he rude?"

"No, he was polite, just rather aloof. Maybe he didn't want to associate with a lowly hat maker."

"Nonsense. Well, if he truly did believe his social status was above yours, it doesn't matter anyway. I admire you, Cora, for being so brave, a woman running her own business by herself! Don't you belittle yourself. You are a strong, talented woman. Besides, those tourists won't be here very long anyway."

"No. I suppose not." Cora gazed across the yard and sighed. Yet she did care and wanted to be accepted into their class. Facing Katie, she said, "It's his mother I have to please anyway."

"Is the man named Sterling related to the others?"

"I don't think so, but they seem to be traveling together. Actually, I believe the younger Miss Worthington has her sights set on him"

"So perhaps they're courting?"

A thrill rippled through her at the memory of Mr. Cunningham flirting with her. "No, I wouldn't say that. She's a bit young for him, I think. He actually suggested that I might join them sometime." He surely wouldn't show her such attention if he were courting someone else, would he? Apparently, Mr. Cunningham didn't perceive her as being inferior.

A broad grin covered Katie's face. "Ooh. That sounds promising. And would you?"

"Perhaps. We'll see if he asks again or he was just being polite."

Katie reached for Cora's hand and squeezed it. "Nonsense.

Only because Jacob's family fell on hard times. Besides, it's time, Cora. Your grieving period is over and you're free to court again. Now would be a good time to start."

Maybe Katie was right. Next time Mr. Cunningham extended an invitation, she'd take it. If there was a next time.

Chapter Four

Cora woke Sunday morning to the clanging of church bells at the Cathedral. Time to get her and Emily ready for the day. A fresh breeze ruffled the lace curtains of their second-floor boarding house room as Cora sat up and glanced over at her daughter sleeping beside her. Her heart filled at the child's peaceful angelic face. If only Cora could provide a better home for her than this small space. She reached over and gently shook her daughter awake.

"Time to get ready for church."

Emily stretched and yawned before climbing out of bed. "I wish we could've stayed on the island last night."

"I know sweetheart, but there's just not enough room for us at Aunt Katie's. Maybe when they move into the new house, we can stay over."

"I hope so. I don't have anyone to play with here."

Cora regretted not being able to give Emily brothers or sisters. At least when she was a child, Cora had siblings to keep her company. But when the war separated her from her siblings, she learned how lonely it was without them. When Jacob died, and Cora was forced to sell their home to pay his doctor bills, she accepted Katie's suggestion to move to Florida which was an answer to prayer. Now Emily had cousins to play with on the island, but Cora had rejected Katies' offer to move in with them at the keeper's house, thinking it best not to impose. Besides, she needed to be near her new millinery store.

But as an outsider—an unmarried, though widowed, working

woman who wasn't local—she hadn't made any close friends either in the two months they'd lived in town. Even with Katie living nearby, they couldn't visit every day. And although Cora wanted the hat business from the city's society ladies, she also hoped she'd become friends with some of them and worried that they didn't consider her to be of equal standing.

"Let's hurry and get down to breakfast so we won't be late for church."

Cora dressed herself and then Emily in their best Sunday clothes. Twisting the girl's hair around her finger, she made ringlets that framed the pretty petite face. Cora placed the matching bonnet she'd made on the child's head and tied its blue ribbon under her little chin. Holding her daughter at arm's length, Cora beamed at the image of herself as a child. She looked perfect.

"Do I look pretty, Momma?" Emily held out her skirt and swayed.

"Absolutely. You're the prettiest girl in all of St. Augustine!"

"I wish we could wear matching clothes like we used to. Before you started wearing black all the time."

Cora straightened the bed linens. "Maybe we can. I believe I need a new dress anyway."

Emily's eyes lit up. "Really, Momma? I can't wait! I'm so tired of seeing you in those ugly, dull dresses. Can we get a pretty color like pink? Please Momma, can you make us pink dresses?"

"We'll see." Cora wasn't sure pink would be appropriate for herself, but perhaps she could find some material they both could wear, something brighter and more cheerful than her mourning clothes. Maybe Emily and Katie were right—it was time to make a change.

Cora secured her tiny black chip hat to the top of her braided and coiled hair, checking the handheld mirror to make sure the hat rested at the correct angle, tipped down toward the face. Satisfied, she placed the mirror on the dresser, picked up her Bible, reticule and umbrella and opened the door for Emily. As they walked along the veranda to the dining room for breakfast, they watched a heron stalk fish beside the pond in the yard. The enormous bird with blue-tipped feathers was like a pet at the boarding house, and prowled the grounds on its stilt legs, hoping for a handout. The "grouchy bird," as Emily called it because it squawked when a person got too close, was taller than Emily. When a fellow boarder walked through the yard to the house, the bird lived up to its moniker by flapping its large wings and complained with a loud squawk before flying to another, less disturbed location.

After breakfast, Cora and Emily strolled down the narrow street toward the plaza, passing the Confederate monument in the bishop's yard. Cora gazed up at the tall memorial, placed there when the city's military governor denied the Ladies' Memorial Association the right to place the shrine on the plaza, which was city property. To Cora, the monument was a testament of what a group of women could do when they set their minds to it, raising funds and garnering support from the Catholic Bishop to accomplish their goal.

Taking Emily's gloved hand in hers, Cora and her daughter crossed the street to reach Trinity Episcopal Church on the opposite side. Strains of organ music sounded through the open doors, inviting all who heard to come in and worship. Cora nodded to others entering as she and Emily settled in a pew, observing the woman playing the organ. Miss Lucy Abbott, the church organist, was so petite her gray voluminous skirt and jacket practically consumed her, but her size belied her ability.

Cora admired the woman's musical talent, but what she appreciated even more was the fact that Miss Abbott was one of the most powerful women in town. In addition to being a member of the Ladies' Memorial Association, she was a real estate entrepreneur, building new homes on property she had purchased north of the fort. Cora was pleased that the lady was one of her first customers when she opened her millinery store. A middle-aged woman, Miss Abbott had never married. Apparently, the lady had been considerably wealthy when she moved to St. Augustine. But she was a businesswoman now, and if she could earn a respectable living without a husband, then so could Cora.

Movement out the corner of her eye drew her attention and Cora glanced over her shoulder. Her pulse quickened at the sight of Daniel Worthington entering the church with his mother and sister—her future customers. The man removed his tall silk hat revealing chestnut-brown hair, then motioned to his family to sit in the pew before he stepped in beside them. His striking features— tall cheekbones, the cleft in his chin, and chiseled jaw—gave an air of dignity to his handsome face, an impression he sustained with his proud stature. She spun back to face the front lest she be caught staring, the image of the trio in her mind. Much as she tried to remember the details of the women's hats, the somber face of Mr. Worthington kept blocking her memory.

Why was he so distant? Why didn't he smile more, like Sterling Cunningham? Speaking of Mr. Cunningham, he was missing from the group. She stole another glance at the group to see if he had arrived. But he wasn't there. Perhaps he was a Catholic and had gone to the cathedral instead. No doubt that's where he was.

When the music ended, the minister preached about showing love and kindness to one another. Cora nodded along with his message, approving the need for people to be nice and show decent manners. Wasn't that the way she lived her life, teaching her daughter to be the same? The minister ended his sermon, but before he gave the benediction, he changed his tone.

"I'd like to make an announcement on behalf of Lieutenant Pratt from Fort Marion."

Oh no, what rules would the military give the citizens now—a new curfew? Cora had no animosity toward the government, but she was tired of the lingering effects of the war on everyone, especially, here in the South. The minister's next words surprised her, however.

"Lieutenant Pratt would like volunteers willing to go to the fort and teach the Indians things like arithmetic, spelling, and reading. We'll also teach them about Christianity. Naturally, I offered my services, but since there are so many Indians, they will be divided into groups for daily classes, and neither I nor the bishop at the Cathedral can be there so often. When the new bishop, Bishop Henry Whipple, arrives here in a few months, he will preach to them on Sundays. If you're interested in helping, please see me after the service, and I'll inform the lieutenant."

Teach the Indians? She shuddered. What an absurd idea. How could these heathens understand God? How could anyone communicate to them unless they knew the Indian language? No thank you. She planned to stay as far from those savages as possible and was grateful for the sturdy walls around the fort. She had her own matters to handle, taking care of her daughter and running a business.

After the benediction, she rose to leave, but heard her name called from the front of the sanctuary. She turned to see Miss Abbott coming toward her.

"Mrs. Miller." Miss Abbott hurried up to Cora, her gray skirt sweeping past other congregants as she passed. "I wanted to speak to you."

"Yes, Miss Abbott?" Cora smiled at the well-dressed woman and admired her choice of hat, particularly because it was one of Cora's own creations. "Would you like me to make a new hat for you?"

"Oh no thank you. I don't need another one right now. What I did want to speak to you about is a benevolence group we are forming. Some of the ladies in town thought you might like to join us."

"Why, I would be honored to join you." Cora displayed her warmest smile as her chest swelled at the offer to be associated with the town's prominent women and prospective customers.

"Oh, that's wonderful. Mrs. Anderson will be in touch with you about what you need to bring."

"Bring? Oh, you mean refreshments for the meetings?"

A confused look crossed Miss Abbott's face. "No, no. Things you can bring to the fort for the Indians. I'm sorry I didn't explain our purpose. We're going to visit the Indians on a regular basis and take them provisions to help make their lives better, whether it's blankets or medicine or even food. We hear some of them haven't weathered their journey well and are ill."

Cora gulped and tried to suppress her surprise. Her face warmed and she opened her fan.

"Momma, you're going to see the Indians? Aren't you scared they could scalp you?" Cora glanced at her daughter, wishing to put a hand over the child's mouth. "If you go, can I go too?"

"No!" Cora took a deep breath and exhaled slowly. "I mean, I don't think the fort's a proper place for little girls to go. And you'll be in school." She shuddered at the sights she imagined her daughter would see—half-dressed men staring with coal-black menacing eyes.

"But you said they—"

"Sorry to keep you, Miss Abbott," Cora blurted out. Her

daughter didn't understand that some things spoken in private weren't meant to be repeated. "Please tell Mrs. Anderson to come by the shop. Thank you for including me." She pushed her daughter down the aisle toward the vestibule. "We must hurry, Emily, or we'll be late."

Once outside, Emily stared up at her mother. "Where are we going?"

Cora had no idea. But at the moment, she was willing to go anywhere to get away from the church. Well, anywhere but the fort. *Lord, what can I do to excuse myself?* She didn't want to endanger her chance to gain these women as customers, but she simply couldn't bear the thought of mingling with the savages. She lifted her eyes to the sky and uttered a silent prayer. *Lord, what should I do?*

A tap on the shoulder startled her and she turned around.

Mrs. Worthington and her daughter stood before her. The elder woman smiled. "Mrs. Miller, so nice to see you in church today."

Judith nodded, her lips barely turning upward at the ends.

Cora straightened and nodded in return. "Good morning Mrs. Worthington, Miss Worthington. Say 'hello,' Emily." She resisted the urge to scan the crowd looking for their male escort. When she heard no response from her daughter, she glanced down and was startled to discover no Emily beside her. "Emily?" Cora spun around, searching for her daughter.

"Over here, Momma!"

Cora's gaze traveled to the side of the church where Mr. Worthington held Emily aloft. "I'm getting a flower." Her daughter reached toward a magnolia blossom on a limb of a tree in the churchyard.

Cora's head spun trying to make sense of what she saw. The other ladies turned to look and laughed at the scene while Cora rushed over to the tree.

"Emily Miller!" Cora stared up at her daughter, then let her gaze drop to the man holding her. She addressed him. "How … why …?"

Mr. Worthington's sincere smile was a surprising change to his normally serious face. "She told me she wanted that blossom, so I offered to help her reach it."

Cora's stomach flipped as she stared at the way the smile

transformed his appearance as his eyes lit up and face relaxed.

"I got it!" Emily cried out, hoisting the blossom like a victory flag.

Mr. Worthington set Emily down, but he kept his lips upturned as he looked at Cora, further unsettling her. His mother and sister approached, welcome company to break the spell.

Cora stammered an apology. "I'm so sorry my daughter has imposed on you this way."

"She didn't. I offered." His penetrating gaze seeming capable of reading her thoughts.

Mrs. Worthington spoke up. "I thought perhaps you'd join us for lunch at the hotel dining room. Do you have any plans?"

"I …" Cora's mouth went dry as she struggled to answer.

"Momma, let's go! We've never eaten there before."

Cora wanted to crawl into the nearest hole and hide.

"Then you must join us," Mrs. Worthington insisted.

Cora drew herself up and assumed an air of confidence. Wasn't this what she wanted— to associate with the wealthy?

"Yes, we will. Thank you very much."

"Wonderful! Come on, Emily, you can hold Judith's and my hands." The little girl grabbed each of the lady's hands and they set off across the plaza toward the hotel.

Mr. Worthington extended his elbow, and Cora accepted, placing her free hand in the crook, the other holding her parasol aloft. The close contact with him reminded her of times past when she'd strolled with her late husband, setting off long-lost senses she'd forgotten. She shoved those feelings aside, embarrassed that the gentleman's polite gesture had awakened a longing she didn't realize she carried.

As they entered the grand dining room of the St. Augustine Hotel, she was captivated by the elegance of the tables, each decorated with a white linen tablecloth and fresh-cut pink and lavender azalea blossoms. Mr. Worthington pulled out chairs on either side of his own, Cora on his right and his mother to his left. Emily was seated beside Cora, and Judith was next to her mother, leaving one seat empty at the round table.

After they ordered, the conversation turned to the minister's message.

"I thought it appropriate that the reverend spoke about love and kindness before he asked for volunteers to teach the prisoners. Don't you agree, Mrs. Miller?" Mr. Worthington's gaze searched her face for a response.

Cora hadn't connected the two and didn't understand what one had to do with the other. Being loving and kind to each other was perfectly acceptable among people who were alike, but including Indians? Surely the Bible didn't apply to them, yet she suspected Mr. Worthington thought it did.

"I'm afraid I don't have the training to be a teacher." Teaching had never been one of Cora's ambitions, especially teaching Indians.

"Momma's gonna bring blankets and food to the Indians!" Emily chimed into the conversation.

All eyes turned to Cora while her blood rushed to her face.

"Is that true?" Judith asked. "All by yourself?"

"No, no, not by myself. In fact, I'm not sure I'll go at all. What I mean to say is, Miss Abbott just asked me if I'd be interested in joining the ladies' benevolent association. They're planning to visit the Indians and bring them items they might need."

Mr. Worthington's serious expression had returned, and he raised an eyebrow at her response. "Perhaps I'll see you there."

"You will? You're going to teach there?" Cora never suspected someone of his standing would get so involved with the natives.

"Maybe. What I'd really like to do is sketch the Indians. But perhaps that would be a conceivable way to communicate with them. I plan to ask the lieutenant when I visit the fort tomorrow."

So he *was* holding a sketchbook when she saw him on the balcony. "You're an artist?"

"Yes, he is. And a very good one too." Mrs. Worthington beamed with pride.

Cora studied Mr. Worthington who ran his finger around the inside of his collar. Did she detect a blush in his cheeks?

"Daniel studied art in Europe." Judith nodded as she bragged on her brother. "In Paris. He worked with some famous artists."

"Is that so? Which artists?" Should she mention seeing him on the balcony?

"Manet, Monet, Renoir, Degas—the avant garde artists, the so-called Impressionists." Mr. Worthington's tone had an air of admiration and perhaps a tinge of regret.

High-pitched giggles erupted from the door of the dining room, and everyone at the table turned to see Sterling Cunningham talking to one of the waitresses. Cora glanced at Mr. Worthington, noting the crease between his brows. Mr. Cunningham spotted them and waved before he swept through the room, garnering the attention of all the other diners.

His cheeks were bright, and his eyes sparkled as he approached the table with a flashing smile. "There you all are! I've been looking for you."

"Sterling, what gets you out of bed so early today?" Mr. Worthington dripped sarcasm as his face resumed its stony appearance.

"My dear Daniel, I've been up since the crack of dawn."

Mr. Worthington looked as though he wanted to say something but restrained himself. "Sterling, you remember Mrs. Miller? And Emily?"

"Ah, yes, of course. How are you lovely ladies this morning?"

Settling into the chair next to Judith, Mr. Cunningham's gesture sparked color in her cheeks and a shy smile.

Cora also smiled at the charming man between her daughter and Judith Worthington, but sensed tension from the man next to her.

"I'm famished!" Mr. Cunningham signaled a waiter, then scanned the group at his table. "Shall we start with some champagne?"

"Champagne?" Cora gaped. Was this common for wealthy tourists to drink spirits at Sunday lunch?

Mrs. Worthington shook her head, glancing from Mr. Cunningham to Cora as if reading her mind. "No, Mrs. Miller, I assure you we don't drink champagne for lunch. Sterling, you're giving our guest the wrong impression of us." She lifted her gaze to the waiter standing beside the table. "Would you please bring us a pot of tea?"

"Oh well, if you people won't join me, I suppose we'll save the champagne for another occasion." Mr. Cunningham's brow wrinkled as he peered down at the menu.

"Are you a Catholic?" Emily peered up at the man beside her. Cora gulped at her daughter's blunt question.

"Hmmm?" Mr. Cunningham studied the young girl. "Catholic?

No, why would you ask that?"

"You weren't at our church this morning, so you must've been at the cathedral instead."

The man grinned. "Ha! You're a very smart girl." He leaned down and lowered his voice as he spoke to Emily.

Cora strained to hear what he told her daughter.

"Actually, Emily, I had some very important business this morning which unfortunately kept me away from church."

Mr. Worthington had a sudden coughing attack.

Mr. Cunningham slapped his palms down on the table, startling the others. "Say, I have a marvelous idea! Why don't we all have a game of croquet after dinner?"

Judith beamed and batted her eyes at him. "I'd love to play."

Would the girl go to the moon if Mr. Cunningham offered to take her?

"Me too!" Emily piped in. "Can we, Momma?"

"Why yes, that does sound like fun." She turned to look at Mr. Worthington. "You'll play too, won't you?"

He fixed his gaze on her face, his soft brown eyes unreadable. "Why not? Sterling needs some competition."

Heat rushed to her face at his comment. Why did she think he was talking about more than the game of croquet? She tore her eyes away from his by turning to his mother.

"And are you going to play too, Mrs. Worthington?"

"It will depend on how I feel after lunch. I may just want to rest and watch you young people. I can enjoy listening to the regimental band on the plaza at the same time."

"So, it's settled! Let's order, shall we?" Mr. Cunningham motioned to the waiter as he set down the pot of tea.

Cora surveyed the dining room, noticing how fashionably dressed the diners were. And she was among them, even though her Sunday dress was black. She watched Mr. Cunningham tease her daughter, pleased that the man paid attention to her little girl. What an entertaining person he was. She looked forward to the afternoon spending time playing croquet on the plaza with him. With all of them, even the moody man beside her.

But what did he mean about giving Mr. Cunningham competition? Did his comment have anything to do with her, or was she just hoping it did?

Chapter Five

The guard stopped Daniel at the ravelin, the stone structure built to protect the entrance to the fort.

"Your business, sir?"

"I need to see Lieutenant Pratt." Daniel stared down the young soldier standing with his gun across his chest.

"Wait here, sir."

The soldier marched across the bridge over the dry moat to the sally port and spoke to another soldier. They both looked back at Daniel, then one left and the other returned to his station beside Daniel.

As he waited, Daniel studied the ancient fort named Fort San Marcos when it was constructed under Spanish rule. He admired the design of the Spanish coat of arms over the main entrance, placed there hundreds of years before the territory was part of the United States.

A few moments passed before another soldier appeared at the entrance and motioned Daniel over. "The lieutenant will see you now." Daniel followed him through the opening into the open parade ground of the fort. He scanned the grassy area looking for evidence of the Indian prisoners. The soldier led him to a corner where a photographer was set up.

Lieutenant Pratt posed alongside a group of Indians, his foot propped on a cannon, a pile of cannon balls nearby. The native men stared expressionless at the camera, flinching when the flash popped, no doubt thinking they were being shot at. Did anyone explain to them what they were doing? Daniel clenched his teeth at the mockery and pretentiousness of the scene, angry at the lack of concern for the prisoners' feelings.

When the photographer stopped to replace the plate, the lieutenant strolled over to Daniel. "I'm Lieutenant Richard Pratt. Did you want to speak with me? What is this about?"

Daniel pulled his gaze away from the Indians to focus on the man in front of him. "Yes, sir. My name is Daniel Worthington. I understand you're looking for people to help teach these prisoners. I thought I might be of assistance."

Lieutenant Pratt looked him up and down, then spoke over his shoulder. "Mr. Carter, you may proceed with your photographs. I'll be back after a while." Turning to Daniel, he motioned to him to follow, leaving the prisoners with their guards. "Let's go to my office."

They entered a door on the opposite side of the parade ground and stepped into a stone room occupied by a simple desk and three wooden ladder-back chairs. Hanging his cap on a peg, he sat down behind the desk and gestured to one of the chairs opposite him. "Have a seat. Mr. Worthington, did you say? So, you're a teacher here?"

"No sir, I'm not teacher nor am I from here. My family is visiting from Boston for the season." Daniel drew himself up, assuming a determined posture so Lieutenant Pratt would see the value of his offer. "I'm an artist and I'd like to sketch the prisoners."

"I thought you said you wanted to teach them." A scowl creased the lieutenant's face.

"Sir, I believe art is a means of communication. Perhaps by drawing, I can teach them our language."

Pratt leaned back and stroked his chin. "Hmm. We do have a problem getting the Indians to understand us. A few know some English, and we have an interpreter as well, but they don't all speak the same language."

Daniel leaned forward. "They don't? Why not?"

"They're from different tribes—Kiowa, Comanches, Arapahos, Cheyenne, and one Caddo. We have seventy-two prisoners plus two wives and their children, so you see communication can be a problem. Maybe this idea of yours would work."

"Yes, sir. I believe it can help."

"You know, Mr. Worthington, many people think I'm wrong to try to civilize these people. They think it's a waste of time and that the Indians aren't able to learn our ways. I disagree, though, and I'll prove it. With the right training, they can become more like us."

Daniel pondered the statement. *More like us?* What if they didn't want to be *like us*? They didn't have a choice in the matter, though.

"When would be a good time for me to start?" Daniel would begin right now if possible, but it wouldn't be likely on a Sunday.

"Tomorrow afternoon is fine. Miss Sarah Mather and Miss Rebecca Perit, two teachers from town, are coming too. They'll be setting up classrooms. First, though, we'll start the prisoners on drills in the morning—teach them how to march, line up. Even got uniforms ordered for them."

Daniel swallowed hard. "Uniforms, sir?"

"Absolutely. I'll let them wear their Indian clothes today for pictures, but once we get the uniforms, they'll dress like soldiers." He waved his hand. "They won't have need for those Indian trappings, the necklaces and so forth. However, you can come after lunch and draw them in their native attire like you suggested." Pratt rose from his seat.

Taking the cue that the conversation was finished, Daniel stood as well and extended his hand. "Thank you, Lieutenant Pratt. I'll be here right after noon tomorrow."

~

Daniel sat on a wooden bench in a vaulted chamber lighted by a small window high up the heavy stone wall. Across from him, a group of Indians sat on the hard dirt floor, their backs against the wall. They stared at him as he took his charcoal and sketched. The straight noses and prominent cheekbones were easily defined by straight lines. Even though they had been conquered, most of them showed a semblance of pride, a characteristic he wanted to denote in his drawing. If only the Indians knew he could be trusted, but they acted afraid to move, casting glances at the armed soldiers standing in the doorway. How could he convey to the Indians that he meant no harm?

After he'd been drawing about an hour, he stood and crossed the room toward them. They drew back, eyeing him with suspicion as he approached. Daniel attempted a smile and extended his sketchbook to show what he had drawn. Furtive looks shot between the men, his tablet and himself, but eventually, two of the men leaned forward to study the picture. They pointed to it and commented to the others in their language. One responded with a comment that made his neighbor chuckle. The sound filled Daniel with a burst of excitement. He had made a connection.

The tension in the room dissipated as they mumbled amongst each other, giving occasional nods and gesturing to the drawing. Daniel breathed a silent prayer. *Thank you, Lord.*

Behind him, someone cleared his throat. "Sir, your time with the prisoners is over for today." Daniel turned and faced the guard who continued, "You may return tomorrow at two o'clock."

Daniel nodded, then looked back at the Indians and tried to communicate with his hands, then spoke. "I'll return tomorrow and draw some more."

Blank expressions responded. Daniel's heart sank. They didn't understand, but he smiled and waved goodbye anyway, hoping to convey a little cheer.

Before leaving, he gazed at one of the men who coughed often and sat curled up with an Indian blanket wrapped around him. Although the weather outside was warm, the dank stone room felt much cooler. Perhaps the man would feel better if he could get out in the warm sunshine. Daniel would tell the lieutenant he needed more natural light and hope the officer would acquiesce and allow him to draw them outside. Yes, that's what he'd do. At least there was one way he could improve their conditions.

As he walked out of the fort, he pulled his watch from his vest pocket and checked the time. Two thirty. By now, Mother and Judith must be finished with their visit to Mrs. Miller's millinery shop. When he left them at the hotel after lunch, the women's conversation was dominated by hat design. However, he had no idea when they arrived at the shop or how long it would take them to accomplish their business. He'd stop by the milliner's on the way back to the hotel and see if they were still there. As the image of Cora Miller's bright smile appeared in his mind, he couldn't help but contrast her lively expression to the somber faces he'd just drawn. What a refreshing change of scenery that smile would be right now.

Chapter Six

"I believe this fabric would be a good match with your coloring." Cora held up a swatch of pale green material in front of Judith.

Judith frowned and shook her head. "Oh no, I don't think so. I prefer browns."

Cora bit her tongue. A pretty pastel would do wonders to improve the girl's appearance over the drab brown she always wore. The door opened, and Cora glanced back over her shoulder, startled by the unexpected arrival of Mr. Worthington. Her thoughts jumbled as she tried to remember her idea for Judith's hat. What had she been thinking about?

"Good afternoon, ladies." Mr. Worthington removed his hat freeing his chestnut hair. "I see you're still conducting business." He walked to his mother who was seated in one of the two small, upholstered chairs, and bent down to kiss her on the cheek.

His mother faced him and smiled. "Mrs. Miller has been suggesting some wonderful designs for my hat. I'm really looking forward to see what kind of masterpiece she can create."

Cora beamed at the compliment. "Good afternoon, Mr. Worthington. Yes, we've discussed several attractive styles for your mother." The man offered a smile, but worry lines creased his brow. He could be so serious.

"And you, Judith? What have you chosen?" Mr. Worthington glanced at his sister.

"Nothing yet. Mrs. Miller thinks I should try some new colors instead of my usual ones." Judith shook her head. "I don't believe

40

I'd be comfortable in any other colors though."

Mr. Worthington strode over to study the fabric Cora held. "Judith, I think you'd look very nice in this shade of green." He took the swatch and held it up by Judith's face and hair. "Oh yes, very nice indeed."

Was he agreeing with her? Cora held her breath waiting for Judith's response.

"Do you really think so, Daniel?" She looked over at Mrs. Worthington. "What do you think, Mother?"

"Let me see, dear." Mrs. Worthington leaned forward to see the fabric Cora carried over. "I think Daniel's right." She shrugged. "Why not give it a try? If you don't like the finished hat, Mrs. Miller can make you another."

She could? "Of course. Your mother's correct. If you don't care for the bonnet, you don't have to take it." Somehow, she'd create a design that would appeal to the girl. Otherwise, she'd be wasting her time and supplies, which she couldn't afford to do.

"In that case, I'll agree to try it."

"Good!" Mr. Worthington headed to the door, apparently in a hurry to leave. "Are you ladies ready to return to the hotel now?"

"Not just yet, son. Mrs. Miller needs to finish up with Judith."

Cora moved to the cabinet where she kept her hat accessories, pulled out a narrow drawer and placed it on the countertop. "What do you think about these?" Judith followed her to investigate the assortment of brooches and pins, while her brother engaged their mother in quiet discussion. Cora kept her ear tuned to their conversation while trying to maintain a dialogue with Judith at the same time.

"What was the condition at the fort, Daniel? Were the Indians cooperative?" Mrs. Worthington asked.

"Cooperative? Do they have a choice?" Cora detected angry frustration in his voice. "Sorry, Mother, I just can't help feeling sorry for them. I didn't see all of them, but at least I was allowed to sketch a small group. I showed them what I was doing and thought for a moment we might have bridged the gap in communication, but I won't know for certain until my next visit. They need to get used to me, trust me, and I don't blame them for their reluctance to trust another white man."

"Were you able to finish any sketches?" Cora glanced up as

Mrs. Worthington pointed to the sketchbook under his arm. "May I see them?"

"Of course, but they're very simple."

Cora suppressed the urge to ask to see the sketches too. How talented an artist was Daniel Worthington?

"You're going back tomorrow?" Mrs. Worthington asked her son.

"Yes, after noon. I'm going to ask permission to sketch them outside this time. It's very chilly inside that fort and some of the Indians don't seem well."

What if they had some dread disease that was catching? And the ladies' benevolent society planned to visit the Indians at the fort. No one from the society had come by yet, thank goodness. She certainly didn't want to expose herself to illness. She'd have to find some way to avoid going to the fort if she was asked.

"I like this one." Judith's voice penetrated her thoughts, drawing her attention to an ivory and gold hatpin.

"Hmm? Oh yes, that's a lovely pin, one of my favorites. I can put some netting over the brim like this, and anchor it with the pin." Cora pointed to a straw bonnet mounted on a hat form. "Shall we put some satin trim around the edge?" She picked up a roll of dark green satin ribbon.

"Ooh, how pretty. And may I have a feather or two?" Judith stroked some quail feathers in the drawer. Cora repressed a grin as the girl's enthusiasm emerged.

"Of course. How about these?" Cora selected a cluster of small feathers and picked them up.

Judith nodded. "I like them." She scanned the rest of the contents of the tray. "That should be enough. I don't want to appear gaudy."

Yet she was willing to wear a peacock feather for Mr. Cunningham? What lengths some women would go to for a man. Cora would never allow some man to convince her to do something she didn't want to do. Not even someone as handsome as Mr. Cunningham. Good thing Judith was still young enough to be under the protection of her mother and her brother. As Mr. Cunningham came to mind, Cora wondered where he was. He certainly didn't share Mr. Worthington's interest in the Indians.

"Wonderful, I believe you'll have a lovely hat." Cora nodded to Mrs. Worthington." I'll get started on it and on your mother's right away."

"How long before they'll be ready?" Judith's hazel eyes radiated a spark of excitement.

"I should be finished by the end of the week, if I'm not interrupted."

Mrs. Worthington pushed herself out of the chair as Judith came toward her. "We'll try not to take any more of your time, so you can get to work."

As Mr. Worthington reached for the door, it opened and in walked Mrs. Anderson from the benevolent society. The gray-haired woman was dressed in all black, from her gloves to her old-fashioned bonnet, her clothes proclaiming her widowhood as they had for the past ten years, from what Cora had heard. The only color she wore came from her large ornate pearl and sapphire necklace.

The dignified elderly woman scanned the group and smiled. "Hello, Mrs. Miller. I see you're very busy." Turning to Mrs. Worthington, she said, "I'm Clarissa Anderson. Dr. Andrew Anderson is my son. Are you visiting St. Augustine?"

Mrs. Worthington nodded to Mrs. Anderson and introduced herself and her family. "Yes, we're from Boston, in town for the season and stretching it out as far as reasonable. Mrs. Miller is going to make some hats for us. One of mine met with a tragic end on Saturday."

Mrs. Anderson frowned, then a look of understanding crossed her face. "Oh, I heard about that. Your hat was trampled by one of the poor Indian prisoners."

"Yes, that's the one. Since I can't go back to Paris to get another one any time soon, Mrs. Miller has offered to create a suitable replacement. Can you vouch for her work?"

Cora's face warmed as the ladies discussed her.

"Yes, indeed. Although I haven't had the pleasure of her services yet, I have a very good friend who has and is quite satisfied," Mrs. Anderson said.

"That's good to hear, although based on the examples she's shown us, I'm not surprised." Mrs. Worthington nodded toward Cora.

Cora smiled her appreciation for the compliments, even though she was embarrassed to be the object of their conversation. "I'll be happy to make you a hat too, Mrs. Anderson."

"When I need another hat, I'll be sure to have you design it. However, that's not the purpose of my visit today."

"We'll leave you two to discuss your business then." Mrs. Worthington stepped aside in the small store to allow Mrs. Anderson to pass. "It was a pleasure to meet you, Mrs. Anderson. Good bye, Mrs. Miller."

Daniel put his hat back on and tipped the brim toward Cora as he left the shop with his family. Even though the little store was crowded with all of them in it, Cora wished they could have stayed, if only to interfere with Mrs. Anderson's purpose. Plus, she was curious to see Daniel Worthington's sketches too, but there was neither opportunity nor invitation to do so.

"Lucy Abbott told me you're interested in joining our benevolent society." Mrs. Anderson got right to the point.

"Yes, I am honored to be asked." Not to mention honored to have Mrs. Clarissa Anderson in her store. Mrs. Anderson was a prominent member of St. Augustine, known for her role in building her deceased husband's dream plantation on the outskirts of town, as well as being the mother of the town's principal doctor.

"I'm glad to know you are as concerned as the rest of us are about the poor and needy of our town. As you know, we've been trying to help the freedmen since the war."

Cora nodded, although her motives might not be as admirable as Mrs. Anderson's assessment of them.

"Yes, I've heard of all you've done in that part of town." Cora thought of the area on the south end of town referred to as Lincolnville, where freed slaves lived. "Your charity is quite commendable."

"There's still much to be done, I assure you, to give these people an education and help them become self-sufficient. In fact, that's one reason we need your help."

"Mine?" Cora placed her hand over her chest and lifted an eyebrow. "I'm not a teacher."

Mrs. Anderson laid her gloved hand on Cora's arm. "No, my dear, we don't need you to teach. We have qualified people for that. However, some of our members are so busy with their work with the freedmen that they can't take on more responsibility. And

I'm afraid my health isn't up to the physical strain. We need new members who can share the load."

Cora shook her head. "I'm afraid I don't understand. What do you need me to do?" Cora held her breath, dreading the answer. Truthfully, she didn't have time either. Not to help anyone else. She needed to help herself to keep a roof over her and her daughter's heads.

"What we need you to do is help with our charity to the Indians at Fort Marion. They need blankets and clothes, plus more food than the government gives them. Some of them are weak and appear to be in poor health, but fortunately, my son is looking in on them to see if they need medical aid."

"So … you want me to donate some things for the Indians?" Cora searched her brain for something she could spare. "I might have an extra blanket you can have."

"That would be very nice. We're collecting things at the church to take to them."

Cora emitted a slight sigh of relief. She and Emily could manage without a blanket and would make do with their quilts. If that's all that was required of her, she'd be thankful.

"Good. When I go home today, I'll get the blanket and bring it to the church."

"Thank you, dear. We also need volunteers to deliver the donations to the fort. Wouldn't it be a blessing to personally hand a poor, destitute soul a warm, cozy blanket with a smile showing God's love?"

Cora gulped and tried to conceal her aversion to being in such close quarters with the Indians. Who would do her work while she spent her time visiting Indians?

"A blessing indeed." Cora put on her sweetest smile. She could picture one of the other ladies in the society at the fort handing out charity to the Indians. She wasn't like them. They had plenty of time for such things, but she didn't. She had responsibility—a young child to care for. Plus she was a business woman. "However, I'm afraid I cannot take the time to go to the prison." She waved her hand across the array of hat makings spread out on the counter. "I have hats to make for my patrons, and they expect me to finish in a short period of time." She inclined her head and lowered her voice. "You know, these tourists aren't here very long, and we must accommodate them while they are."

Mrs. Anderson frowned, then nodded. "I see. Well, then, perhaps this isn't a good time for you to join our society."

Alarm raced through Cora. She had to be in the good graces of St. Augustine society ladies. What could she do?

"Please don't misunderstand, Mrs. Anderson. I truly do want to be a part of your charity. Perhaps there is something else I can do to help?"

"Well if you're genuinely interested in the plight of our poor and needy, come to our meeting at the church Wednesday morning. We'll discuss the situation and how we can best address it."

"I'd love to attend the meeting. Thank you for inviting me. What time will it be?"

"Nine o'clock."

"I'll be there as soon as I take my daughter to school."

"Very well. Then we'll see you on Wednesday."

As Mrs. Anderson turned to leave, Emily bounded into the store.

"Momma! Guess who I …?" Emily fell silent when she saw another person in the store.

"Emily, please say hello to Mrs. Anderson."

Emily grinned and gave a quick curtsy. "Hello."

Mrs. Anderson smiled down at the little girl. "Hello, Emily. Did you have a good time at school today?"

"Yes, ma'am." Emily studied the ornate jeweled necklace on Mrs. Anderson's neck.

"You're a big girl to walk all the way home by yourself," the matron said.

Was Mrs. Anderson's remark meant as a rebuke? "I usually meet her at school, but I was tied up with some new clients today." Did Mrs. Anderson think her negligent?

Emily's eyes brightened, then she blurted out. "Oh, but I wasn't by myself."

Cora raised her eyebrows. If she didn't meet Emily, who did?

"Who were you with?"

Emily turned around and pointed to the store door as Mr. Cunningham entered.

"Him! Mr. Cunningham walked me home."

Cora's face flamed at the sight of the man standing in the doorway, his dazzling smile gleaming at her.

Mrs. Anderson looked toward Sterling Cunningham, then back at Cora as if to ask a question but shook her head instead and moved to the door, headed to the carriage waiting outside.

"Mrs. Anderson, this is Sterling Cunningham. He's a friend of the Worthingtons."

Mr. Cunningham doffed his hat and bowed. "The pleasure is mine, Mrs. Anderson."

Color rose in the woman's cheeks as she acknowledged the introduction. Apparently, the gentleman's charm extended to women of all ages.

"Mr. Cunningham. Please excuse me. I was just leaving." As she went out the door, she peered back over her shoulder at Cora.

"You certainly are busy, Mrs. Miller."

The glass in the door rattled when it closed as Cora stared after Mrs. Anderson. What did she mean by that remark? Beads of perspiration popped out along her hairline and she scanned the countertop for a fan. Was Mrs. Anderson implying something improper? What more would happen today?

Chapter Seven

"Isn't it about time to close business for the day?" Sterling Cunningham sauntered up to Cora, his gaze fixed down on her face. "All work and no play make Jack a dull boy. Isn't that right, Mrs. Miller? However, I find you anything but dull."

His penetrating stare was like a torch sending flames through her body. She glanced away and surveyed the work on her counter waiting to be done. Eager as she was to begin designing the hats, it was impractical to start at this time of day.

Cora looked at the clock on the shelf. "I suppose you're right. All this can wait until tomorrow."

"Of course it can! You must take time for more pleasurable endeavors."

"Actually, I enjoy what I do, Mr. Cunningham, so it scarcely seems like work at all." She reached for the tray on the counter. "As soon as I straighten up, I'll close the shop."

Mr. Cunningham touched one of the jeweled brooches. "Did Mrs. Worthington choose one of these for her hat?"

"No, she didn't, but Judith chose this ivory one." She pointed to the pin for Judith's hat.

"Hmm. Nice choice, but I'd prefer one of these with the more colorful jewels. They're very good imitations."

"Well, some of them are."

"Would you put a real jewel on a hat?"

"If the hat and the customer called for it." She touched a dainty diamond and ruby pendant brooch. "This one's real, and that one's real emerald. I would only use them on very special hats." Gently rubbing a dark blue stone in a gold filigree setting, she said, "This is lapis. It belonged to my late husband's mother. I'm not sure why I brought it here, actually. I doubt I would use it on a hat because it's more meaningful."

"They all show excellent workmanship, especially that one."

Cora's thought drifted to her mother-in-law, who had passed away the year before Jacob did. "Yes, it is." She shrugged. "Perhaps I'll use it on a very special hat." She lifted the drawer and returned it to the chest. Mr. Cunningham had quite an interest in jewels.

"No peacock feathers?"

Cora pursed her lips. "I'm afraid not. But Judith did make some good choices." Cora collected the ribbons and other accessories and put them away.

After donning her gloves and grabbing her parasol, Cora extended her hand to her daughter. "Come on, Emily. Let's go home." She turned to Mr. Cunningham. "Thank you for accompanying Emily."

Sterling Cunningham held the door for her and Emily to step outside before he did, then waited while she put the key in the lock. "Actually, I confess to having ulterior motives."

Cora's eyebrows lifted as she gazed up at the charming man and tilted her head, ready for an explanation. My goodness, what kind of motives did he mean? Should she be concerned?

He assumed a forlorn demeanor, lowering his head and feigning guilt. "Yes, I'm afraid I did. I knew that if I went with Miss Emily, I'd get to see her lovely mother. And then I hoped she might join me for dinner."

"Thank you for your invitation, Mr. Cunningham, but we normally take our meals at the boarding house." The idea of him taking her out to dinner was tempting, but she couldn't accept his offer and leave Emily alone.

"Why don't you do something out of the ordinary, then? Dine with me, please. Both of you. I hate to eat alone."

Cora didn't believe for a minute that Sterling Cunningham ever had a problem finding a dinner companion, but he definitely could be convincing. And he'd invited both she and Emily, an appealing suggestion.

"Don't you usually dine with the Worthingtons?"

"My dear lady, the Worthingtons are my friends, but we are not conjoined. Would you please allow me to escort you two lovely ladies? The restaurant at the Florida House has very good food."

One of the best restaurants in town, Cora had heard the food was excellent. And expensive.

"The Florida House." Emily clapped her hands, her face aglow with excitement. "Momma, you said you wanted to eat there! Can we go? Please?"

Cora's face warmed at her daughter's disclosure. Yet seeing the hopeful faces of the two, she knew she was outnumbered. "I suppose we can accept Mr. Cunningham's invitation, as long as we don't stay out too late. You have to get up early for school, young lady."

"Yippee!" Emily bounced down the sidewalk ahead of them.

Mr. Cunningham extended his arm and Cora accepted by placing her hand inside his elbow. For the second time this week, she'd had the pleasure of a gentleman's company. Yet the two gentlemen were as different as a top hat and a Panama hat. But this man appeared to be interested in her company while the other one preferred the company of Indians. Such a realization could hurt her self-confidence if it weren't for Sterling Cunningham's attention, and she intended to enjoy it.

As they proceeded down the street, a man hurried around the corner and headed straight toward them. Cora stiffened when she recognized the short, portly fellow, his red face dripping with perspiration. She and her escort stopped abruptly to avoid colliding with him.

He stopped too and squinted in the sunlight as he focused on the pair.

"Ah, Mrs. Miller. I was just coming to see you."

Cora steeled herself. Why did she have to run into her landlord Mr. Beasley now?

"I'm afraid we've closed for the day, Mr. Beasley. But I'll be open tomorrow."

"Yes, you do that. You know rent's due on your shop this week. I don't suppose you have it with you now?"

"No, Mr. Beasley. But I will have it for you later this week, I assure you."

Mr. Cunningham extended his hand. "Sterling Cunningham, sir."

Cora didn't want to introduce her landlord but knew she must. "This is Mr. Beasley, my landlord at the shop."

The two men assessed each other with their eyes as they shook hands. Then Cora's escort pulled her aside. "Please excuse us, Mr. Beasley. We have a dinner engagement."

Mr. Beasley glanced between Cora and Mr. Cunningham, then nodded and passed by, calling over his shoulder, "I'll call on you later this week to collect your rent."

Cora burned with embarrassment. How dare he speak to her about such things in front of Mr. Cunningham?

"He's a rather unpleasant fellow," Mr. Cunningham declared, waving the air with his hand as if to shoo a pesky insect.

"He is, but I'm afraid I have to deal with him since he owns the building my shop is in."

"Why don't you just buy the building?" Mr. Cunningham's suggestion made the transaction sound as simple as buying a piece of fruit at the market. Did he think she had that kind of money?

"I'd like to … some day. We haven't been in St. Augustine that long ourselves and I'm still deciding on where we will live permanently, among other things."

He shrugged as if the matter was no longer interesting, then assumed an undignified, ape-like posture and began tromping down the sidewalk.

"What in heaven's name are you doing?"

Emily turned around and giggled. "You look funny, Mr. Cunningham!"

He glanced over his shoulder at Cora. "Remind you of anyone? Your landlord, perhaps?"

Cora gaped. "Mr. Beasley!"

Emily danced on her tiptoes. "Momma, he looks funny like Mr. Beasley!"

"Mr. Cunningham, please behave yourself." Cora blushed as she glanced around to see if anyone she knew was nearby, witnessing the scene. What if Mr. Beasley saw?

Mr. Cunningham straightened his jacket and recovered his posture. "Yes, ma'am. At least I got a smile from Emily. No smile from you, my serious beauty?"

Cora couldn't hold back the smile that responded to his teasing. Mr. Cunningham's behavior bordered on the outrageous, but she found herself relaxing in his company. Did she present such a serious attitude? Perhaps she did. After all, she had important responsibilities with a child to raise by herself and a business to run. His carefree attitude might annoy her if he wasn't so entertaining.

"There it is. There's your lovely smile. You should show it more often."

"I wasn't aware that I appeared so solemn."

"We'll put an end to solemnity, then. For the rest of the evening, I want to see that gorgeous smile that lights up your face so brilliantly."

If she could only hide the color that crept up her neck when he heaped such effusive compliments on her. As they strolled along Treasury Street, they passed a home where a tree branch heavy with oranges hung over the garden wall. Mr. Cunningham pulled off an orange, whipped out his pocket knife and cut a hole in the end.

"What are you doing, Mr. Cunningham?" Emily asked.

"I saw a man do this the other day, so I tried it." He cut a hole out of one end of the orange and put it to Emily's mouth. "Open your mouth, and I'll squeeze the juice in."

Emily obeyed, and her eyes rounded as the sweet nectar filled her mouth. "That's good! Momma, you should try it like this." She took the orange from his hand.

"I don't think ..." Her words were cut off when Mr. Cunningham grabbed another orange and repeated the process, putting the fruit to her lips this time.

"Shhh. Taste it." The fresh juice squirted into her mouth, both startling her and refreshing her at the same time. "You see? Don't you like it?"

Cora nodded. "It is indeed delicious. I never knew you could eat them like that."

"Life is full of surprises if you look for them," Mr. Cunningham said with a wink.

They continued to the entrance of the Florida Hotel as Mr. Cunningham regaled her with funny stories. A welcome breeze blew off the bay, lifting Cora's spirits and lightening her burdens along with it. A soldier trotted by on horseback, and Cora smiled as the man tipped his hat to her. Maybe she could allow herself to relax and simply enjoy a gentleman's company, if only for a little while. Still, she was thankful Emily was with them. Not much of a chaperone, but somehow a protective barrier between her and Mr. Cunningham. Curious to think she needed a barrier, yet comfortable to have one nonetheless.

Dinner was quite enjoyable as expected. Cora allowed her escort to order for her, since he was well-known at this hotel's restaurant as well. He certainly had a way of making himself familiar in town. It was a good thing she wasn't the jealous type, or she might have been bothered by the attention he both gave and received from other ladies. However, Cora didn't have any claims to the man and wasn't sure she wanted any.

It wasn't only women that knew him though.

A distinguished gentleman escorting a well-dressed woman passed their table while the three of them were enjoying their meal. The man paused to slap Mr. Cunningham on the back.

"Shall I see you at the card table tonight? Give me a chance to win back some of that money you took from me last night."

"Sure, I'll give you a chance." Mr. Cunningham laughed. "If you truly want to lose more money trying."

"We'll see, won't we? See you later, Sterling."

As the gentleman walked away, Emily spoke up. "Do you play Happy Families, Mr. Cunningham? I want to play!"

Their escort cocked an eyebrow at the child then glanced at Cora, as if to seek explanation.

"Her great-aunt was from England and had a card game called "Happy Families" that was popular there."

"I see." Mr. Cunningham pulled on his goatee. "I'm sorry, but I don't have those kinds of cards. However, if you did, I'd play with you!"

Emily's face drooped as her gaze fell. "I don't have any either. Aunt Winifred took them back to England with her."

"Well, if I'm ever in England again, I'll buy you a deck."

Emily's face brightened as hope reclaimed her features.

"You've been to England before?" Cora wasn't at all surprised but hoped to discover more about this intriguing man.

"Yes, yes, visited all the interesting places, saw the Queen, did all the customary things that everyone does." He waved a waiter over and pointed to his empty wine glass, which was promptly refilled.

Everyone does? Perhaps everyone in his circle, but not in hers. She could only dream of such a voyage.

"Did you see a castle?" Emily asked wide-eyed.

He leaned over to the perky child. "I did indeed. In fact, I saw several, even visited some distant relatives that live in one."

"Truly? Are they kings or princes?" Emily bounced in her chair.

"No, just a duke and duchess."

"Did they wear crowns?"

"Emily, you mustn't ask so many questions." Cora admonished her daughter, even though she was keenly interested in the answers herself.

"I don't mind the questions. It's far more interesting to her than to me. I found it rather boring."

Emily tapped his arm. "Do they have knights in armor?"

Mr. Cunningham laughed out loud. "Not anymore, I'm afraid. Just gardeners and servants and maids—the usual."

The usual. To him, that was normal. "So, your parents are from England?"

"No, my great-grandparents were. My parents are both deceased now, but they were born in America."

"Please forgive me. I'm sorry." Cora patted her mouth with her napkin. "I'm doing the same thing as Emily."

"Don't be. They were killed in a carriage accident when I was very young. I was raised by my grandmother in Boston."

"And that's how you know the Worthington family, I assume, since they're also from Boston."

"That's right. Daniel and I went to boarding school together, then university."

"Are you going to marry Miss Judith?" Emily blurted out.

"Emily! I'm so sorry, Mr. Cunningham. Her manners are sorely lacking tonight."

His laughter rang out across the dining room as he leaned back, resting his arms across the backs of the two chairs on either side of him.

"No, dearest Emily. Miss Judith and I are not betrothed." He faced Cora, a sparkle in his eye. "I've known Judith since she was Emily's age. She's like a little sister to me. I prefer grown women, especially pretty little blonde ones."

"Like Momma? She's pretty and blonde too!"

Cora cringed and hoped the gaslight hid the deep crimson her face must be.

"You're absolutely right about that, Emily. She most certainly is, just like you!"

"Momma says she used to look like me."

Eager to change the subject, Cora exclaimed, "It must be getting late. I'm afraid Emily and I need to get home."

Mr. Cunningham pulled an ornate gold watch with a pastoral scene on the front from his vest pocket and flipped it open. "Seven-thirty, and not even sunset yet. But I mustn't keep you young ladies out too late." He snapped his watch shut and replaced it in his vest. "Shall we take our leave?"

"Yes, please." Cora knew she needed to get Emily to bed, but almost hated for the evening to end so quickly.

Mr. Cunningham stood and pulled back both her chair and Emily's. "I've enjoyed our dinner immensely, and I hope we can partake together again."

Cora ushered Emily in front of her between the tables as they moved to the door. When they stepped outside, Mr. Cunningham retrieved a cigar from his inside coat pocket. Cora shot him a disapproving glance.

He held the cigar aloft, then saw her reaction. "You dislike cigars?"

"Yes, I'm afraid I find the smell offensive."

"What a pity." He tucked the cigar back inside his coat. "Your cigar makers here produce the finest I've ever had. Tobacco straight from Havana, I understand."

"I've heard they are very popular among the gentlemen." For what reason, she didn't know. She'd never cared for the odor. "Please don't let me interfere with your pastime."

He shrugged. "For you, my dear lady, I will wait until I am not in your presence. I do not care to offend you."

How considerate of him to respect her wishes.

The sun had begun its descent behind the trees casting an amber glow on the world below as they strolled several blocks to the large, two-story boarding house. When they reached the gate of the whitewashed picket fence, he opened it, and Emily skittered inside, running across the yard.

"Emily! Please tell Mr. Cunningham good night!" Cora sighed and faced him. "I must apologize for my daughter's manners, Mr. Cunningham. I'm truly trying to teach her to behave more politely."

"She's just a child, a carefree child, like we all once were. Why can't we be more like her than all stuffy and grown up? She has a zest for life and I'm certain has a lot more fun than most adults."

Cora tilted her head, eyeing this man who seemed to be carefree as well, never lacking for amusement. She extended her hand. "Well, I thank you for our lovely dinner. It was quite a nice evening for both of us."

Mr. Cunningham took her hand and lifted it to his lips. "It is my pleasure, Mrs. Miller." Cora held her breath, grateful for the gloves that shielded her from his kiss. "But I must ask you a favor."

Cora lifted her eyes to his smoldering ones. "What is it?"

"Would you please call me Sterling? Mr. Cunningham is far too formal for friends."

"I suppose I could do that." Were they friends?

"And may I please call you Cora?" He searched her face for an answer.

"It only seems fair if I'm to call you by your given name that you should address me by mine. Yes, you may call me Cora."

A brilliant smile stretched across his face. "Splendid. Then I bid you good night, Cora Miller."

Cora stepped inside the gate, and pulled it shut, watching Sterling Cunningham stroll away.

"Good night, Sterling," she whispered.

What would the Worthingtons think about the two of them calling each other by their given names?

Chapter Eight

The soldiers guarding the front of the fort didn't stop Daniel when he approached this time. He tipped his hat and they stepped aside to let him in.

But instead of heading to the room where he sketched the Indians the day before, he spotted Lieutenant Pratt in another part of the parade ground and strode over to him.

Pratt lifted his eyebrows as Daniel approached. "Mr. Worthington, good day. You can find the Indians in the same place as yesterday."

"Sir, if I may make a suggestion. Would you allow them to come outside? Perhaps out in the sun? I think it'd be good to draw them in the sunlight. Plus, it might be good for them to get some fresh air too."

Lieutenant Pratt stroked his beard. "Hmm. I suppose there's no harm in letting them go outside."

"I doubt they'd try to escape, with all your soldiers guarding them."

"No, no, I don't believe they would. They've been pretty docile since they got here."

Docile indeed. More like resigned to their fate.

Daniel pointed to a sunny corner of the grounds. "How about over there?"

Pratt followed Daniel's gesture and nodded. "That will be fine. I'll have the guards bring them out." He called to another soldier, "Private, get Mr. Worthington a chair and place it over there."

"Yes, sir!" the soldier said before marching away.

"Thank you, lieutenant."

"You're welcome, Mr. Worthington. I'm sure the natives will appreciate the fresh air." He clasped his hands behind his back, then strode away.

Daniel settled in the chair and opened his sketchbook. While he waited for the Indians, he made some strokes to capture the architecture of the fort. The Spanish masonry fort had been in many hands over the past two hundred years—the Spanish, the British, and even the Confederates before Federal troops captured it. The fort was built as a simple square, but with four triangular bastions on each corner, leaving the central "Plaza de Armas" open to the sky. No longer a stronghold keeping an enemy from invading the city, the fort had become a prison keeping another enemy from getting out.

As a group of Indians trudged toward him, Daniel was relieved to see the shackles were removed. Like a dog that's been tied too long, the natives moved as if they were still bound. Daniel lifted his hand in greeting and a couple of the men acknowledged with a slight nod of their heads. He gestured for them to sit on the ground, which they did obediently, crossing their legs, eyes focused on him.

Daniel began to sketch, watching the men as they stole glances at their surroundings. He was glad to see the elderly man who had appeared ill in the dank room yesterday. The old Indian, still wrapped in a threadbare blanket, lifted his face to the sun as if absorbing the warmth. At the edge of the group, one of the younger men scratched on the ground with a stone. Another Indian seated beside him watched intently.

After a while, Daniel's curiosity got the better of him. "What's he doing?" He motioned to the Indian scratching on the ground.

The Indians seated nearest Daniel glanced at the other Indian, then back at Daniel and pointed to his sketchbook, nodding.

"He's drawing something too?" He tried to communicate with his hands.

More nods. Daniel stood, and the Indians cowered. He pointed to himself and then to the Indian who was scratching on the ground. The message must have translated, for the man with the stone stopped and looked at him.

"May I see what you're doing?" Daniel pointed to himself and then to the ground.

The Indian nodded, and Daniel edged around the others to take a look.

In the dirt, the Indian had made a crude drawing of an Indian on a horse. Daniel's heart leaped at the sight. This man may not have had Daniel's art education, but he was an artist nonetheless. Daniel smiled. "Good! I like your drawing." The barest hint of a smile crossed the Indian's face.

Daniel was elated. They were fellow artists! What could he do to encourage this talent? What if there were others who wanted to draw? The dirt wasn't a good place to draw, but he couldn't give them his sketchbook. An idea hit him that he hoped Lieutenant Pratt would agree to.

When the guards came to take the Indians back to their quarters, he watched two of the younger men help the older man to his feet. One of the young men was the one who'd been drawing. Respect for the man swelled in Daniel's chest, and he had a pressing desire to get to know this Indian more personally.

Daniel closed his sketchbook and replaced his pencils in their wooden case, then scanned the courtyard for Lieutenant Pratt. At the sound of female voices, he turned to see Lieutenant Pratt exiting an alcove of the fort in the company of two women. Recalling the discussion about Cora Miller visiting the prisoners, his pulse quickened at the prospect of running into her there. However, these two women were nothing like the vivacious Mrs. Miller. These two ladies were more matronly, and dare he say, plain? He shook his head, reproaching himself for the comparison.

He remembered his need to speak with the commanding officer and crossed the grounds toward the group. When Lieutenant Pratt spotted him, he waved Daniel over.

"Mr. Worthington, may I introduce Miss Sarah Mather and Miss Rebecca Perit? They have come to teach the Indians, educate them in our ways."

Daniel tipped his hat and bowed. "Very nice to meet you ladies. I'm sure the prisoners will appreciate your teaching."

"Mr. Worthington here is an artist, visiting from Boston. He wanted to draw the Indians."

The ladies smiled and nodded. Miss Mather, the more mature

lady, motioned to the sketchbook under Daniel's arm. "I'd like to see your sketches some time."

"They're very rough now, but perhaps when I've worked on them a little more, they'll be good enough to see."

"I'm sure they're good enough now. But I'll be happy to see them whenever you're ready."

"The ladies were just leaving. They've been setting up their classrooms. They'll be back tomorrow to begin lessons." Pratt motioned toward the gate. "I see you're finished, Mr. Worthington. Would you like to accompany them out?"

Daniel cleared his throat. "I'd love to, but I need a few words with you before I leave."

"Of course. I'll have the guards escort them then." Pratt motioned to a soldier to come over. "Thank you, ladies, for coming. We'll see you in the morning."

The women smiled and nodded, and Daniel did the same before the guard ushered them out.

"So what did you need to discuss with me, Mr. Worthington?"

"Sir, I have an idea that I'd like your approval for." When Pratt crossed his arms over his chest, Daniel continued. "While I was sketching the Indians today, I noticed one of them was drawing on the ground. I'd like to offer them some paper to draw on. I only have one sketchbook with me, but perhaps we can find something else they could use—ledger books, maybe? I'm sure I can find some of those in town at the mercantile."

"Excellent idea! I can requisition some ledger books and pencils as well, but it will take a couple of weeks before they arrive. You know, some of the Indians drew pictures on their teepees, so they might like to draw on paper. Yes, I like that suggestion. See what you can get in town, and I'll order the rest."

"Thank you, sir." Daniel shook Pratt's hand, then started to walk away, but halted and turned back. "Sir, do you know any of the Indian's names? It might help if I called them by their names."

"Of course. I have a list, although I don't know them all. Were there any in particular that you wanted to know?"

"Yes, the young man that drew the picture. Seemed like an honorable type—well-liked by the others. In fact, I observed him helping the elderly man who seems ill."

"Ah. That's probably Sun Dancer. He's Cheyenne and his

Indian name is Okuhatuh. I've got my eye on him too. Appears to be pretty smart and is adapting well here. He'd make a good leader. I might even put him in charge of the others. They'd probably respond to him better than to white soldiers."

Daniel considered the possibility of making one of the Indians a soldier over his fellow-prisoners. Sun Dancer would have to be very trustworthy for that responsibility, that is, if he was willing. "Based on what I've seen, he'd be a good choice. Appears to have an agreeable attitude."

Pratt nodded. "It would be better if his family was with him."

Daniel raised an eyebrow. "His family?"

"Yes, most of the families are at Fort Sill, Oklahoma, left behind when the men were taken away, except for Black Horse's wife and children who came along, refusing to be separated, and Buffalo Calf, the other woman, who is also a prisoner and married to another prisoner. I believe Sun Dancer has a wife and one or two young ones back at Fort Sill. I hope someday to be able to bring all the families here and reunite them."

Daniel's gut wrenched at the thought of the Indians being so far apart from their families with no hope of seeing them again. With renewed determination, he decided he would do all he could to help the men. They might not be free, but their living conditions could be better.

"I'm sure if you did, the men would trust you much more."

"Certainly would. Right now, they all think we're going to kill them. That's what always happened when one tribe defeated another. The men were killed, the women and children sold or made slaves. It'll take some time before they believe we're not planning to do any such thing."

"Maybe the teachers will help convince them. I heard the benevolence society is coming by as well. Surely, their charitable actions will prove good intentions."

"I agree. I'm encouraging the townspeople to get more involved, and not just as curiosity seekers."

"I'll do what I can to that end as well." Daniel extended his hand. "Thank you for your cooperation, Lieutenant. I'll see you tomorrow, hopefully, with ledgers in hand."

As Daniel walked away from the fort, he had a sense of being given a mission. Did God delay his family's return to Boston so he could be in St. Augustine when the Indians arrived? Was this why he had studied art and how God wanted him to use his talent? Moisture dampened his eyes at the thought. He had always thought he had a greater purpose than practicing law in the family firm, but he didn't know what it was. Had he found it here in a prison?

~

Cora slipped into the back of the church and spotted the group of ladies seated near the front corner. She recognized most of them as the town's prominent socialites, even though she hadn't met them all.

On the front row sat Clarissa Anderson, talking quietly with Sarah Peck, the elderly widow of Dr. Seth Peck. Mrs. Peck lived in the impressive house dominating the corner of St. George and Treasury streets that Cora walked past every day. Behind Mrs. Peck were the Gibb sisters, Laura and Julia, widows of brothers who were both killed in the War, and beside them was Jane Farley, wife of Thaddeus Farley, who owned the haberdashery and the men's furnishings store.

Cora didn't know the other women congregated there for the meeting, but their faces were familiar. Two nuns from nearby St. Mary's Convent were also present, denoting how the benevolence society crossed all religious barriers. Cora seated herself in a row behind the other ladies and waited for the meeting to begin.

"Sorry I'm late, ladies." The voice of Miss Abbott came from the back of the church and all the women turned to see her hurry down the aisle toward them. "One of my builders had to see me first thing this morning." She strode to the front of the first pew, then stood before Mrs. Anderson. "Shall we begin, then?"

With some effort, the elderly Clarissa Anderson rose to her feet and faced the other ladies.

"Thank you all for coming, today. We have some new business to discuss about the Indians at our fort." She scanned the faces of those listening and stopped on Cora's. "I see Mrs. Miller has joined us. Welcome to our group. I look forward to working with you to help the less fortunate of our town."

Cora nodded and gave a polite smile to the others. What was she doing here among these wealthy benefactresses? Miss Abbott had inherited wealth from her family, but not from a husband. Mrs. Farley was the only other woman who worked outside the home, making plain hats for women in her husband's haberdashery, but she looked down her nose at Cora as if she were well above her in social standing. Perhaps the ladies assumed Cora had inherited wealth too. Oh, if only that had been the case. Instead, Jacob had left her virtually penniless after paying his many doctor bills. She'd come to town with just enough to get by, or she might be considered one of the "less fortunate" herself. What did she have to give others?

Chapter Nine

As Sun Dancer fumbled with the pencil he'd been given, Daniel moved beside him.

"May I help you?" Daniel extended his hand, motioning to the pen.

Sun Dancer's eyes registered understanding and he offered the implement to Daniel. Daniel positioned the pencil in his own hand.

"Hold it like this." He held the pencil aloft as he scanned the group of Indians around him, hoping they'd pay attention. Then he took his sketchbook and demonstrated making strokes. The Indians attempted to copy his actions by marking on the ledger books they'd been given. Daniel handed the pencil back to Sun Dancer who cradled it the proper way this time.

"Yes! That's it." Daniel nodded approval, then looked around to see how the other Indians were doing. He grasped his own pencil and walked around the circle of Indians to illustrate further to those still struggling with the device. Each one who succeeded to hold the pencil correctly and make a mark filled Daniel with a spark of celebration. Just the fact that they were making the effort was an achievement he relished.

Some preferred to simply sit and watch the others, but Daniel was content to know they had something worthwhile to occupy their time. He hoped more of the Indians would participate, but it would take time, patience, and commitment to see success. Commitment and patience he had, but time? How long would he be able to stay in St. Augustine before his mother was ready to return to Boston?

His eyes focused on Sun Dancer, creases crossing his brow as he concentrated on his drawing. If only this man's interest would spread among the others. Meanwhile, the native had acquired a following of admirers who had positioned themselves around him. Daniel studied the firm set of Sun Dancer's strong jaw, his straight nose and high cheekbones. He had the demeanor and carriage of a leader. What was his background? What had he done to land here in this prison? With a jolt, Daniel realized he was probably the same age as the Indian, yet Daniel's life had been one of ease while Sun Dancer's had been anything but. Worlds apart, yet, thank God, they shared a love for expressing themselves in art.

Wracking coughs from the old Indian diverted Daniel's attention. The man was still not well. Daniel heard that one of the town doctors had visited the Indians. Had he seen this man or tried to help him? Surely sleeping on the cold floors of the prison only worsened his condition.

Sun Dancer stopped drawing, got up and strode over to the old man, then crouched beside him and spoke quietly, drawing a sparse blanket more tightly around the shaking shoulders. Daniel shivered as well in the dank cold of the fort. Morning drizzle had prevented them from going outside today and had further dampened the stone casement where the men were held. The sickly man must be miserable.

Voices echoing off the hollowed walls diverted Daniel, who glanced at the open archway as Lieutenant Pratt appeared with another man not dressed in military uniform. Daniel strode toward the men as Pratt approached.

"Mr. Worthington, this is our interpreter, Mr. George Fox. He has some knowledge of the language these Indians speak and can help you communicate with them."

Daniel shook hands with the man. "Very nice to meet you, Mr. Fox." What a relief to have someone who could understand the Indians. Thank God, there was a man who knew their languages. As much as Daniel wanted to form a bond with the prisoners through art, there was sometimes difficulty conveying what he meant, as well as what the natives tried to tell him.

"I'll leave you men, then." Lieutenant Pratt turned and strode away.

"So you're teaching them to draw?" Mr. Fox stuffed his hands in his pockets and rocked back on his heels. "No doubt some of them have experience with that already, having drawn on their teepees and inside caves."

"Yes, it does appear some have more skill than others." Daniel nodded toward Sun Dancer. "That one over there near the old man—he seems to know how to draw, even if he does have difficulty holding a pencil correctly."

"Of course. Where he came from, he probably used buffalo bone to draw with."

Mr. Fox faced the Indians and spoke a few words which Daniel assumed was a greeting. A couple nodded their heads.

"Do they all understand you?" Daniel watched the Indian's reactions.

"Most. I can speak Cheyenne and Kiowa—that's the two biggest groups here."

"Sun Dancer is Cheyenne, isn't that right?"

"Yes, and so are the others with him." He pointed out the group sitting around Sun Dancer. Nodding to another group, he said, "Those over there are Kiowa."

"No wonder they stay separated."

Fox crossed him arms. "They've fought each other before."

Daniel eyed the different groups. "I hope they'll be able to live together in peace now."

"They're on their best behavior here."

Sun Dancer's voice came across the room where he squatted beside the older man wrapped in the blanket. The younger Indian looked at Mr. Fox as he spoke and motioned to the sick man. Although the words were unintelligible to Daniel, he surmised the Indian was talking about the ailing man. Fox nodded and replied in the Indian's language.

"Is he saying something about that old Indian? He doesn't seem well."

"Yes, his name is Lone Bear. Sun Dancer said he's sick, needs medicine man."

"Isn't there a doctor coming to check on them?"

"Dr. Anderson has been here a couple of times. Don't know that he's been able to help him though. Too bad we can't make him more comfortable."

"I agree. Sleeping on these floors would make anyone sick. Not to mention how cold it is in these damp stone rooms."

"I'll speak to Lieutenant Pratt and see what we can do." Fox spoke a few more words to Sun Dancer who in turn spoke to the ailing man beside him. Then patting Lone Bear on the shoulder, Sun Dancer stood and walked back to his drawing.

Daniel and Fox strolled around the room watching the Indians who sat cross-legged on the ground drawing on the ledgers in front of them. Daniel and the interpreter stopped beside a group where one Indian worked on a scene.

"Tell him he's doing good job," Daniel said to Fox.

Fox spoke a few words and the Indian acknowledged him with a nod.

"His name is Zotom. He's Kiowa."

"Looks like he's trying to draw a train."

Fox propped his elbow on the opposite arm as he studied the drawing. "Yes, I believe you're right."

Zotom painstakingly drew straight lines as he made a row of train cars on what appeared to be tracks.

"Fascinating. Wonder why he's drawing a train?" Daniel restrained himself from giving the Indian instruction. Perhaps when they trusted him, he would offer to help. Right now, though, he didn't want to interfere with their creativity.

"Who knows? The only train he's been on was the one that brought him here."

The train took shape as Zotom drew what appeared to be the engine at the front of the train.

"He's quite talented." Daniel noted the symmetry of the drawings, the perspective of the scene. Next, Zotom drew a row of trees lined up behind the train. The black and white sketch was impressive, but some color would be nice. Daniel would bring some color pencils next time.

Zotom raised his head and studied the soldiers standing near the doorway, then he began to draw some stick figures in the foreground of the train, clothing each one in a uniform.

"Ah, soldiers guarding the train, no doubt." Fox assessed the connection between the drawing and the Indian's focus on the life-size models.

Soon all the soldiers in the picture held rifles chest-high.

"Are the soldiers aiming at the train?" Daniel cringed inside as the peaceful scene took on a hostile tone. Did the Indians expect to be shot?

Zotom sketched a couple of figures behind the train next. One was another soldier with a gun. The other was lying down. When Zotom picked up a sharp rock and made a thin gash across his forearm, Daniel gasped.

"What…?" But before he could finish his sentence, the Indian squeezed a few drops of blood from his arm and applied it to the figure lying on the picture. Alarm raced through Daniel at the implication. The soldiers had shot someone.

"Grey Beard," Fox stated. He spoke to Zotom in his native dialect, and the Indian responded with a slow nod.

"Mr. Fox, please tell me about this drawing."

"We had an incident on the way here. One of the Indians, Grey Beard, attempted to escape from the train and run away. He was shot and killed."

"Dear God." Daniel shook his head. "No wonder they're afraid."

"Guess they think a soldier could shoot them any time. However, Grey Beard wanted to die."

"What makes you say that? If he was trying to run away, maybe he wanted to live free instead of being in prison."

"You're right, but he knew he'd get shot. He told Lieutenant Pratt he didn't want to live if he was going to be a prisoner. When he ran, Pratt didn't want the soldiers to kill him, but he couldn't stop them from shooting. Shortly before his death, he'd asked Pratt to write a letter to his wife."

Zotom looked up at Fox and murmured something in his language.

"What did he say?"

"He said 'Grey Beard is free now'."

Chapter Ten

"Mrs. Miller, your workmanship is remarkable." Mrs. Worthington held out the new black straw hat festooned with purple satin folds, revolving it slowly in her hand as she studied the details. She touched the satin bows nestled in the brim and stroked the soft ribbon streamers that ran down the back.

"So you're pleased with the hat?" Cora resisted the urge to jump up and down like her daughter would, clapping her hands like a schoolgirl.

"It's wonderful, stunning. You have exceeded my expectations."

"I'm so happy you're pleased with the hat." What an understatement. "Here, let me help you try it on."

The older woman untied her own bonnet in preparation. Cora set the new hat atop the puffs and thick braids of her patron's hair, tilting the brim forward so that the rear of the hat rose several inches higher than the front. Cora tied the purple ribbon in a large, soft bow at the woman's neck, then stepped back to admire the result.

"Here's a mirror so you can see for yourself how well it becomes you." Cora handed Mrs. Worthington a silver handled mirror, her heart fluttering at the smile on the woman's face when she saw her reflection.

"Judith, let's see yours." Mrs. Worthington turned to her daughter, who had already taken off her dull brown hat, replaced it with the new beige straw one and was standing in front of the wall mirror.

Judith turned to face the other ladies, a shy smile working its way onto her lips. "Do you approve, Mother?"

"Oh, my, yes. Absolutely! It is just perfect for you. Highly complementary."

"May I adjust the elastic?" Cora accepted Judith's nod as an answer and slipped the large elastic loop behind her head and under the girl's thick braids to hold the hat on. Judith had chosen the doll-hat design that was popular with the younger women. The small hat's brim was barely visible beneath two hues of green satin ribbon adorning the top. A large bow accented the back of the hat and featured the ivory pin Judith had chosen. Two quail feathers emerged from the ribbon on one side of the hat.

Judith's cheeks flushed with pride. "Mother, I really do like it. Do you think I can have a dress made to match it?"

Mrs. Worthington chuckled, something Cora hadn't seen her do before.

"That's a marvelous idea, Judith. When we return to Boston, we can have our seamstress create a dress suitable for such a lovely hat."

Judith's lip formed a pout. "Must we wait so long? I'd like to wear the hat sooner than that."

"Dear, it won't be so long. We'll probably go home next month."

Next month? Cora's heart stopped. They mustn't leave so soon.

"Maybe I can find a way to help in the meantime. Tell me what the wardrobe you brought here with you looks like, and perhaps I can add a touch that will work with the hat."

"You could do that?" Judith's eyes widened.

"Of course. I can add a flower, ribbons or something else to one of your dresses or blouses that match these on the hat."

"What a brilliant idea." Mrs. Worthington nodded approval.

"But how… I can't bring my trousseau here."

"Mrs. Miller will have to come to our room at the hotel and take a look at your clothes. Would you be so kind to do that for us, Mrs. Miller?"

"I…of course." Cora stammered to reply as she tried to digest the invitation to their hotel room. "When would you like me to come by?"

"Can you meet us for tea this afternoon? Judith can show you her clothes then."

"Do you mind if I bring Emily with me? She'll be out of school by then."

"Of course, we don't mind! She's a charming child. In fact, she reminds me of my two granddaughters, my older son Henry's girls."

"Then, yes, I'll be delighted to come. I'll bring some ribbons and a few accessories that might help coordinate the hat with your clothes."

"Wonderful!" Mrs. Worthington reached into her bag and pulled out a handful of bills and presented them to Cora. "I believe this will adequately compensate you for your work, Mrs. Miller. This will cover the hats, and I'll also pay you for embellishing Judith's wardrobe when you finish. Let me know if you disagree."

Cora accepted the money, afraid to count it. She could tell from just the size of the stack that the payment was generous.

"I'm sure it's sufficient." Cora closed her hand over the money to make sure it wouldn't take wings and fly away before placing it in the pocket fold of her dress. She didn't want to appear too eager to count it but would do so when she moved it to her cash box after the ladies left. "Thank you very much, Mrs. Worthington. I do appreciate your letting me design the hats for you and Judith. I truly have enjoyed doing that for you."

"Oh, thank you! You're a very talented woman. I could keep you quite busy if you lived in Boston. My friends would love to receive your services."

Satisfaction bubbled up in Cora. She never considered moving somewhere else. After all, she'd only been here a short time, but the compliment was beyond her expectations. Maybe Mrs. Worthington would send her friends to St. Augustine.

"Why, what a nice thing to say." Cora helped the ladies remove the new hats, then placed each of them in a hat box. "I doubt I'll be leaving St. Augustine though." She handed the black corded handles of the round boxes to each woman. As they turned to leave, Mrs. Worthington addressed Cora.

"We'll see you at four o'clock. Ask the hotel clerk where to find our room, and we'll have our tea out on the balcony."

Cora nodded. "I look forward to it."

As the door closed behind them, Cora's heart thumped against her rib cage. Like a miner striking gold, she could hardly contain her excitement. She carefully removed the bundle of dollars from her pocket and went behind her glass case to count it, just in case someone walking by her storefront saw her. She opened the stack and gasped at the total—$25.00. She could pay for two months' rent on the store as well as their room at the boarding house with that much money. Taking a key from her reticule, she opened a drawer and pulled out her cash box, unlocked it and tucked the money inside before relocking the box and returning it to the drawer. Only then did she allow herself to breathe.

The bell on her door startled her as it opened and in rushed Lucy Abbott.

Chapter Eleven

"Mrs. Miller! I'm so glad to see you're not busy! I—we need your help!"

Cora's mouth gaped. "My help?"

"Yes!" The woman was breathless, as if she'd been running. "Dear Mrs. Jones has taken ill, the other ladies went to Lincolnville, and there's no one else we can turn to. Then Mrs. Anderson remembered that you said you wanted to help us."

A heavy weight pulled down inside Cora's chest with the dread of realization. "That's true, I did." Taking a deep breath, she said, "What do you need me to do?"

"Why, help me take things to the Indians at the fort, of course. I'm so glad you agreed to participate in our mission."

Cora's stomach began to get queasy. "Oh. Well, if I have time, of course. When did you need me to go?"

"Right away. My buggy is waiting outside."

Cora gripped the edge of the countertop. "Right now? But ..."

Dressed in a brown and black striped jacket and skirt with a black lace choker on which was suspended an exquisite ivory cameo, Miss Abbott glanced around the store. "What a fortunate time, when you're not busy with customers!"

Cora wanted to lie to the woman, tell her she had something to work on, but truth was, she didn't. She had no plans except for tea that afternoon with the Worthington ladies. And nothing would interfere with her keeping that commitment. Nothing. But she was trapped. She'd offered to help, yet she'd hoped they wouldn't ask her to go to the fort in person.

"I do have a commitment later this afternoon that I must keep, plus I'll need to be back before my daughter gets home from school." Surely, those were reasonable excuses.

"Don't you worry. You'll be back in plenty of time. It shouldn't take more than an hour to go to the fort and handle our affairs there. So, can you leave now? My buggy is loaded with the blankets we'll take." She motioned toward the street.

Cora followed her gaze and saw the horse-drawn buggy through the glass window, a trunk strapped on behind the cab.

"I suppose I can spare a little time." Cora took her hat and shawl off the peg and put them on in front of the wall mirror, then grabbed her reticule and trailed Lucy Abbott out the door. As Miss Abbott climbed into the buggy, Cora locked the front door, then went around and climbed in the other side of the vehicle.

The morning drizzle had ended, but the heavy clouds that brought it still hung over the city, cloaking the atmosphere with humid air. As they rode the short blocks to the fort, Miss Abbott continued to thank Cora for her help.

"It's volunteers like you that make such a difference in the lives of the less fortunate. God will surely bless you for your charitable acts."

Cora stared out at the bay beside them as they rode past, guilt haunting her conscience. She didn't deserve any praise and was thankful Miss Abbott couldn't see her true feelings. How could she say "no" though, especially if she wanted to stay in the good graces of the women in the organization? *Lord, please forgive my selfish motives.*

A humid breeze blew off the water, doing little to dry the moisture on her face. Each step of the horse's hooves crunching seashells that comprised the road pounded her heart in dreaded anticipation. When she turned to face the front of the buggy, the huge masonry fort loomed ahead, sending a shudder rippling through her. What horrors lay inside the imposing structure?

Miss Abbott guided the horse to the front of the fort, pulling in the reins to a stop at the foot of a small hill. The petite woman climbed out and bravely walked up to the drawbridge leading to the demi-lune, the small fort-like building that led to the larger fort behind. Two uniformed soldiers stood at the entrance as Miss

Abbott approached.

"Sir, Lieutenant Pratt is expecting us. We're bringing blankets to the Indians. Can you please help us carry our trunk in?" She indicated the buggy.

Cora marveled at the woman's boldness, a characteristic she'd also like to master.

"Yes, ma'am." The soldiers approached the buggy and walked around to the rear.

"You can get out now, Mrs. Miller."

Cora jumped at the sound of her name being called and noticed Miss Abbott motioning for her to come. She stepped out of the buggy with leaden feet and joined the other woman to wait for the two soldiers carrying the trunk.

"If you'll follow us, ladies." One of the soldiers waved his hand to the short drawbridge which led into the stone walls of the ravelin. On the other side, the walls ended at another drawbridge. The soldiers walked across, then placed the trunk on the ground beneath the sally port, the main entrance to the fort. What measures the early builders of the fort had gone to in order to keep their enemies from getting in. Much less effort would have kept Cora out.

The soldiers with the trunk spoke to the soldiers standing guard at the entrance, who nodded and took over at that point. The odor of stagnant water reached her from the moat below that separated the fort and the ravelin. She looked up to catch fresh air and eyed the Spanish coat of arms engraved into the wall above the entrance. When she'd first arrived in town, she was as attracted by the mystique of the medieval fortress as other tourists who came to the area. No longer did she find the place attractive.

God, let this be over quickly. As Cora entered the sally port and gazed up at the heavy iron gate that comprised the portcullis, she shivered at the possibility that it could come down and she might not get back out. *Cora, you must stop thinking like that.* Why would they want to keep her? She wasn't a criminal.

Miss Abbott's voice caught her attention. "Does Lieutenant Pratt know we're here?"

"Yes, ma'am, someone's gone to tell him. Please wait here."

"I expect he'll escort us to the Indians," Miss Abbott said.

Just the reminder of the natives she was about to see made

Cora's stomach flip. How close to them would she have to be?

The soldier nodded, then focused his attention on the figure walking across the open courtyard. He snapped to attention and saluted as the man drew near. The officer she recognized as Lieutenant Pratt approached.

"Ladies. Miss Abbott, nice to see you again." The officer touched the brim of his hat. "I understand you've brought some things for the Indian prisoners."

"Yes, sir, Lieutenant Pratt. I'd like to introduce you to a new member of our benevolent society, Mrs. Miller."

Cora liked the way "new member" sounded. She gave a slight bow as Lieutenant Pratt nodded. "Nice to make your acquaintance, Mrs. Miller." Lieutenant Pratt motioned across the courtyard. "If you'll follow me, I'll take you to the prisoners. I'm sure you'd like to hand out your donations yourselves." As if reading Cora's mind, he added, "We'll be with you, so you needn't be afraid of these people. They haven't tried to harm anyone since they've been here."

Why did Cora think he left out the word "yet?"

Cora and Miss Abbott hurried to keep up with the lieutenant as he strode across the open area as soldiers carrying the trunk followed behind them. When they reached one of the arched entries, the lieutenant entered and motioned for the others to come in as well. The soldiers placed the trunk on the floor, then were dismissed.

With a start, Cora realized she was in a room with Indians sitting cross-legged on the bare floor. She stared at the sullen faces who returned her stare with as much enthusiasm as she conveyed herself.

"Mr. Worthington, Mr. Fox, I'd like to introduce you to Miss Lucy Abbott and Mrs. Miller. These ladies are from the benevolent society and have brought some things to the Indians."

Cora gaped at the sight of Daniel Worthington. Their gazes locked, and a smile eased across his strong features as heat rushed to her face. Something akin to relief at seeing his familiar face settled her nerves a bit. Yet these surroundings must be so foreign to the life he was accustomed to.

The two men crossed the room to the ladies. "Welcome," Mr. Fox said. "I'm an Indian interpreter, and this gentleman here is an art teacher." He swept his arm around the room. "The Indians have been busy drawing."

For the first time, Cora noticed that the Indians held books in their laps. She glanced at Mr. Worthington and caught a twinkle in his eye. He had accomplished what he set out to do and seemed pleased with himself.

"So what did you ladies bring?" Mr. Fox eyed the trunk with interest.

Miss Abbott knelt beside the trunk and opened it to reveal blankets and quilts folded inside. "We have something we hope will make them more comfortable." She retrieved a blanket and handed it to Cora. "Cora, why don't you give one of these to that Indian there?"

Cora shrank back. She was actually supposed to hand the cover to an Indian?

Mr. Worthington must've sensed her fear, because he stepped forward and took the blanket from her. "I'll give it to him."

Cora thanked Mr. Worthington with her eyes, but she hated herself for being so fearful and helpless. She reached into the trunk for a thick quilt, this time praying for the right person to give it to. One of the Indians stood and approached her, hand extended. She tensed as the tall young Indian reached for the quilt. With the trepidation of feeding a wild animal, she forced herself to hand it to him. His dark eyes penetrated her own as if he could read her mind as he took the quilt and nodded what she assumed was a thank-you, then retreated back across the room.

What he did next startled her.

He carried the quilt to an older Indian lying on the floor, removed the ragged blanket the man was wrapped in and covered him with the new blanket, tucking it in tightly around him. The older Indian coughed, then mumbled to the young one who patted him on the back before returning to his spot on the ground. She and Mr. Worthington exchanged glances, a hint of sadness in his eyes.

When all the blankets and quilts had been passed out, Miss Abbott closed the trunk and stood.

"We'll bring some more as soon as we can gather them. Many of our ladies are working on others. I do hope they help. It's quite chilly in here."

"We were just discussing the situation before you ladies

arrived," Lieutenant Pratt said. "I'm going to secure approval to build some sleeping quarters for these prisoners on top of the wall."

"Is that so?" Miss Abbott eyed the officer with surprise. "That would be very humanitarian of you, Lieutenant Pratt."

The lieutenant shook his head as he motioned to the soldiers by the door. "Humans should be treated as humans. These are people, not animals."

"And God loves us all," Miss Abbott added, with a nod of affirmation as the soldiers came to get the trunk.

As Cora and Miss Abbott moved toward the door, Mr. Worthington stepped alongside Cora.

"It was a nice surprise to see you here."

Despite the damp chill of the structure, heat flushed through her body.

She glanced at Mr. Worthington, then behind him at the old Indian, whose frame shook each time he coughed. What kind of ailment did the man have?

"Is he very sick?"

"Yes, I fear so." Mr. Worthington turned to look at the Indian. "I hope Lieutenant Pratt can provide better housing for them soon." His serious expression softened as he faced her again. "Thank you for the warm quilt. I'm sure it will provide some comfort."

Cora stepped out of the room following the others, then glanced over her shoulder at Mr. Worthington, who had stopped at the opening. He raised his hand in farewell before she turned back around and followed Miss Abbott and Lieutenant Pratt toward the sally port.

Sun rays pierced the clouds as they walked back to the buggy, promising an end to the gloom of the morning. As Cora climbed into the vehicle, she watched the sun glisten off moisture trickling down the walls of the fort, brightening the dull gray stones. She exhaled a sigh of relief that she had survived the experience. Yet, instead of being happy to be outside the confines of the prison, the image of the young Indian taking the quilt to the old Indian lingered in her mind, the tenderness of the act stirring her emotions. Daniel Worthington had given her credit for bringing the quilt, but her effort was anything but charitable. It was the young

Indian who truly exemplified charity.

Could it be possible that a savage could be more caring than a civilized woman like herself?

~

Daniel stood in the entrance of the casement for some time, still focused on the place he'd last seen Cora Miller as she left the fort. The woman was an enigma. His first impression of her had not been very favorable. Not that she wasn't attractive. On the contrary, the little blonde woman was interesting, if not puzzling. Outside the confines of the fort, she was spirited and assertive, maybe even courageous. She had stood up to his mother with confidence and self-assurance.

Yet, here within the walls of the fort-turned-prison, a different personality presented itself. She'd seemed fearful and timid among the Indians. At first, she'd even appeared to be somewhat condescending toward the natives. However, he sensed a change in her attitude as her dainty gloved hands handed out the blankets. Especially when Sun Dancer committed such a kind gesture toward Lone Bear. He'd never forget the wide-eyed expression on her face when she observed the deed. She'd even expressed concern for the old Indian before she left. Was she showing sympathy or curiosity?

He'd wanted to have further discussions about the Indians with her, now that she'd seen them firsthand. But he wasn't certain she wanted to have such a conversation. She'd left in a hurry, as if she feared being left behind. He stared at the memory of her walking away, her shawl held tightly around her shoulders. Then he dropped his gaze to the ground and kicked some loose stones at his feet.

Why did he care to know her better? Was it because he wanted to share his burden for the Indians with someone else? Considering her hasty exit, one might assume she had no interest in the Indians' affairs, much less returning to see them again. Yet, he'd seen a spark of compassion in her eyes. Perhaps he could kindle that spark, if he had a chance.

"Mr. Worthington?" Mr. Fox's voice interrupted his thoughts. "The Indians need to get to the classroom now. What would you like for them to do with these ledger books?"

"Can you tell them to write their names on the bottom of their work, so we'll know whose drawings are whose?"

Mr. Fox interpreted the question in native dialect, holding up one of the books and pointing to the bottom.

The Indians nodded, then wrote something on the paper. As Daniel strolled around observing their work, he noticed they wrote with symbols.

"Can you read these?" Daniel pointed to the marks on one book.

"I'll ask them their name, then write it in English beside it. Perhaps someday, they'll be able to write in our language."

Daniel stood over Sun Dancer, studying the crude drawing of a horse with an Indian astride. The Indian wore a long headdress and carried a lance.

"Is this you?" Daniel pointed to the figure and then to Sun Dancer. "Sun Dancer?"

The Indian nodded and pointed, then spoke.

"Did he say, 'Sun Dancer'?"

Mr. Fox asked the Indian to repeat, pointing to the picture.

"No, he said his name is 'Making Medicine.' He doesn't wish to be called Sun Dancer anymore."

"Making Medicine?"

The Indian nodded and pointed to Lone Bear, who was sitting up and watching.

"So he wants to make Lone Bear well?" Daniel asked Fox.

"Yes. He said he made medicine in his village and would do it again if he had the right ingredients."

"I wish we knew what the ingredients were. Perhaps we can procure them."

"I'll try to find out, but we may not have anything comparable in this part of the country, especially if they're herbs and such."

"Tell him we'll see what we can do to find the right supplies."

"Shouldn't we ask Lieutenant Pratt first?" Mr. Fox stuffed his hands in his pockets.

"I suppose we should. But why would he resist the idea? He wants to treat the Indians humanely, doesn't he?"

Mr. Fox shrugged. "Yes, he does, even though many disagree with his reasoning."

Fox helped Daniel collect the ledger books, then spoke to the Indians who rose to their feet. They formed a crude line and waited for the next command.

Mr. Fox extended his hand to Daniel. "I'm impressed with your work with these men. Their willingness to participate is encouraging."

Daniel shook his hand. "I suppose no one expected there to be artists among them."

"Not in prison, anyway." Fox called to the soldiers at the entry, who took their place at the front and back of the line of Indians. "Take these men to the classroom."

Making Medicine helped Lone Bear to his feet and join the others. As they filed out, Making Medicine looked at Daniel and pointed to himself.

"Making Medicine." The words came out slowly and deliberately in broken English.

Daniel nodded. "Making Medicine."

Sometimes acts of kindness were as good as medicine.

Chapter Twelve

Cora couldn't get out of Miss Abbott's carriage fast enough. There. She'd done her good deed, so now they couldn't exclude her from the society. After all, hadn't Miss Abbott said she was a new member? With the task behind her, she could concentrate on more pleasant endeavors. Thank goodness, she had her meeting with Mrs. Worthington and Judith to look forward to this afternoon. The prospect of having tea with the women in their rooms and seeing their fine wardrobe sent a thrill through her.

She unlocked the shop, then reached for her box of ribbons to find the spool she'd used for Judith's hat. Looking about her, she considered what other accessories might coordinate that she could add to a dress. As she surveyed her button drawer, the glint of colorful glass buttons caught her eye. The multicolored buttons resembled jewels when they caught the light and sparkled, a perfect complement to a variety of fabrics. She'd always fancied these buttons she'd bought on a whim, saving them for a special creation. But they weren't right for Judith, as she was accustomed to real jewels instead of shiny buttons.

She glanced at her Seth Thomas shelf clock, one of the few items she'd brought from her home in Philadelphia, stuffed the notions in her reticule, and rushed out. There was scant time to get Emily from school and make one more trip before she was due at the St. Augustine Hotel for her meeting with the Worthingtons. She locked the door and hurried down the street to the school, arriving just in time for the dismissal as children dashed out of the building. She waved Emily over, who exited while chatting with another little girl.

"Momma!" Emily ran across the yard. "Bye, Anna!" She raised her hand to her friend before reaching her mother and embracing her with a hug.

Cora patted her daughter on the back. "Did you have a good day at school?"

"Yes, Momma! And I met a new friend—Anna. She said her family has lots of money."

Cora frowned. How odd that a child would mention something like that.

"That's nice, Emily." She steered the girl toward the square. "Is she new in town?"

"Yes. Her family moved here to be near her grandmother."

"Is that right? Do you know her grandmother's name?"

"I forget, but she's that lady that was in your shop when Mr. Sterling brought me home."

"Mrs. Anderson?"

"Yes, that's her." Emily watched the other children leave. "Can I go to her house and play someday?"

"Perhaps. If you're invited." Would her child be invited to play with Mrs. Anderson's grandchild? Or would she frown upon a child that lived in a boarding house? Cora wondered if her status as a new member of the benevolent society would matter. She took Emily's hand and headed down the sidewalk.

"Where are we going, Momma?"

"I have a surprise for you."

"You do? What is it?" Emily looked about Cora for a clue.

"We're going to pick out some material for new dresses—one for you and one for me!"

Emily's bright smile warmed Cora's heart. "Oh, Momma! Pink, can we have pink?"

"We'll have to see what kind of piece goods the mercantile has in stock. I'm sure we can find something pretty."

"Can we have matching dresses?"

"Maybe. We'll see. But we mustn't take too long there. We are joining Mrs. Worthington and Miss Judith for tea at the hotel."

Emily danced around her. "Ooh. Will they have cookies?"

"I'm sure they will."

At the Smith's Mercantile, Cora and Emily searched through

bolts of fabric stacked on the shelves. Neither could agree on one they liked, especially something suitable for both of their dresses.

Cora shook her head. "I don't really see anything here I care for, and we don't have time to look any more. Perhaps we should see if the other mercantile has some material." She turned to leave, her heart twisting at the look of disappointment on Emily's face.

"Ma'am," the store clerk called out from the back of the store, hurrying toward them carrying some bolts of cloth. "These just arrived. Perhaps you'd like to look at them before you go." He laid the bolts on a table beside Cora.

Cora pushed aside the first, then the second bolt, but stopped at the third, her heart lifting at the beautiful light shade of violet. Running her hand along the soft lightweight muslin, she smiled, envisioning the lovely dresses it would make for herself and Emily.

"Emily, what do you think about this one?"

Emily turned her attention away from the display of parasols and looked. "Oh, Momma. It's so pretty! Can we get it? Please, please?"

"Yes." Cora considered the design she planned to make, allowing for the bustle and ruffles, as well as, Emily's smaller dress. She turned to the clerk. "I'll take eighteen yards, please."

"We're going to be the most beautiful momma and daughter in town!" Emily pirouetted and curtseyed, assuming her "most beautiful" poses.

"You're already the most beautiful daughter." Cora adjusted the ribbon on Emily's bonnet while waiting for the clerk to cut the fabric.

"Can we get a new parasol too?" Emily pointed to the display.

"Not today. I'll take a look at ours and see if they need some fresh lace." Some nice lace would accent the dresses too. Cora moved to the lace display and found a wide, ruffled edge ivory lace that would work well for the collar and cuffs of the bodice. "I'd like to get this too. I'll take the whole roll." She handed the lace to the clerk, thankful for the money Mrs. Worthington had paid her.

Much as Cora wanted to spend more time perusing the accessories, she didn't want to be late for tea time. She paid for her purchases, then asked for the heavy bundle to be delivered to the boarding house. Cutting off a piece of the fabric in case she needed to match it to anything, she stuffed it in her reticule before she and Emily headed across the plaza. Truth be told, she was as excited as Emily about having a new dress. The more she considered shedding the somber colors of widowhood, the more eager she grew. After her experience at the fort, pretty colors were a welcome change. The day seemed brighter as she squashed the dismal image of the Indians and replaced it with visions of strolling through town wearing something fashionable and attractive.

After considering Katie's comment, she was ready to add more joy to her life. Even though she was already thirty years old, she didn't need to appear like a somber old matron. Would anyone notice her change to brighter colors? The scene of Daniel Worthington at the fort flashed through her mind, the intensity of his eyes as he looked at her, as if trying to read her thoughts. Thank God, he couldn't. But why think about him now? All he was concerned about were the Indians. He wouldn't even notice if she changed her dress style.

As they stepped into the hotel lobby, she heard laughter coming from the direction of the billiards room. Was that Sterling? She smiled as she anticipated his reaction when she wore her new clothes. Surely he would take notice. Now she was anxious to get home and begin working on them. At the front desk, the hotel clerk gave her the room number for the Worthingtons and pointed to the stairs. She and Emily climbed to the top floor and found the correct room. Hot from hiking up the stairs, she stopped to fan herself before tapping on the door. She knocked twice and waited for a response.

A voice inside called, "Come in!" But as she reached for the knob, it opened, and Judith greeted them.

"We're out on the balcony. Please join us." Judith appeared genuinely glad to see them showing a change in her former jealous attitude to Cora. No doubt she was more interested in whatever Cora had in mind for her wardrobe.

Emily skipped in ahead of Cora, eyes wide as she took in the room and headed for the open balcony doors.

"Emily, would you like a cookie?" Mrs. Worthington lifted a plate of cookies from the small table beside her chair on the balcony. "Judith, please pour our guests some lemonade. Or would you prefer tea?"

"Lemonade is fine for both of us." Cora smiled at Judith. "Thank you."

"Ooh. Tea cakes. My favorite!" Emily inspected the cookies before selecting the right one from the plate as Cora followed her out onto the balcony.

A breeze of salty air from the bay greeted her outside. "Good afternoon, Mrs. Worthington. How refreshing it is up here."

"One of the best features of this hotel. Even when the heat is stifling down on the street, it's cool up here."

"Momma's going to make us new dresses that match!" Emily announced.

"Is that right?" Mrs. Worthington smiled at the little girl. "What color are they going to be?"

"It's a very pretty color!" Emily pranced along the railing, nibbling her cookie.

Mrs. Worthington cocked an eyebrow. "That so? May we see it?"

Cora was glad she asked, hoping the woman would approve. "Certainly, if you'd like. I have a piece of it with me." She opened her reticule and withdrew the fabric sample.

"Emily, you're right. It *is* a pretty color—reminds me of our lilacs back home." Mrs. Worthington touched the fabric, feeling it between her thumb and fingers. "This soft texture should be very comfortable and a nice weight for this tropical weather."

Sitting back, the woman gazed up at Cora and asked the inevitable question. "When did you lose your husband, Mrs. Miller?"

"It's been almost two years since Jacob passed away." She answered quietly so Emily wouldn't hear. As Judith felt the fabric, the thought occurred to Cora that Jacob's death seemed so long ago. Somehow, life had gone on without him.

Mrs. Worthington nodded. "So this will be your first dress out of mourning?"

"Yes. My cousin convinced me it's the proper time." Hopefully Mrs. Worthington would approve.

"She's right. And I'm sure you're ready to wear a more cheerful color. The material should make a lovely dress, and the color will complement both your and Emily's complexions and your blonde hair. Don't you agree, Judith?"

Judith nodded, a wistful look on her face.

"Thank you, I hope so." Cora set the bundle down, then seated herself and faced Judith. "Judith, I've been looking forward to seeing your dresses and how we can coordinate them with your new hat."

"Enjoy your refreshments first." Mrs. Worthington gazed out toward the bay. "Did you say your cousin lives over there on the island?"

Cora looked out toward the island, the black-and-white striped lighthouse standing tall above the foliage. "Yes, she lives on Anastasia. Her husband is the lighthouse keeper."

"I'd like to take an excursion over there. Do you think she'd mind?"

"Oh, no, of course not. There are tourists on the island all the time."

"Perhaps so, but I'd like you to introduce us." Mrs. Worthington sipped her lemonade. "I understand they're building a new keepers house. She must be pleased to have a new home."

"Maybe she'll show it to you!" Emily reached for another cookie. "May I have another, please?"

Cora wished her daughter hadn't suggested something that could be an imposition on Katie. "She's very pleased to have more room to accommodate a family with five daughters."

"Five? My, she does have a houseful." Mrs. Worthington faced Emily. "I'm sure you like to go visit them, don't you?"

"Yes, so we can play." The child's countenance dimmed. "But we can only go over there on the weekend when Momma doesn't have to work."

"Don't they ever come over here?"

Cora spoke up. "Yes, their father rows the older ones over for school every day, and they come to church on Sundays when possible."

"But it's more fun to go over there and play on the island." Emily pouted.

Rising from her chair, Cora adjusted her skirt, then moved toward the open door. "Judith, are you ready to show me your dresses?"

"First, I'll show you my day dresses." Judith rose and entered the room with Cora following. "We had them made for daily strolls and leisure activities. I'd like to wear the hat with at least one of these."

Cora remembered when she'd had dresses for every occasion too. But it hadn't seemed practical for her since she moved to St. Augustine. She hadn't been a lady of leisure for some time.

Judith moved to a large trunk and opened the lid. One by one, she pulled out five dresses and laid them across the bed. As Cora suspected, they were all in shades of brown. Cora studied them, tapping her finger on her chin.

She lifted the lightest colored bodice, a beige one that was trimmed with a satin lace collar in a deeper tan color. Her mind worked through the possibilities, regretting the time it would take to make the necessary changes and take away time from making her own dress. However, she wouldn't be paid to make her own dress.

"I have a couple of suggestions. I could embroider some flowers on this collar which would add color and add green leaves to match your hat. Or, I could find some buttons that have green in them and replace these down the front. Another idea would be to add a ribbon trim that matches the ribbon in your hat around the edge of the collar. Which would you prefer?" Cora hoped she'd choose the buttons, the quickest solution.

"All of those sound like good ideas to me," Mrs. Worthington said, standing at the open doorway to the balcony.

"May I see?" Emily bounded into the room, stopping to gawk at the dresses on the bed. "You have a lot of dresses!"

Cora frowned at Emily, hoping she'd get the hint that her comment was not appropriate.

"How would it look if you made all those changes? Would it be too much?" Judith smiled at Cora.

Cora groaned to herself at the prospect. "Yes, I suppose I could." Why hadn't she made Judith a brown hat instead? "Perhaps I can add the embroidery to this bodice and add the ribbon and buttons to that other one." She pointed to another, taupe-colored bodice. "That way, you could wear it with two outfits."

Judith answered with a huge smile. "I would love that. Don't you think so, Mother?"

A tap on the door was followed by the creak of it opening.

"Sorry to be late for tea, Mother." Mr. Worthington entered, then halted as he took in the scene before him. "Did I interrupt something?" He removed his hat, glancing from Cora to Judith to his mother, then back to Cora. "Excuse me. Good afternoon, Mrs. Miller. Nice to see you again so soon."

"Mrs. Miller came by to look at Judith's dresses."

Cora's pulse quickened at his gaze. "I'm going to embellish Judith's dresses to match her new hat."

"I see." Mr. Worthington faced his mother. "So I missed tea?"

"Not really. Too hot for tea, but we have some lemonade in a pitcher on the balcony." Mrs. Worthington turned to Emily. "Did you leave him any cookies?" At the girl's nod, she said, "Why don't you go outside with him and show him where they are?"

Emily smiled and skipped to the door of the balcony, beckoning Mr. Worthington to follow.

~

The cool lemonade soothed Daniel's throat. He hadn't realized how thirsty he was. When had it become so dry? When he saw Mrs. Miller? His pulse quickened when he saw her in the room, most likely from surprise at finding her there. He gazed across the open water watching pelicans dive, landing with a splash.

"You should see the pretty material Momma bought today. She's going to make me a dress and make one for her too."

Daniel started at the sound of the tinkling voice from the little girl beside him. He glanced down, seeing a miniature of the girl's mother in the same bright blue eyes and blonde ringlets. "Is that so?"

"Yes!" Emily ran over and picked up the scrap of fabric, then took it to Daniel. "You can look at it if you want."

"Oh, it is a nice color." He was surprised it wasn't black and couldn't imagine a pretty black, much less making the child a dress that color.

"Momma says the color is orchid, like a flower."

"Orchid, huh? Well, that does sound pretty. And your mother's going to have a dress the same color?"

"Uh-huh. We're going to match!" Emily beamed as she spread her arms wide.

Mrs. Miller was shedding her widow attire? How interesting.

His mother's voice behind him caught his attention as she

stepped out on the balcony.

"What did you mean about 'seeing Mrs. Miller again so soon'? Where did you see each other?"

"She came to the fort today while I was there. She and another lady from the benevolence society arrived to give blankets to the Indians. I was conducting an art class with them at the time."

"Is that right?" She looked over her shoulder at Mrs. Miller talking with Judith. "Mrs. Miller is a busy lady."

"Indeed she is." Daniel admired such an enterprising woman. And apparently, a caring person as well, if he'd interpreted her reaction to Lone Bear today correctly. His first impression of her was quite the opposite.

Mrs. Miller looked up, then blushed under his gaze when she caught him looking at her.

She lifted a bodice, folded it carefully. "Do you have something I can carry this in? I'm afraid I forgot to bring anything larger than my reticule."

His sister glanced around the room, then spotted a carpetbag. "Yes, you may use this. Or we can have the hotel deliver them to you."

Mrs. Miller took the bag and placed two folded garments inside. "I can carry this. I'll return it tomorrow."

"Oh, no hurry. We won't need that until we leave."

Mrs. Miller walked to the balcony door avoiding Daniel's gaze. "Emily, we must go now." Turning to Mrs. Worthington, she said, "Thank you for having us for tea. I'll get right to work on Judith's bodices. I think she'll be pleased with the results."

Daniel stepped forward. "May I escort you home?"

Mrs. Miller's eyes met his. "Thank you, but that's not necessary."

"It'd be my pleasure." He reached for the carpetbag. "Let me carry that for you."

"Thank you," she said, handing the bag over. "Come, Emily. Say 'thank you.'"

"Thank you!" Emily skipped in from the balcony and across the room.

Daniel followed Mrs. Miller to the door and opened it, motioning her to exit in front of him. Maybe now they could have the conversation he'd wished for earlier.

Chapter Thirteen

"Emily, please don't run down the stairs." Mrs. Miller called to her daughter as she disappeared around the landing.

Daniel chuckled as he watched the top of the pert straw hat vanish from view. "Can't keep up with that pace."

In front of him, Mrs. Miller shook her head, talking back over her shoulder. "Sometimes I wonder if I'll ever make a lady out of her."

"Of course you will. But surely, you've run down stairs before?" An image of Mrs. Miller as a child looked just like her daughter.

"I'm afraid to admit that's true. In a houseful of five children, we were always scrambling up and down, in and out. I can't imagine how my mother survived all the ruckus. It's difficult enough with just one child."

"So I suppose you never wanted that many children too."

"I'm afraid that decision was out of my hands."

Daniel mentally kicked himself for such a personal statement. He cleared his throat as they reached the bottom of the stairs where young Emily waited, looking up at them. He stuffed his hands in his pockets. "I'm sorry, I didn't mean to be so impertinent."

"I won!" Emily pranced away, skipping through the lobby toward the front door.

"Emily Miller, you wait right there." Mrs. Miller hurried to reach her daughter's side.

At this rate, Daniel feared his desired-for conversation might not occur. A few strides and he was abreast of Mrs. Miller. The doorway stood open so the fresh ocean breezes could invade the hotel space and cool the interior. Daniel nodded toward the two men behind the long front desk counter on his way out the building.

"Are you going to your home or your shop?" He wasn't certain where the boarding house was, but was willing to accompany her to either, if it allowed extra time to find out more about her.

"We'll be going back to the boarding house, but you don't have to accompany us."

"Please, allow me. Would you like to take a little detour and walk beside the water on the way? The temperature is much more pleasant by the bay."

"Yes, that would be nice." Mrs. Miller motioned to Emily. "Emily, let's go this way."

The afternoon sun shone golden across the water as it gilded the edges of puffy clouds. Seagulls squawked and hovered over fishing boats out in the bay as people strolled along the top of the seawall, a favorite pastime of tourists.

"Momma! May we walk on the seawall too?" Emily headed for the low coquina and cement wall that separated the bay from town.

"Emily, please don't. I wouldn't want you to fall in."

"But Momma. Look at all those people. They're not falling in."

Suddenly Emily started giggling and pointed toward someone on the seawall.

"Emily, that's not good manners."

"It's Mr. Sterling, Momma! Look how funny he looks!"

Sure enough, Sterling Cunningham sauntered along the seawall toward them, twirling a cane like a baton.

"Hello!" He waved his cane at them and Emily ran to meet him.

"Mr. Sterling! Your hat is funny!" Emily pointed to Sterling's large palmetto hat draped in Spanish moss.

Daniel gritted his teeth. Why did Sterling have to show up at such inopportune times?

And why did he have to act so absurd? He always had to be the center of attention.

"Don't you like my hat, Emily? Isn't it as nice as one of your mother's creations?"

Emily giggled. "No, it isn't! Why did you put moss on your hat?"

"It's fashionable, don't you know? I rather like it." Sterling winked at Emily, then gazed up at her mother. "Don't you like it, Cora?"

Cora? Daniel's insides cringed. What right did he have to use her given name? Were they so familiar with each other?

"It suits you, Sterling. However, none of my customers desire Spanish moss on their hats or bonnets." Mrs. Miller's eyes twinkled as her hand covered her mouth, as if suppressing a giggle. "They prefer something more exotic."

"More exotic? My dear lady, from where I hail, this moss *is* exotic." Sterling swaggered atop the seawall pointing his cane at Daniel. "Daniel, why the long face? Are you sad because you don't have a hat like mine? Or maybe you'd like one of these fine orange-wood canes."

"I don't need a cane to keep my balance, Sterling, but I can see you do." Surely, Mrs. Miller could tell he was tipsy. Yet, she appeared to enjoy his theatrics. "Where's the cigar box with the baby alligator in it?" Daniel muttered under his breath. If Sterling was buying all the popular tourist souvenirs, he'd probably buy one of those disgusting things too.

"Wouldn't you all like to join me for a stroll along this fine promenade?" Sterling swept his arms and gestured to the seawall stretching out a mile before him. "Tis the thing to do, especially during the moonlight." Sterling punctuated his statement with a wink at Mrs. Miller.

Her face matching the rosy hue of the sunset, Mrs. Miller's eyes widened.

"Momma, can we? Can I get up there with Mr. Sterling?" Emily headed toward the seawall.

"No, Emily." Mrs. Miller caught Emily by the shoulders, halting her progress. "I'm sorry, Sterling, but perhaps another time. We need to get home now."

Sterling gazed out at the water where sailboats floated along the wind in the bay, then spun around to face them. "How about a sailing excursion?"

"Right now?" Mrs. Miller asked before Daniel had a chance to.

"How lovely it would be. However, I was referring to this

Saturday. How about it? We can sail to North Beach or down to the ruins of the Old Fort or perhaps over to Fish Island—wherever you'd like to go."

"Momma, can we?" Emily peered up at her mother with a pleading pout.

"Daniel, you must tell your mother and Judith they should come along as well." Sterling gestured with his cane toward the hotel. "What say you, we could have a nice picnic!"

"I'll ask them if they'd like to go." And if they did, Daniel accepted the fact that he would not only be their escort, but Sterling's chaperone, a role he'd performed many times in their lives.

"And you, Cora, would you and Emily do me the honor?"

"Momma, please!" Mrs. Miller gazed down into her daughter's eyes and sighed.

"Thank you for your invitation, Sterling. We accept." Then she glanced at Daniel. "And I do hope all of you will come along too."

"Splendid! I'll come for you around eleven o'clock Saturday morning. I'll ask the chef to prepare some delectable delights for our picnic." Sterling tapped his cane on the seawall.

Daniel placed his hand on Mrs. Miller's back to steer her away. "Good evening, Sterling. I'll see you later—after I return from seeing Mrs. Miller home." He emphasized her formal name, reminding himself that he and the woman were on less familiar terms, as they should be.

"Challenge me for a game of billiards tonight?"

Daniel shrugged, then turned from Sterling to face Mrs. Miller. "Shall we proceed?" He gestured ahead.

Mrs. Miller glanced at Sterling, then back to Daniel as if reluctant to leave. "Yes, of course. We need to get home. I must get started on my sewing." She reached for her daughter's hand. "Come, Emily. We will see Mr. Sterling again on Saturday."

"Bye!" Emily waved to Sterling.

Sterling gave a grandiose bow, then straightened and pointed his cane toward the Capo Bath House over the water. "I see the white ball is hoisted," he said, referring to the signal atop the bathhouse which indicated swimming time for men. "I think I'll go for a swim."

"So you're taking in sewing?" Daniel attempted to change the subject and divert Mrs. Miller's attention from Sterling.

She jerked her head toward him, a spark in her eyes as if she'd been slapped. "No. I'm a milliner." She lifted her chin. "I'm merely accessorizing Judith's clothes to match the hat I made for her."

Was it possible for him to say the right thing? He hadn't meant to insult her. She obviously took great pride in her chosen work. "Ah, yes, of course. You are quite talented, I see."

Her shoulders relaxed. "Of course I do sew my own clothes—and Emily's."

"Speaking of such, I look forward to seeing the new dresses that Emily has told me about."

She gave him a sidelong glance, lifting an eyebrow. Why on earth was he talking about clothes?

He ran his finger along the inside of his tightening collar. "Actually, women's fashion is not a subject I'm that familiar with other than what I hear from my mother and sister."

Mrs. Miller smiled and appeared amused by his comments. As they turned the corner, she gestured ahead.

"That's the boarding house at the end of the block."

So close? He slowed his steps to have more time to speak about what was foremost on his mind.

"What I'd really like to talk about is your visit to the fort today. I was pleasantly surprised to see you there. I'm glad you've become involved with aid to the Indian prisoners."

She shuddered, then drew herself up straight. "I was just helping the benevolent society."

"Yes, and helping the Indians as well. Surely you saw how pitiful they were, what barren conditions they live in."

"I scarcely noticed. I wasn't there very long." She focused straight ahead, as if she didn't want to look at him.

His heart dipped as his hope of sharing his concern for the Indians with her dimmed. Was she so unmoved by her visit? She'd appeared to be touched by their plight. Wasn't that compassion he'd seen in her eyes? So why would she pretend not to care?

"Do you remember when the young Indian took that quilt and gave it to the older Indian?" She couldn't have forgotten that poignant scene.

She nodded and answered in a soft voice. "Yes, that was a

thoughtful gesture. Was the older Indian his father?"

"No. But Indians treat their elders with great respect." He continued, committed to engage her. "That young Indian is very interesting, very smart. Talented too. He was called Sun Dancer when he arrived, but he told us today his name is Making Medicine."

They'd reached the entrance to the courtyard of the boarding house. Emily pushed open the gate and ran inside in pursuit of the yellow tabby cat sauntering across the lawn. The sweet aroma of trailing jasmine enveloping the side of the building filled his senses as Cora Miller looked up at him, her brow creased. "Those names have nothing in common. Is he a medicine man?"

"I understand he was a leader, but I think he was trying to tell us he wants to help or be known as one who helps others, especially Lone Bear."

Mrs. Miller arched an eyebrow. "Lone Bear?"

"Yes, that's the name of the older Indian."

"Well, I hope he can."

She turned away and placed her hand on the gate. He reached out to offer assistance and inadvertently placed his hand over hers. A rush of warmth ran up his arm, but he didn't remove his hand, even though he should have. She glanced up at him, a surprised look on her face as her eyes searched his.

Easing her hand away, she said, "Thank you for escorting me home, Mr. Worthington."

He sucked in a breath, then exhaled. "Mrs. Miller, I would prefer that you call me Daniel." Did he really or was he simply jealous that Sterling had that liberty?

She tilted her head, regarding him. "Would your mother approve of such informality?"

Why did she think he had to get permission from his mother? Yet he wondered about her reaction. She liked Cora Miller, even if their social status was different. And he also believed Mother admired her spunk. He'd just have to risk her opinion.

"She'll have to."

Cora Miller arched an eyebrow, then glanced at her daughter running through the garden. Squaring her shoulders, she said, "Then goodbye, Daniel. I need to get Emily washed up for supper."

"Of course. I didn't mean to keep you. Will you be going back to the fort soon?"

A shadow crossed her face and she looked away. Daniel sensed tension in her demeanor.

"If the society needs me again, I'll go back." She pushed the gate open. "But I don't know when that will be."

"I see. Then I'll see you on Saturday."

"Saturday?"

"Yes. I think I'll take Sterling up on that sailing expedition, whether Mother or Judith want to go or not."

Cora Miller slipped inside the gate, eyeing him with curiosity. A smile eased across her face. "I can't remember when I've looked forward to a Saturday more."

Daniel returned her smile. "Me too. Good evening, Cora."

"Good evening, Mr. Worthington."

His heart descended like a rock at the sound of the formality. He shook his head and she put her gloved hand over her mouth.

"I'm sorry, I forgot. Good evening, Daniel. It'll take me a little time to get into the habit of calling you by your given name."

He was charmed by her apologetic look. "You need more practice then. Just say it over and over again—Daniel, Daniel, Daniel. Like the man in the lion's den."

Cora offered a wry smile. "If you insist. However, I might make the mistake of calling someone else by your name if I practice it too much."

"Perish the thought!" He chuckled, then bowed and left her, hoping she would make that mistake.

Chapter Fourteen

Cora pulled the thread through the back of the button and tied it into a knot, then snipped the extra thread with the sewing scissors from a nearby table. There. Judith's bodices were ready. From her chair by the window, she gazed into the garden of the boarding house and inhaled the scent of orange blossoms and jasmine from the courtyard. A rustle in the room caught her attention and she turned to gaze at the form of her sleeping daughter.

Stifling a yawn, Cora's heart swelled as she looked at Emily. She was the one gift Jacob had given her that she still had, except for the cameo brooch he'd given her for their engagement. Selling most of her jewelry had been necessary so she could afford to move south and open her shop. Katie had offered her a room at her house, but Cora knew how crowded it was there already and didn't want to take advantage of Katie's generosity. Besides, after growing up helping her father in the mercantile back in Apalachicola, she knew how to run a store. Surely, she would succeed and be able to provide a home for her and her daughter.

She'd only kept a few jeweled hatpins to be used for special clients who wanted extraordinary hats. Opening her millinery shop in St. Augustine had been both a dream and a risk, especially since there was already a store that sold ladies' hats, Farley's, but she believed her hats, original creations far superior to the ones sold at the other store, would bring in enough business. It had to, and the Worthingtons' patronage confirmed her belief. Hopefully, they would recommend her to other wealthy tourists who would take their place when they returned to Boston.

She sighed, tired from staying up so late. It must be past midnight by now, but she had been determined to get finished with the bodices, so she could start working on her own clothes. After dinner, she and Emily had gone back to her shop where she gathered the rest of her supplies, then hurried back with them to their room.

While at the shop, Cora had an uneasy feeling, like she was being watched. She had glanced out the display window but seen no one looking back. Perhaps it was only the fact that is was getting dark, and she wasn't comfortable going places that late, but Emily had been with her, so she wasn't alone. Still, she was tense and anxious. In her hurry to leave, she was afraid she'd forgotten something, but searching her memory, she couldn't recall anything. Still, something seemed amiss. What on earth was it?

She was grateful to have Emily's company, if not for protection, for distraction. She had been full of questions tonight. Did she like Mr. Sterling? Did she like Mr. Daniel? Which one did she like the best?

Once they'd returned back at the boarding house, Cora had done her best to assuage the girl's curiosity, but the questions alone were tiring. While she worked by the light of the kerosene lamp, she'd asked herself some of the same questions. Yes, she did like them both and was flattered by their attention. Both men were interesting, yet so dissimilar. Sterling was amusing, entertaining and enjoyable. When she was around him, she laughed, and her concerns about business and making money disappeared for a while, lifting a burden from her shoulders. He was never serious or morose, and didn't worry about what people thought, even when he acted foolishly. She envied his freedom of restraint. And she was pleased that he appeared to enjoy her company.

She stood and stretched, her legs stiff from sitting so long. A late moonlight walk with Sterling was appealing at the moment, but she'd never agree to something so scandalous. Wouldn't the tongues wag if anyone she knew saw her?

Daniel, by contrast, was as serious as Sterling was not. Daniel would never consider a moonlight stroll, let alone ask her to accompany him for one. Although he smiled sometimes, his eyes conveyed a depth that frightened her, and the intensity of his gaze made her wonder if he could see what she was thinking. But his concern with the Indian prisoners was more important to him than more pleasurable activities. Despite his efforts to be relaxed when he walked her home, he still had the Indians at the forefront of his mind, which she didn't care to discuss at all. His frown had indicated that he wasn't pleased with her response to the topic.

Yet, his tenderness toward the Indians showed a softer side of his personality, especially his worry over the sick old Indian. Daniel wanted to know the Indians personally, a notion that unsettled her. Why did he think she did as well? She shook her head. Why would she trouble herself about Indian prisoners? They were barely civilized, dirty and frightening. They were prisoners for a reason, weren't they?

An image of Sterling strutting on the sea wall crossed her mind, and she giggled. Even with his head practically hidden beneath the preposterous palmetto hat, he was still handsome. His clownish behavior contrasted so much with his European flair, and his constant smirk suggested he harbored a secret joke. Should she believe the attention he'd given her was special or just his friendly character?

And why didn't Daniel like Sterling? Even though they'd known each other for a long time, they didn't seem to like each other. Was it because their personalities were so different?

A nighttime breeze ruffled the lace curtains on the window and Emily stirred. Cora turned down the wick and blew out the lamp, then tiptoed over and pulled the covers up around her daughter's shoulders. Was she wrong to accept the invitation to go sailing? Even though Emily needed a father, neither of these men would consider marrying beneath their class. Why did the thought even cross her mind? She wasn't romantically involved with either of them and never would be. Besides, they'd be leaving as soon as the temperatures climbed, like all the other tourists. However, while the Worthingtons were in town, she did want to stay in their good graces, if only for the sake of business.

She must face the reality of her situation. She was a laborer, albeit a step above most, in her opinion. Yet, she was nothing more than a tour guide to the Worthingtons. And if that was the case, then, she might as well let them entertain her while they were in St. Augustine.

She climbed into bed next to Emily and closed her eyes, anticipating an interesting day of sailing on Saturday.

~

"Mrs. Miller?" Mr. Beasley entered the shop without a courteous greeting.

Cora glanced up from a hat she was designing for a window display. "Good day, Mr. Beasley."

He grunted and glanced around the shop as if looking for other people he'd missed. "Came for your rent." He crossed the room to the counter, resting his palms on the top of the case. She'd have to clean it after he left.

Cora turned around and withdrew the key from her reticule, opened her cash box, and withdrew the few bills inside. Her breath caught as she realized there was far less money than she'd put in. With her back to Mr. Beasley, she counted it, her stomach clenched in a knot. She didn't have enough to pay him. Where had it gone? She hadn't spent that much on other things. She was very careful to make sure she covered all her expenses.

"Mrs. Miller? I need to get on my way." The impatient man huffed behind her.

She slowly turned and held out the cash. "I'm sorry, but I'm a little short right now."

His face turned red and eyes narrowed. "You don't have the money?"

"I have half of it. I can give you all I have and pay you the rest later."

"Later? I told you I was coming to get the rent."

"Mr. Beasley, I have not yet collected for some of my work, but as soon as I do, I assure you, I'll have the money."

"Hmmph!" He snatched the bills out of her hand. "You have until Monday to get me the rest or you'll have to surrender this space. Do you understand?"

Cora's anger burned at his rudeness, but she couldn't let herself show it. "Yes, of course. I will have it."

As he stormed out, she wanted to crumple onto the floor. Where did the money go? She couldn't lose the shop. She just couldn't.

~

Daniel spent the rest of the week going to the fort every day.

He bought all the colored pencils he could find in town at the mercantile and ordered more. He also hoped to find some real sketchbooks to take the place of the ledgers the Indians currently used.

The Indians were pleased with their new implements and wasted no time using them to add more character and design to their drawings. Medicine Man and Zotom were the most productive artists, each with his own style. Zotom worked in painstaking detail. When he completed the picture of Grey Beard's shooting, he began another drawing that showed a train crossing a high bridge over a valley.

Daniel and Mr. Fox usually supervised the Indians together during the art class. Lieutenant Pratt had allowed them to be outside again, and the Indians responded by being more relaxed. Those not engaged in drawing still cast furtive glances toward the soldiers, but the tension that had been present at first had eased.

"It looks like Zotom is drawing more events of his trip here." Daniel nodded toward the Indian.

Fox rubbed his chin whiskers. "I think you're right. That bridge crossing was out west."

Daniel noticed a border of white space across the bottom of the picture. "Wonder why he left that space there instead of drawing all the way to the bottom?"

"Don't know. I'll ask him."

Fox strode over to the Indian, pointed to the paper and spoke a few words of Kiowa.

The Indian's response made him chuckle.

"He said that's where to put the words. I think he means a title, to name the picture."

"How interesting. He's making a type of journal, you might say."

"Could be."

Daniel lifted his gaze to the surrounding walls of the fort, and an idea struck him.

"Do you think Pratt might allow us to take the men up there?" He nodded toward the steps leading up. "It might inspire them to see more of the surrounding area, especially those who don't seem to know what to draw."

"I don't know. Could be asking for trouble." Fox shook his

head.

"You think they'd try to jump off? Those walls are pretty high. Besides, with those soldiers up there standing guard, the Indians know they'd be shot if they tried to escape." Daniel motioned to the soldiers strolling the wide terreplein on top of the walls.

Lieutenant Pratt emerged from an archway and walked across the parade ground toward them. "Hello, gentlemen. How are our students doing?" He stopped beside them and glanced over at the Indians.

"Coming along nicely, I believe." Daniel cleared his throat. He pointed to the top of the walls. "Lieutenant, I think we should take the Indians up to the parapet and let them see the city and the water. We could give them the English words for what they see, and they could draw them."

"Hmm. Letting them out here is one thing, but up there? Could be dangerous."

"Surely they wouldn't try to escape from there. That's a long way to jump." Daniel extended his arm up to convey the walls' height.

"I suppose you're right. If we allow them up there, they must understand any efforts to get away will get them killed." Pratt faced the interpreter. "Could you make that clear to them, Mr. Fox?"

"Yes, sir. I'll tell them," Fox said.

"All right then." Pratt addressed two soldiers standing nearby. "These men are going to take the prisoners to the parapet. Accompany them and keep an eye out for any attempts to escape."

"Yes, sir!"

Fox spoke to the Indians in their appropriate languages. They responded by standing and forming a line. Making Medicine helped Lone Bear to his feet. When the soldiers motioned them toward the masonry steps leading to the top, the Indians' eyes grew wide with fear.

Daniel stepped forward. "I'll lead the way. Perhaps they'll be less afraid if they follow me."

Fox encouraged them to walk behind Daniel as the guards below called out to the guards above to be ready for the prisoners. When Lone Bear reached the bottom of the stairs, he glanced up, doubt in his eyes. Making Medicine walked alongside, his arm around the old man, practically lifting him up each step. As all the Indians reached the top of the fort, they huddled close together, eyeing their surroundings and the soldiers with caution.

Daniel swept his arm out toward the city and the water. "Look!" He lifted his sketchbook and pointed to it, then simulated drawing. "Tell them to draw what they see."

Fox translated Daniel's message. The Indians looked at him, then at Daniel, then out at the view. Daniel motioned for them to follow again as he walked toward the corner bastion of the fort past the cannons lined up along the wall. The Indians shuffled along, stopping when Daniel did. He pointed toward the bay and across to Anastasia Island where the black and white spiraled lighthouse rose above the foliage, then he gestured south toward the Matanzas River before directing their gaze to the city beside it.

The Indians took in the view, some glancing down at the moat below, then backing up in fear, muttering to each other. Lone Bear slowly lifted his arm, pointing to the lighthouse and mumbled something to Making Medicine. Making Medicine nodded, then spoke aloud to Fox, pointing to the lighthouse as well.

Fox laughed and answered, motioning with his arms.

"What are they saying?"

"They want to know who lives in the large teepee with the stripes. The asked if that's our chief's house."

Daniel looked at the lighthouse, then at the two Indians and smiled. "How do you explain a lighthouse to them?"

"I'm not sure, but I'm trying."

"Maybe one day we can take them there and show them firsthand."

Fox eyed him with a frown. "You do have some wild ideas, Mr. Worthington."

Wild? Daniel had never considered himself unconventional, yet perhaps as an artist, he wanted others to see the beauty of the world around them.

"Well, let's have them sit down and see what kind of drawings they can create from this perspective."

The sun shone through a cloudless sky and warmed the terreplein as a gentle ocean breeze kept the temperature pleasant. Daniel watched Lone Bear, who closed his eyes and let his head drop back, exposing his deeply lined face to the sun's heat. He appeared to be feeling better, even though he still had the wracking cough. Making Medicine nudged him, and Lone Bear lowered his chin to look at his sketch. Lone Bear nodded, a faint smile on his face.

Daniel noticed a younger Indian seated on the other side of Lone Bear, intent on his drawing. The older man glanced at the drawing and pointed, calling Making Medicine's attention to the sketch. The two spoke, nodding their approval. Daniel sidled over to get a look. The young Indian had drawn a scene of the water with the island across it. In the water was a boat and on the island were both the old and new lighthouses.

Daniel motioned to George Fox to come over. "Who is he?"

"Ah, that's Bear's Heart. He's Cheyenne too."

"He's very good with proportions." Daniel observed the various sizes of the objects in the drawing.

"So he is. Looks like you've found yourself some artists, Mr. Worthington."

Daniel's heart swelled with pride, not for himself, but for his new apprentices. Fox was right. Daniel didn't teach the Indians their talent. They already had it. But thank God, he'd been able to help them find it. Maybe their art would give them the same pleasure it gave him. He hoped so. They had left their homes and lifestyles out West. But this way, they could keep it in their drawings.

He strolled over to the Kiowa group of Indians where Zotom was drawing a different scene. The Indian had sketched a picture of all the Indians on top of the fort. They stood or sat facing the water with guards standing on either side. Below where the Indians stood, Zotom worked on the features of the fort's interior.

"His detail is amazing." Daniel commented as Fox walked up.

"Certainly is. Look. He drew the cannons, even the stones in the wall." Fox pointed to the sketch.

Each Indian had his own style, just like artists anywhere else. Some focused on people while others on setting, some were detailed like Zotom, others showed a more general view. Not only did they seem to enjoy working on their art, they appeared to be pleased with the results. Another artist came to Daniel's mind, but this one was a different kind of artist. This one created works of art in her hats. If anyone could appreciate the Indians' ability, it should be her. Would she appreciate seeing what the Indians could do? His pulse beat a little quicker at the prospect of showing her.

But then he remembered how she'd reacted when he tried to talk to her about the Indians. Her demeanor had changed from friendly to distant at the mention of the prisoners and her experience at the fort, almost as if she wanted to forget about it completely. He shook his head. She obviously only cared about hats or fashion or something frivolous.

So why did he insist on joining her and Sterling for a sailing expedition and tolerate a whole day of the man's shenanigans? Normally, he disliked women who found Sterling attractive—the ones who fell for his trifling and didn't give a whit about his integrity. Yet he refused to believe Cora Miller was like most women. She was smart. Clever even. She was an interesting woman, and for some reason, he was intrigued by her. Or maybe he just wanted to know for certain if he was completely mistaken about her. Maybe she didn't have any compassion after all.

Chapter Fifteen

Cora and Emily were sitting on the large porch of the boarding house when Sterling arrived Saturday morning sporting the palmetto hat, this time without the moss adornment. Cora planned to enjoy the day and not worry about the rent, if she could. She'd tell Judith her clothes were ready when they were out today and hopefully, could get them to her when they returned later in the afternoon.

"Good morning," Sterling said as he entered the courtyard. "Are you lovely ladies ready for a day of adventure on the high seas?"

Emily jumped up and ran to the man dressed in a white linen suit. Sterling who removed his hat and proffered a sweeping bow. "I am!" she said.

Cora smiled at their escort, pleased with her daughter's joy. Emily was dressed to perfection—white frock with a blue satin sash and a straw bonnet tied with matching blue satin ribbon—ideal clothing for a day of sailing. Cora stood and smoothed her own skirt, then followed the girl to greet the handsome man with the gleaming smile.

"The high seas?" Cora raised an eyebrow. "Let's hope we're staying in the bay and not going beyond the island. That's adventure enough for me."

Sterling laughed aloud. "Don't worry your pretty head. I'll fend off the pirates." He brandished his cane in a sword-fighting stance.

"Pirates? Are we gonna see pirates, Momma?"

"No dear. I'm sure Mr. Sterling is teasing."

"Who knows? Perhaps we will, but I'll protect you, nevertheless!" He extended his elbows on either side. "Ladies? Our ship awaits."

Cora and Emily each took hold of his arms and they headed toward the plaza. "The Worthingtons are waiting at the hotel," Sterling said. "We'll meet them there and collect the delectable fare the chef has prepared for our al fresco repast."

Emily stared up at the man, her brow furrowed. "What are we going to collect? I like to collect seashells at the beach. Do you?"

Sterling laughed again, glancing above the child's head at Cora. "What a delightful child you have!"

"Thank you." Cora beamed, pride mingling with amusement.

"Did I mention how lovely you ladies look today?"

Cora's face warmed at the compliment. Even though she didn't have a fancy day dress, she'd made her first attempt to come out of mourning clothes with a lace-trimmed white blouse and gray skirt. She accentuated the plain clothes by wearing a blue satin ribbon choker with her cameo brooch. Her own straw hat sported the same blue satin ribbons flowing from the back of the high brim.

"Momma and I match!" Emily pointed to the ribbon on her bonnet and at her waist, then to her mother's hat.

"Why, you're practically twins!"

Cora delighted in the praise, despite its nonsense. For a moment, she did feel years younger. The day promised to be a refreshing reprieve from her worry, and she welcomed the entertaining distraction from their escort.

When they reached the hotel, Daniel stepped out onto the steps. Cora was delighted he'd agree to accompany them and hoped he'd be able to enjoy himself as well. Would he be able to relax or was he going to remain somber? Surely, he wouldn't mention the topic of the Indians at the fort today.

"Mr. Daniel!" Emily let go of Sterling's arm and scampered up the steps to greet Daniel.

"Good morning, Emily." Daniel smiled down at the girl, then lifted his gaze to Cora. "Good morning, Cora."

Cora smiled. "Good morning, Daniel." She glanced around. "Are your mother and Judith going to join us?"

Judith came through the open door. "I am, but Mother's staying here." With both hands, she lifted a picnic basket. "I picked up our lunch from the kitchen. It's rather heavy. Wonder what the chef put in here?"

Daniel reached for the basket, but Sterling jumped in front of him. "I'll take that." He grabbed the basket and grinned. "I asked him to put in a secret ingredient."

Shaking his head, Daniel frowned, then relaxed his features when he glanced at Cora. "Are we all ready?" He approached and offered his arm. With the other, he waved toward the water. "Sterling, please lead us to our vessel."

Sterling's gaze traveled from Cora to Daniel, then to Judith. "Come on, Judith. Let's go find our ship."

Cora reached her free hand toward Emily. "Emily, please hold my hand until we get onboard."

Sterling had procured one of the largest sailboats in the harbor. A local Minorcan boatmen waited for them. "Captain! We're ready for our excursion."

"Yes, sir. Let me help you in." The boatman extended his hand, but Sterling leaped onboard, ignoring the assistance and rocking the boat.

Setting down the picnic basket, Sterling reached out to help Judith climb into the boat. The boatman took Emily's hand, then grabbed her around the waist, lifting her onto the boat's deck. Sterling reached for Cora's hand as Daniel steadied her to step in.

"You ladies can sit over there." The boatman motioned to the benches along the sides of the bow.

Would you like me to release the ropes?" Daniel pointed to the thick rope wrapped around a piling.

"Thank you, sir. I'll get the one in the back." The boatman moved toward the rear of the vessel and untied it as Daniel jumped in and pushed the boat away from the dock.

"Where to, sir?" The boatman addressed Sterling.

"That way!" Sterling pointed south. "Let's go down the Matanzas to the Old Fort."

The boatman nodded and turned the boat in that direction as Sterling balanced himself on the edge of the boat midway between the boatman and the others.

Cora's left arm encircled Emily's waist keeping her daughter beside her, while holding her parasol aloft with her other hand to keep the harsh sunlight from bearing down on them. Judith sat opposite them next to her brother, keeping an eye fixed on Sterling.

Soon the wind filled the sails and they were skimming along the azure waters, gliding past the town. Cora took in the scene around them, the fishing boats and other sailboats that dotted the water of the Matanzas River between Anastasia Island and the town on the mainland. Imagine that she, Cora Miller, was sailing with the likes of Sterling Cunningham and the Worthingtons. When they passed other pleasure boats, Sterling waved as if he knew the occupants. Did all the wealthy tourists know each other?

Out of the corner of her eye, she felt Daniel looking at her, but she dared not turn to face him. Was he really staring at her or something else in that direction? Why would he be watching her anyway? It seemed like he was always trying to read her mind. Thank goodness, he couldn't. Still, she was grateful for the cool air that kept her cheeks from blushing under his possible scrutiny.

The bow hit a wave, and the women squealed as a spray of salty water splashed their faces. Hands grasped bonnets as the women attempted to prevent them from flying off.

"Look over there!" Sterling pointed to a group of porpoises rolling through the water some fifty feet from the starboard side of the boat.

"Ooh!" Emily leaned against the side to get a better look. "There's a baby one in the middle of those two!"

"I think you're right, Emily." Cora's heart thrilled with the sight as well as her daughter's delight. "The two adults must be protecting it by being on either side." As it should be in a normal family. The family scene was bittersweet, reminding Cora there was a missing adult in Emily's family.

The boat hit a large wave, almost bumping Cora off the bench. She lost her grip on Emily, who landed on the bottom of the boat, wet from the water that sloshed inside.

"Oh dear." Cora dropped her parasol to help her daughter up as Daniel rushed over to assist.

"I'm all wet!" Emily got to her feet, her dress dripping. Cora frowned at the limp clothes. Why didn't she think to bring a change of clothes for Emily in case she needed them?

"Well, thank God, you didn't fly overboard." Daniel offered his hand to steady the little girl.

Cora glanced up at him. "Thank you. I'll have to hold onto her better."

Their gazes held a moment before he returned to his place in the boat.

Did he think she was too careless by allowing Emily to fall? Her heart raced from the incident and the embarrassment of his judgment.

"Momma! There's the lighthouse. Do you think Captain Harn sees us out here?" Emily waved as they passed the tower.

Cora glanced over at the island, thankful for the diversion. "Perhaps so." What would Katie think if she saw them in the company of these people?

Soon the town was behind them. To the east, the mangrove marshes of Anastasia Island bordered the river. On the west bank, groves of orange trees covered the land south of St. Augustine, an occasional roof line poking through the tree line. As they headed south toward the Matanzas Inlet that opened out into the Atlantic, the orange groves gave way to marshes on that side of them too. The gentle rhythm of the waves lapping the side of the boat relaxed Cora, and she found herself trying hard to stay awake. If not for the entertainment of pelicans diving into the water and gulls crying overhead, she might have drifted off to sleep. The family of porpoises accompanied them for a while before they swam out of sight.

"Land ho!" Sterling shouted, standing and pointing ahead. "That's Rattlesnake Island."

Cora shuddered at the name of the island. She glimpsed at wide-eyed Judith whose skin had paled even whiter than her normal light tone. Was the island justly named? Hopefully, they wouldn't find out.

"Is that the fort?" Emily pointed to an ancient stone tower coming into view.

"That's it. Fort Matanzas." Sterling nodded. "Built by the Spaniards to keep the enemy from coming in the back door."

"Shall we stop here, sir?" The boatman addressed Sterling.

"Indeed! We'll enjoy our repast over there in the shade of the building."

The boatman aimed for the small beach in front of the fort where a white egret stalked its prey in the shallow reeds nearby. Daniel stood, his gaze fixed upon the shore. As the boat hit the sandy bottom, Sterling leaped out, his feet landing in shallow water.

"Daniel, toss me the rope."

Daniel picked up the end of the rope and threw it to him. As Sterling held onto the rope, the boatman lowered the sails, then jumped out to help Sterling pull the boat farther up onto dry land.

Daniel helped the women out, lifting first Emily and handing her to Sterling. As he put his hands around Cora's waist, she sucked in her breath, the strength of his touch startling her senses. He passed her over to Sterling, who hoisted her higher before putting her feet on the ground.

"You're not much heavier than Emily, dear lady!" Sterling laughed as he let go of her.

Cora's cheeks burned while she tried to regain her composure, embarrassed to be handled like a sack of flour. The men helped Judith out in like manner, then Daniel handed the basket to Sterling before he, too, climbed out.

"Emily! Wait!" Cora cried out to her little girl who was running toward the Old Fort. "That might be dangerous!"

Emily halted at the foot of a twenty-foot ladder leading up to the gun deck of the ancient fort. The others caught up to her.

"Can't we go up, Momma?" Emily's eyes pleaded.

Cora studied the old fort, unsettling with its abandoned appearance. It was an unusual shape, with one tall side which formerly housed soldiers and the wide gun deck in front which boasted two cannons. The fort wasn't nearly as large as Fort Marion, but its old walls were crumbling and its ancient tower foreboding.

"Oh, I'm sure it's fine. People go up there all the time." Sterling chuckled, leading the way. Indeed, another group of tourists appeared above them, looking down over the edge of the deck.

"Is that ladder safe?"

"Of course. It wouldn't be here if it wasn't safe." Sterling grabbed hold of the ladder. "I'll go up first and show you how safe it is."

Sterling climbed up the tall ladder which leaned against the coquina wall. At the top, he called down to them. "See? I told you it was perfectly fine. Come on up!"

"Momma, please!" Emily begged Cora with a pouty expression.

Cora's gaze traveled up the ladder to Sterling, then over to the taller part of the fort behind him. She shuddered at the thought of being so high above ground, and fear gripped her heart imagining her daughter falling from those heights.

"I'll take her up if you don't want to go." Daniel stepped beside Emily.

"All right, thank you. But please keep an eye on her."

Emily grinned, clapping her hands. She grabbed the sides of the ladder and began to climb while Daniel climbed right behind her, his arms on either side of the girl. Slowly they made their way to the top, the ladder shaking with their weight while Cora held her breath. At the top, they climbed off the ladder and Emily waved down at her mother.

"Come on up, Momma!"

"Yes, do come, ladies." Sterling called down.

Cora glanced at Judith who shook her head. "No, I can't do it. I'm terribly afraid of heights."

"I'm not fond of them either," Cora said. But as she looked up, Emily disappeared, making Cora anxious to see where she had gone. Daniel disappeared from view as well, and Cora hoped he had gone to check on her daughter. Only Sterling stayed in sight, smiling and motioning for her to come up.

"I hate to leave you down here by yourself." Cora was tempted to join them, despite her fear, but wasn't comfortable leaving Judith by herself.

Judith gazed wistfully up at Sterling, then turned to Cora. "You go. I'll be fine right here."

Sterling shouted down at them. "Bring the picnic basket and we'll eat up here!"

Cora and Judith looked at each other wide-eyed, then laughed.

"I'm afraid he overestimates our courage," Cora said.

"And strength," Judith said, eyeing the basket. Apparently, there were some limits to Judith's desire to be with Sterling.

"I suppose if he gets hungry enough, he'll come get the basket himself." Cora shook her head, studying the ladder. "I certainly won't try to carry it up."

Emily's head appeared at the top again.

"Come see, Momma! You can climb all the way up there!" The girl pointed to the top of the tall tower.

"No, Emily. Don't you dare!" Cora felt sorry for Judith, but she had no choice. "I'm afraid I must go, just to keep an eye on Emily."

"I'll wait here…with the basket." Judith smiled. "Be careful."

Cora grasped hold of the ladder's sides, her hands perspiring as she slowly climbed the shaking ladder and holding her breath until she reached the top. Sterling grabbed her as her feet stepped on the top rung and put her down on the gun deck, where the old cannons pointed out to the Matanzas Inlet, originally to guard against enemy invasion.

On one end facing the water was a round turret with a small window. Emily ran over to it and peered inside.

"Momma, it's like a castle."

Sterling laughed loudly. "That's a sentry box so the soldiers could spot the enemy coming."

"Can I go inside?" Emily waited as Cora hesitated. Sterling rushed over.

"Certainly! Let's go look out the window and pretend we're guards." The two disappeared inside the deteriorated corner of the parapet, which perched precariously off the corner of the wall, looking as if it might fall off any moment.

Cora eyed the cracks in the building. "How old is this fort? It must have been here longer than Fort Marion."

Daniel pulled a guidebook out of his pocket. "Says here it was built around 1740. I believe Fort Marion was built the century before."

"I would've guessed this one was older. It seems to be falling apart."

"It's probably been abandoned a hundred years."

"I'm surprised those cannons are still there." Cora walked over to one of the two rusty cannons facing the water.

"The book says the Spanish left in 1821. Apparently, they didn't care to take the cannons with them."

Emily raced toward Cora. "Let's go in there. Mr. Sterling says there's another ladder that goes all the way to the top!" She pointed to an open doorway of the tower.

"That doorway leads to the soldiers' quarters. There's a ladder that goes up to the former officer's quarters, then up through the roof of the observation deck." Daniel quit reading and looked up, his hand shielding his eyes as he gazed at the top of the building above them. "It's pretty high, at least three stories."

Cora followed his gaze, the height making her dizzy. "No, Emily! This is as far as you can go."

"Please... Mr. Sterling said he was going up there."

As a grinning Sterling sauntered toward them, Cora frowned. "Perhaps Mr. Sterling has changed his mind."

"Emily, I'm getting pretty hungry. Aren't you?" Daniel patted his stomach.

The diversion worked, and Sterling looked around. "Where's the picnic basket?"

Cora pointed down. "Down there. With Judith. She didn't care to climb up."

"What a pity. She's missed the view from here." Sterling swept his arms around.

"Let's go join her and find a place to eat." Daniel motioned toward the ladder.

Cora didn't know what she was more afraid of—going up the ladder or going down.

Chapter Sixteen

Daniel saw the terrified look on Cora's face. Either she was afraid of climbing down or afraid of her daughter getting down the ladder safely. Before he could react, though, Sterling bolted for the ladder.

"Come on, ladies! I can assist you." Sterling grinned, motioning for Cora and Emily to follow.

Daniel clenched his fists. He'd seen the silver flask Sterling slipped out of his pocket when he thought no one was looking, taking a swallow before returning it to its hiding place inside his coat. Sterling might be able to hide behind a jovial façade, but Daniel could see the increasing inebriation. He couldn't trust Sterling's stability and wouldn't allow him to jeopardize the safety of Cora and her daughter.

"Wait." Daniel stepped forward. "I'll take Emily down. Cora, would you mind waiting here until I come back for you?"

A look of relief crossed Cora's face, but she glanced at Sterling who stood waiting with his hands gripping the ladder.

"We shouldn't all get on the ladder at once. I doubt it can hold that much weight." Daniel glared at Sterling. "Why don't you go on down, Sterling, and help Judith with the lunch basket?"

Sterling opened his mouth to protest but shut it when his gaze met Daniel's.

"See you at the bottom!" Sterling disappeared over the edge of the roof. Daniel glanced over as Sterling's shaky descent ended when he jumped and fell the remaining distance to the ground.

Daniel blew out a breath as Sterling got back to his feet and brushed himself off, looking up as if he'd hoped no one saw him. Seeing Daniel, he waved to indicate he was fine.

Cora held Emily's hand as they stepped to the edge of the roof. "Emily, why don't you let Mr. Daniel help you down the ladder?" She glanced toward him with a look of gratitude.

Daniel positioned himself on the second rung of the ladder, leaning forward to reach for the little girl. "Come on, Emily. Get on the rung above me and we'll go down together."

Cora helped Emily onto the ladder, then let go of her hand. "Hold on to the sides, Emily."

"I will, Momma. Don't worry, I climbed up here all right, didn't I?"

Daniel backed down the ladder with one arm around Emily and the other on the ladder. When he reached the bottom, he found Sterling rummaging through the picnic basket.

"Sterling! Would you please wait until we can all partake of our refreshments?" Daniel looked at Judith standing nearby and pointed to a grassy area near the back corner of the fort. "Judith, why don't you find a nice shady spot for us to spread out our things? I'll be right back after I retrieve Cora. Sterling, please carry the basket for Judith." Daniel leaned over to Emily. "Would you please help Miss Judith get things ready for our picnic?"

Emily nodded and hurried to take Judith's outstretched hand.

Sterling frowned at him, then shrugged. "Judith, shall we follow Daniel's orders? I believe your brother has spent so much time around the fort, he's beginning to act like an officer." Sterling laughed aloud, and Judith giggled.

Daniel scrambled back up the ladder as Cora peered down at him. At the top, he took her hand and helped her over the edge. He'd intended to escort her down the same way he'd done for Emily, but he hadn't expected the close proximity of their bodies to distract him so. However, he couldn't place himself too far below her and risk her the embarrassment of seeing up her skirts, so he stood on the rungs just beneath, with his arms on either side of hers.

The sweet scent of lavender wafted in the space between them, and he turned his head to clear his mind. She seemed to weigh about the same as Emily, the ladder not shaking much more as they climbed down. He was tempted to put his arm on her waist as he had her daughter's, but that wasn't necessary. They were not on such familiar terms. All he wanted was to know her better and see if they shared any common interests.

Once their feet were safely on the ground, Cora tugged down on her bodice to straighten it, a slight blush on her cheeks. She glanced around. "Where did the others go?"

"Should be around the back of the fort. I expect they'll be setting out the picnic." Daniel motioned in that direction and Cora went ahead of him. How did she manage to appear so immaculate, as if she'd just stepped off the pages of a magazine? He couldn't help but contrast her appearance with the dismal image of the two squaws back at the fort. Yet, he couldn't imagine them dressed like her. In a way only an artist could appreciate, they portrayed their own type of beauty.

Behind the old fort, the tablecloth from the hotel was laid on the ground with Judith and Emily removing items from the basket and setting them out. Sterling lay on his back, a blade of grass between his teeth. Cora hurried to help arrange the food.

"Make yourself comfortable, Daniel." Sterling turned his head and pointed to a spot on the tablecloth.

"I see you already have." Daniel turned to the women. "Can I help you with anything?"

"We have everything ready, don't we, Emily?" Judith smiled as she handed the girl some napkins. "Why don't you hand one of these to everyone?"

Emily eagerly obeyed, counting out each napkin. Bowls of ham sandwiches, fried chicken, and boiled eggs attracted Daniel's stomach, which growled a response. Judith unwrapped the cloth from a plate of biscuits and pulled a jar of orange marmalade out of the basket along with some serving utensils while Cora passed out plates.

"Here's a jar of pickles!" Emily lifted it out of the basket. "Umm. I love pickles!"

"It's really tight." Cora tried to twist the lid off the Mason jar. "Can either of you gentlemen open it?"

"I'll do it." Sterling pushed himself up to his elbow and reached for the jar.

Daniel held back, waiting to see if Sterling would fail in his attempt. However, he opened the jar, pulled out a pickle, then handed the jar back.

"And here's some lemonade. No wonder the basket was so heavy," Judith said, as she lifted out two jars of the sparkling liquid.

"Oh, goody. I'm so thirsty!" Emily sat with her hands resting on her knees, eyeing the lemonade.

"These must be the glasses." Judith retrieved an object wrapped in a napkin and opened it to reveal one of the hotel glasses. Cora helped her get the rest handed out, then poured the lemonade, still cool from the chunk of ice wrapped next to it, before passing the drinks out to each person.

"Thank you, ladies." Daniel took a sip. "Very refreshing."

Across from him, Sterling sat up and twisting away from the others, poured some liquid from his coat flask into his lemonade before taking a sip.

"Ah, yes. Very refreshing indeed!" He lifted his cup in the air. "A toast to our excursion!"

The others responded in kind, but Daniel lacked Sterling's enthusiasm as he followed suit.

"What is that loud noise?" Judith inquired, glancing around them. As they listened, the noise increased.

"Cicadas," Cora said. "They're a type of insect."

"A cacophony of cicadas!" Sterling raised a toast to the unseen noisemakers.

"Do they bite?" Judith's forehead puckered as she searched for the insect.

"No, ma'am," Emily said. "I like to look for their shells. Would you like me to find you one?"

Judith shook her head vigorously. "No, thank you."

"Emily, finish your lunch, please." Cora looked around. "Shouldn't we offer the boatman something to eat too? Surely he's hungry as well."

"That's very hospitable of you," Daniel said, pleased to see the woman did have a charitable spirit, perhaps more than he'd first thought.

"Oh, don't bother. I'm sure he brought something for himself." Sterling waved the notion off with a flourish of his hand as he lay back on the tablecloth.

Daniel stood and brushed off his clothes. "I'll take him something. We have plenty to share." Cora assembled a plate of food and handed it to him.

When he found the boatman sitting near the shore, Daniel gave him the food. The man thanked him, then nodded toward the sky.

"We should head back soon, sir." He took a quick bite of his sandwich. "We might run into some rain."

Daniel followed his gaze and confirmed the boatman's assessment. "Of course. I'll tell the others to prepare to leave."

The singing of the cicadas rose to a clamor as Daniel hurried back to the group and motioned to the approaching clouds. "Our boatman thinks rain could be headed our way. We should start back." He looked around him to see what he could help gather.

"I was just showing Emily how to whistle with a blade of grass." Sterling put the grass in his teeth and blew a noise.

Emily searched for a piece of grass nearby. "I want to try!"

Cora's brow knit as she glanced up. "Perhaps later, Emily. We must get our things together and leave as Mr. Daniel suggested."

With a pout, the little girl handed things to her mother who wrapped them in the napkins and placed them back in the basket. Daniel and Judith helped with the task before everyone stood and Cora lifted the tablecloth to shake it. Judith grabbed the other end as the two women folded it and returned the cloth to the basket.

The wind had intensified as clouds rumbled overhead when they returned to the boat. The boatman held the boat as steady as possible while waves knocked it about, then Sterling clambered aboard and tried to maintain enough balance to assist the women Daniel helped from the shore. Once Daniel climbed aboard and they were all seated, the boatman shoved them away from the shore, hopped in and assumed his position at the stern to operate the tiller. The sail filled with air and soon they picked up speed.

Angry waves jostled the boat as the passengers bounced on the benches. The women squealed each time the boat hit a swell, splashing the passengers with salty sea spray. Lightning flashed as the black clouds rumbled, further frightening the women. Daniel sat across from them, wishing he could do more to make them comfortable, while Sterling gripped the edge of the boat closest to the boatman.

"Sir, you need to sit down lower before you fall off." The

boatman addressed Sterling.

"Nonsense. I can ride this thing like a bucking bronco!"

The words had barely left his mouth when a large wave smacked into the boat. Sterling fell forward, sitting hard on the bottom of the vessel. Cora and Judith gasped, but Emily giggled as if he was clowning as usual.

Sterling's laugh sounded forced as he tried to stand, and Daniel wondered if he could even stand on solid ground in his condition.

The boatman extended an arm out to him. "Sir, you mustn't. The sails might hit you."

"Let *me* handle this boat." Sterling stumbled toward the stern and reached for the tiller. "I can do a better job than you."

Daniel jumped from his seat. If Sterling wanted to make a fool of himself, that was his choice, but Daniel couldn't sit by and let the man endanger the rest of the group.

"Sterling! Stop!" Daniel yelled above the noise of the blowing wind and the water. He moved across the boat to pull Sterling away. However, as he reached the center of the boat, Sterling grabbed the tiller and jerked it, causing the boat to make a sudden shift. With a loud noise, the boom released and swung around, jarring the boat as the sail switched from one side to the other. Before he could get out of the way, the boom hit Daniel in the head. He lost his balance and fell overboard, grasping for something to hold on to. Just as his body hit the chilly water, he latched hold of the gunwale, securing himself to the side of the boat.

The women screamed and ran to help him. Sterling laughed as he let go of the tiller and stumbled over to the spot where Daniel hung onto the boat. The boat tipped low to the water with all the weight on one side, and arms reached out to pull him in.

"Please, ladies go back to the other side before we capsize!" The boatman called out, waving them off as he came to help. Daniel struggled to stay alert, his head throbbing from the blow. He pulled up with all his might while the boatman and Sterling hauled him back in.

The boat righted as the boatman recovered control of the tiller. "Please, ladies and gentlemen, sit down before anyone else gets hurt or falls out!"

Daniel sat in the bottom of the boat, taking deep breaths,

shivering as the wind assailed his wet clothing. The women knelt beside him, worried looks on their faces.

"Are you all right?" Judith patted Daniel on his back as he coughed.

A soft hand touched his forehead, and Daniel squinted to see whose it was. Making eye contact with Cora, he saw her look of concern.

"You've a nasty bump." Her soothing soft voice calmed him in such a way that he relinquished his pride and accepted her sympathy.

Sterling sat on the floor of the boat as well, his knees bent with his back against the side of the vessel.

"Why, Daniel, I didn't know you wanted to go for a swim!" Sterling's wide grin accompanied the mirth in his eyes.

Daniel glowered at him, a volume of words wanting to come out and attack the man but wouldn't. He was tired, sleepy and too spent for a battle. The urge to grab Sterling by the throat and throw him overboard was suppressed by a sense of overwhelming lethargy. His eyelids were heavy, and he wanted to collapse right where he was.

"You should rest," Judith said.

Daniel started to lie back and take her advice, but the boatman stopped him.

"Do not let him fall asleep! It is very bad for someone who's been hit in the head."

"We should at least bandage his head." Cora pointed to Daniel's forehead. "Judith, why don't you get one of those napkins from the picnic basket?"

Judith retrieved a napkin and handed it to Cora while Emily crouched beside her.

"Sterling, can you please hold this over the side to get it wet?" Cora extended the napkin to Sterling. "I think it will help to put something cool on that bump."

Sterling obliged and ran the napkin through the water before handing it back dripping. Cora wrung it out, then folded it diagonally before gently placing it over Daniel's head and tying it in the back.

"Now you look like one of your Indian friends." Sterling smirked, pointing at Daniel's bandage.

Daniel didn't miss the frown on Cora's face as she looked at Sterling. Perhaps she was beginning to realize the man's flaws.

"Does it hurt?" Emily's face drew close to his as she studied his injury.

"A little," he mumbled, lying. His head throbbed, and the motion of the sea didn't help his discomfort.

A crack of lightning split the sky overhead followed by a loud burst of thunder, jolting Daniel's head even more. For the life of him, he couldn't remember why he was on this boat, but he couldn't wait to get off.

Cold raindrops hit his face, snapping him alert as the wind hurled them like daggers. Daniel shivered inside his sodden jacket, glimpsing Cora who huddled with Emily, their heads lowered to avoid the wet assault. He wished to huddle with them, not just for his own warmth, but for theirs as well. But he was in no position to offer comfort to anyone else in his feeble condition.

He glanced toward Sterling whose hat was pulled low over his eyes. Was the man sleeping? Did he have any idea what trouble he'd caused? Or did he even care?

Daniel thanked God he had been able to hold onto the boat. He was a good swimmer, but that whack on the head could've impaired his ability.

Soon the rain ceased, and the wind slowed as well. Rays of sunlight pierced the clouds like arrows bringing welcome warmth to his cooled skin. His hat long gone, Daniel's hair dripped down his face, despite the napkin bandage. He brushed it back with his hand, lifting his face to the sky. The sudden brightness hurt his eyes, and he was forced to close them. The waves resumed a gentle rhythm, and he drifted in and out of sleep, afraid to give in due to the boatman's warning.

"Look, Momma! A rainbow!"

The child's voice brought Daniel out of his drowse and he opened his eyes to search for the colorful arch.

"Yes, I see it." Cora spoke from the bow of the boat. "What a nice way to signal the end of the storm."

Daniel spotted the rainbow and reflected on Cora's words. God's symbol of hope should bring him peace as well. So why did a storm still rage in his heart?

Chapter Seventeen

The day had gone nothing like Cora expected. Although it began with such promise, the trip home was dismal, dangerous even. It wasn't only the weather that had changed though. Something else happened while they were at the fort, and she couldn't put her finger on what exactly it was. She had been having such an enjoyable time as a guest with such prestigious company. Sterling was his usual, amusing self, at least for a while.

Yet, when he took charge of the boat resulting in its sudden tilt and Daniel's injury, the situation was no longer humorous. Sterling appeared remorseful by the way he slumped in the boat after the accident. Even though he and Daniel sparred often, they were friends, and she was certain he meant no harm. At least she thought they were friends. According to Sterling, they'd known each other since childhood. So why did Daniel always seem so angry with good-natured Sterling?

Cora eyed Daniel when they disembarked on their return.

Sterling extended a hand to him. "Need some assistance, old man?" He chuckled, pointing to the napkin around Daniel's head. "Quite the fashion statement. Perhaps now that you've lost your hat, you can set a new style."

Daniel glowered at Sterling, knocking his hand away, a motion that caused him to sway and grab his head. Judith rushed to his side to steady him.

"Are you all right, Daniel?" His sister put her arm around him. "Try leaning on me."

He allowed himself to use her for support and took a few staggering steps. Was he unsteady from the motion of the vessel or was it the blow to his head? Cora wanted to help him too, but was afraid he'd refuse. Daniel paused, glancing around. When his gaze met hers, he frowned as if he were trying to think. Straightening, he blew out a heavy breath.

"I assure you all I am fine. I'll ask for some ice at the hotel to put on my head." Daniel's words were slurred like he was inebriated. The blow had definitely affected him.

Cora took Emily's hand and followed a short distance behind. They weren't family and Cora believed the man was embarrassed by the situation. Much as she wanted to be of some assistance, it seemed best for she and Emily to leave and let Daniel's family take care of him. Thank goodness, the hotel was just across the street from the basin where the boat anchored.

She hesitated in front of the hotel as Daniel slowly mounted the steps, Judith by his side. He glanced over his shoulder and gave her a weak smile, attempting to lift his hand to signal goodbye before he entered the building. Cora had forgotten about Sterling until his voice startled her.

"May I see you home?" She jerked her head as he leaned down next to her ear.

Any other time, Cora would've loved to have his company. But not now. She was damp and disheveled and must look a fright, especially if she looked anything like Emily, whose hat ribbons hung like wet laundry, her hair and dress drooping as well. Truthfully, Cora's previous excitement before the outing had been replaced by a pall of disappointment, and she was no longer in a jovial mood. How could she make pleasant conversation in such a state? Tendrils of wet hair plastered her face, and she patted her hair to see if her hat was still attached to her head.

"Don't worry. You're still as lovely as you were this morning." Sterling grinned, peering down at her. "Wasn't that fun? We should do it again someday."

Cora frowned. "Fun? I hardly think Daniel had fun." Did he not care about Daniel's injury?

Sterling laughed. "Perhaps not. But you must admit our outing was exciting."

"Maybe so, but I'm afraid it was a bit too exciting for us,

though, and we need to go home and rest."

"Perhaps later, after you freshen up, you'd join me for dinner?"

Cora shook her head. "Thank you, but I must refuse your offer today. We're both tired, so we'll turn in early tonight, so we can refresh ourselves before church service tomorrow. Will we see you there?"

Sterling's eyebrows knit together, then he glanced over her head. "Excuse me. I need to have a word with that gentleman over there." He took her gloved hand and kissed the back of it. "I bid you adieu, dear Cora. We shall see you soon, hmmm?"

Before Cora could answer, Sterling hailed a man who had just stepped out of the hotel and headed the other direction, then hurried to catch up to him.

Chapter Eighteen

Daniel woke the next morning with the worst headache he'd ever had. As the room came into focus, he blinked and tried to sit up. "Uh!" He grunted and fell back on the bed.

Mother stood at the foot of his bed, straightening the bed covers. "You better stay put a while and let that knot on your head go down."

"What time is it?" Daniel shielded his eyes from the sunlight coming in the window.

"It's nine o'clock on Sunday morning. Judith and I were about to leave for church, but we wanted to see how you were first."

He hadn't noticed Judith standing in the room until Mother mentioned her. Her worried expression made him want to demonstrate that he was perfectly fine. Daniel tried to sit again, but his mother came around the side of the bed and placed her hand on his chest, pushing him back.

"No, you don't. You stay right here. We'll come back to check on you after church. Maybe by then, you'll be able to eat something."

Food? His head had taken priority and eating didn't sound appealing.

"Would you like me to pour you a cup of tea before we leave?"

He attempted to shake his head, but the motion hurt. "Not right now, thank you."

"All right then." Mother pulled on her gloves. "We'll be back in a couple of hours. You just rest."

As the door closed behind them, Daniel stared at the ceiling, scenes from yesterday's outing running through his mind. What a fool Cora must think him. He had gone along to protect her from Sterling and hadn't even been able to protect himself. What a poor example of chivalry. He touched the lump on his forehead, wincing at the pressure. Would his hat even cover it? His hat. It must be floating out to sea by now or sitting at the bottom, a new home for sea creatures. Too bad Cora didn't make men's hats. He'd have a reason to speak with her. At the moment, he had none. Just as well, though, since she'd rather spend time with that fool Sterling.

Tired of languishing in bed, Daniel slowly pushed himself up to sit on the side. His stomach churned at the movement. Perhaps he did need some tea. He stood, gripping the bed rail until he found his balance. Maybe he could borrow Sterling's cane. Daniel grimaced at the thought of Sterling twirling the cane. No, he didn't want to copy the man. As long as he'd known Sterling, Daniel had tried to keep the man out of trouble. But trouble followed Sterling or else he just attracted it.

Daniel used to have sympathy for his friend when they were younger, and Sterling was still struggling with the loss of his parents. But Daniel's sympathy had reached his limits when Sterling became old enough to be responsible for himself. With the fortune he'd inherited from his grandparents, Sterling spent excessive amounts of money on liquor, gambling and women. And even though he appeared to be happy and carefree, Daniel believed Sterling had not found happiness. Daniel had tried to reason with him, and turn his life around, but Sterling just laughed him off and shooed him away.

When Daniel left for Europe, Sterling had no one to supervise him anymore and his bad habits continued. Why he wanted to accompany Daniel's family to St. Augustine was a mystery, but Mother was still sympathetic and wouldn't deny him. Yet Sterling showed no interest in reforming yet. Would he ever change his ways? Daniel wondered if God had gotten as tired of Sterling's shenanigans as he had?

Daniel managed to balance well enough to pour himself some tea from the pitcher Mother left on the dresser. The open door to the balcony beckoned him outside for fresh air. Grasping the cup with one hand, he noticed his Panama hat and snatched it from the wood valet stand, gently placing it on his head before facing the bright sunlight. An invigorating cool morning breeze greeted him from the water, and he inhaled deeply, drawing in refreshment. He settled into a chair and took in the peaceful Sunday scene. Observing Sunday as a day of rest, the fishermen weren't out, and it was too early for most tourists' excursions. Across the Matanzas Bay, the lighthouse on Anastasia Island stood solitaire, yet regal above the foliage.

Where was his sketchbook? He glanced around and remembered its location in the room. But he wasn't up to retrieving it at the moment. He tried to memorize the details of the view— from the pelicans diving into azure water to the beach on Anastasia. Church bells pealed from town, reminding him he was missing the service today. No doubt Cora Miller would be there with Emily. And here he sat alone. He identified with the lighthouse that also appeared alone above the world with none other like it for company.

Daniel took a sip of the tea, feeling it trickle down to his empty stomach. An unfamiliar longing urged him to dress and join Mother and Judith, but why? He didn't miss their presence. Did he miss being in church? Or did he miss others that might be there? He shook his head, and the movement made him dizzy. He hated being useless, but when did he hate being alone?

Lone Bear's grizzled face came to mind. What must it be like for him? His home and his family were gone. Surely, Daniel had never experienced the same level of loneliness. Thank God, Making Medicine stayed with him. Daniel blew out a frustrated breath. There must be something more he could do for them. He downed the rest of his tea, then stood, tired of his own self-pity. He went inside and fetched his sketchbook, then returned to the balcony with a new concept. He would draw a picture of the area and then show it to the Indians and encourage them to copy his drawing. With renewed enthusiasm, Daniel decided it was time to resume his life and his mission, the one God had called him to when he landed in St. Augustine.

~

Cora glanced around the church, hoping to spot the Worthingtons. She needed to speak with them and was relieved to see them seated a few rows back. Daniel was not with them today.

Had he been hurt so badly? Her heart stung with regret that he had suffered the injury during their outing. She'd been frightened when he fell overboard and terrified that he might drown. Thank God, they'd gotten him back in the boat.

She'd forgotten to tell Judith her clothes were ready and needed to return them, but would telling her today be akin to working on Sunday? Perhaps taking them to her wouldn't be appropriate, but at least she could let her know. Cora had to get that money by tomorrow morning. Whispers and giggles came from behind her. Who on earth was causing such a ruckus? Thankfully, the service hadn't yet begun, but she hoped the offenders would quiet down. Before she could turn to look at the source of the commotion, Ruby, Molly, Charlotte and Katherine slid into the pew beside her and Emily, accompanied by Katie holding Ida. Captain Harn squeezed in beside his wife and everyone inched over to make room.

The excited girls tried to restrain themselves as they greeted Cora and her daughter. Cora leaned forward to catch a glimpse of Katie whose smile spread to her entire face. Cora soon forgot about the Worthingtons while she dealt with the unexpected arrival of her cousin's family. Emily was beside herself with joy, but Cora kept her hand on her daughter and a finger to her lips to shush the girls.

When the service ended, the family hurried out through the vestibule, trying not to knock over the minister at the door. As she edged past him, the minister caught her arm.

"Mrs. Miller. I heard that you went to the fort to help provide blankets for the Indians."

Stunned, Cora said, "Yes, sir. I accompanied Mrs. Anderson."

"Well, I just want to thank you for being so unselfish and considerate of our fellow man. God will bless you for your efforts."

Cora grasped for words, but uttered "Thank you" before slipping outside. If only he knew the truth about her "unselfishness." Guilt gripped her conscience knowing her motive had been quite the opposite. Would God really bless her efforts, since He did know the truth?

Once out the door, she pressed her way through the crowd to speak with Katie while her husband corralled the children, including Emily who had already joined them.

"I didn't know you were coming to church today," Cora said, giving her cousin a hug. "What a pleasant surprise."

Katie handed her squirming toddler to her husband, who spoke to Cora before he sauntered away to supervise a game of tag. "I'm happy we could make it too. We were up early, so I told William I wanted to go to church today." She looked across the churchyard at the children. "The weather was so nice, it didn't take long to row across."

"I'm so happy you came. I wish you could come every Sunday."

"I do too, but you know it isn't always possible. I've missed attending though." Katie glanced around at the people exiting the church. "Where's your 'new' friends?"

Cora cocked her head. "Friends?"

"You know, the ones you're making the hats for, the tourists."

"Oh, the Worthingtons." Cora turned to look over her shoulder as Mrs. Worthington and Judith approached. "Right here."

Cora nodded and smiled at the two women. "Mrs. Worthington, Judith, how are you today? I'd like to introduce you to my cousin, Katie Harn."

Mrs. Worthington extended her hand as did Judith and Katie shook them. "My pleasure, Mrs. Harn. I noticed your family when you entered the church."

Katie laughed. "I'm sure you did. I hope they didn't disturb you too much."

Mrs. Worthington smiled. "Actually, they were very well-behaved." She glanced over at the children. "So you live at the lighthouse? I'd hoped to visit it while we're in town."

"We actually live beside it, but yes, my husband is the keeper. That's Captain Harn over there with the girls."

"He appears to be outnumbered."

"Yes, poor man. We kept hoping for a boy, but the Lord sends us girls."

"And lovely ones too. I only have Judith here. I can't imagine so many girls."

Judith looked at her mother, frowning. "And you have two sons too. Are you forgetting Daniel and Henry?"

"I was referring to having daughters, but yes, I do have two sons. One is back in Boston and Daniel is here. He was under the weather today, though, and couldn't make it to church."

Cora was dying to ask. "Is Daniel still suffering from his injury?"

"Yes, I'm afraid he needed more rest today."

Katie glanced from Cora to Mrs. Worthington, eyebrows raised. "What happened to him?"

"I'm afraid it's a long story," Cora said. "I'll tell you after lunch. I think we need to relieve Captain Harn before he gets too exasperated."

"You're right. I'll go get the baby. We brought a picnic, so we'll go over to the square and find a shady spot." Katie turned to leave. "It was nice to meet you, Mrs. Worthington, Judith. Oh, and you're welcome to come visit at the lighthouse any time."

When Katie walked away, Cora faced the other two women. "I wanted to tell you that I've finished adding the trims to Judith's clothes. I can bring them over tomorrow if you'd like."

"That would be splendid," Mrs. Worthington said.

Judith's eyes sparkled. "I can't wait to see them."

"Why don't you join us for breakfast in the morning?" her mother asked.

"Thank you, but I need to get Emily to school first."

"Then come to the hotel after you drop her off. We'll wait for you in the dining room."

"I'll do that." Cora breathed a sigh of relief that she'd be able to get paid in time to give Mr. Beasley the rest of the rent. She needed to catch up with Katie's family, but a question loomed in her mind. Just how injured was Daniel? "Please tell Daniel I hope he'll be better soon."

"We will. Thank you for your concern."

When Cora rejoined the rest of the family, Katie had the food spread out, and the girls were sitting in a tight circle on the quilt she'd brought. The meal wasn't as fancy as yesterday's picnic, but the atmosphere was much more comfortable for Cora. Katie had brought biscuits with homemade blackberry jam, boiled eggs and oranges cut into slices. Captain Harn blessed the simple meal and the girls were finished practically before the adults had started. The children were excused to go play, leaving the adults a chance to converse without interruption. Captain Harn stepped away, giving the women some privacy while he supervised Ida's attempts to walk.

Katie and Cora watched some tourists play croquet in an area of the plaza, then Katie tapped Cora on the shoulder. "Cora, tell me what happened to Mr. Worthington."

Cora explained as best she could. "And so our picnic yesterday didn't turn out as well as this one."

"I had hoped to see the gentlemen you spoke of. What about the other one, Mr. Cunningham?"

"I don't know. I haven't seen him in church, so I don't know what he does on Sundays."

Katie motioned to a group of men standing in front of the hotel. "That's a nice-looking man over there, the one twirling a cane. He's pretty good at that."

Cora's gaze followed Katie's, knowing before she saw him that Sterling was the one Katie was referring to. With a cigar in one hand and the cane in the other, Sterling held court among a group of gentlemen. Laughter came from the group as Sterling threw the cane in the air, catching it while it was spinning.

"That's Sterling Cunningham."

"Oh? Well, he puts on quite a show."

Katie was right, Sterling did always seem to be performing. Perhaps he had been an actor at some point. She would ask him the next time she had a chance.

"Yes, he is entertaining, like I mentioned before."

"Do you like him?"

"Of course. Who wouldn't?" Images of Daniel's reactions to Sterling came to mind. Cora wasn't certain if Daniel did like Sterling.

"Your friend, Mr. Worthington, was he angry about the accident?"

"I don't know if it was anger or embarrassment. But it doesn't seem fair that Sterling is enjoying himself while Daniel can't leave his room."

Katie began gathering things to put back in the basket. "I see you're on familiar terms with these gentlemen, calling them by their given names."

"They asked, separately though, but I can't claim to be 'familiar' with either of them." Cora moved the picnic basket while Katie shook out the quilt.

Katie studied her. "Do you want to be?"

"I'm not sure I want to make that decision. They'll be leaving soon anyway, so it's best to keep my feelings at bay, where they've been for a long time."

Katie held the folded quilt, pausing to reflect on Cora's words while the military band from the nearby soldiers' barracks started playing a lively tune on the plaza.

"Perhaps you're right. I just wish you could find someone to be happy with."

"Maybe I will, but perhaps it shouldn't be a tourist."

"Well, there are soldiers here. You could always meet one of them."

Cora put her hands on her hips. "Katie, please stop trying to match me with someone. I'm perfectly happy with just Emily, with the two of us."

"All right, cousin. But I'm still praying for the right man to come along for you."

Would God listen to such a prayer? She thought Jacob had been the "right" man. Now that he was gone, could there be another "right" man?

"Cora, I meant what I told Mrs. Worthington. They are welcome to come to the island. Why don't you offer to accompany them and help me show them around?"

Cora crossed her arms. "Katie, you're impossible."

"Nothing is impossible with God, you know," Katie said with a twinkle in her eye.

Cora waved her off, turning away to see what the children were doing. A sensation of being watched made her scan the area. Then she saw him, a solitary figure standing in the shade of one of the massive oak trees at the far edge of the square. The erect stance was familiar, but it took her a moment to realize the man wearing a Panama hat was Daniel. He gazed at the water beyond the seawall and not at her, at least not at the moment. Had he been watching her?

Chapter Nineteen

Making Medicine studied Daniel's drawing, glancing up to view the actual setting, then back down at the sketch. He pointed to part of it and spoke to the other curious Indians gathered around.

"Would you like to draw this too?" Daniel said, making motions with his hands to explain his meaning.

Making Medicine grunted and nodded, handing back the sketchbook to Daniel before moving to a place on the terreplein and settling down where he could see across the bay. Zotom approached Daniel, his hand extended toward the sketchbook. Daniel passed it over, and Zotom examined it while Daniel motioned to Anastasia Island, hoping the Indian made the connection.

Zotom pointed to his chest, looking at Daniel. "I do."

If men could be giddy, Daniel could think of no other word to describe the feeling of hearing the Indian communicate with him. Mr. Fox had been delayed today, so Daniel was on his own to convey understanding to the men this time. Sometimes he wondered if he made any sense to the Indians, but Zotom's response affirmed his efforts. Daniel was eager to see how the Indians saw the same scene that he did. And unless he was mistaken, they showed some enthusiasm for the project as well.

Lone Bear sat by himself, staring ahead, but still bothered by coughing fits. Daniel approached, and squatted beside the old Indian. Lone Bear didn't acknowledge Daniel's presence, and Daniel wasn't sure what to say. The old man did not attempt to draw as the others had, yet he appeared to be aware of what they were doing. Daniel cleared his throat. "Lone Bear, I hope you are feeling better."

No response came from the man. Daniel assumed he was failing to communicate, so he stood. A noise came from the old man. Did he speak? Daniel leaned down. "Did you say something?"

Lone Bear raised his arm and pointed out beyond the fort's walls. "Big water."

Shock rippled through Daniel. "Yes, yes, it is big water." The Indian had glimpsed the ocean beyond the island. Was this the first time he'd ever seen the ocean? Even more intriguing, was this the first time he'd ever spoken English? Surely not.

Lone Bear made a waving motion with his hand. "Fish."

"Yes, there's fish. Big fish." Daniel expanded his hands to show the size of a big fish.

Something akin to a smile crossed Lone Bear's face. Daniel pretended to eat. "You like to eat fish?"

Lone Bear nodded. "Me catch big fish."

What was he saying? Had he caught big fish before or was he saying he wanted to? What was taking Mr. Fox so long?

Daniel acted like he was casting a fishing line and pulling in a fish. The Indian eyed him with curiosity. Perhaps he didn't fish the same way. A plan took root in Daniel's mind that seemed impossible. Yet, he knew there was a way to make the plan work. And he was willing to do all he could to that end. The only problem was getting Lieutenant Pratt to agree.

Mr. Fox arrived, and Daniel apprised him of the day's events so far. "I didn't know they could speak English yet."

"Some of them know a little English, but they don't want you to know."

Daniel arched his eyebrows. "Do you think he's telling me he wants to go fishing?" Daniel asked, his eyes on Lone Bear.

"Could be. I'll ask, but I don't know how he'll be able to do that."

Mr. Fox went over to Lone Bear and spoke to him. The Indian nodded, and Mr. Fox glanced at Daniel, nodding as well.

He returned to Daniel's side. "You're right. He used to catch fish from a lake out West. He's never seen so much water before and thinks it has many fish."

"He's right, of course. Which is why I intend to take them fishing."

Mr. Fox drew back, his eyes wide. "Mr. Worthington, I do believe you're delusional. Take the prisoners fishing?"

"Why not? I mean, for those who are interested. We can retain a couple of fishing boats to take them over to Anastasia. They can fish from the boat or the shore."

"And you believe Lieutenant Pratt will allow this excursion?"

"I think I can persuade him. I'm confident the men won't try to escape."

Daniel removed his hat and wiped his brow. One of the Indians nearby pointed to him and muttered to his neighbor, then the two chuckled and shared their amusement with others.

"Mr. Fox, why are these men laughing? I believe they're laughing at me."

Fox went over to the Indians and came back laughing as well. He indicated Daniel's head. "It's that big purple knot on your forehead. They want to know if your squaw is angry with you."

Daniel touched the bump that he had forgotten, then laughed along with the others. "Tell them I don't have a squaw, but if I did, she'd probably be angry with me!"

~

Mrs. Worthington and Judith waved Cora over when she entered the hotel dining room.

"There you are. Please, have a seat." Mrs. Worthington motioned to a chair, then scanned the room. "I'll get the waiter to come and take your order."

"Thank you, but I had breakfast with Emily at home."

"Won't you at least have some tea with us?"

"Yes, tea would be nice." Cora settled into a chair at the table, placing the carpetbag on the floor beside her.

"Or would you care for orange juice?" Mrs. Worthington lifted a glass. "How I love this drink. It's quite a treat for us here." She turned to Judith. "Judith enjoys it too don't you, Judith?"

Judith nodded. "Yes, I do. I wish we could have it back home."

"Tea is just fine." Cora glanced around the room. "Are you ladies alone today?"

"Daniel is at the fort and who knows where Sterling is." Mrs.

Worthington spread some butter on her biscuit, then took a bite.

"So Daniel is recovered from his injury?" Cora relaxed as if a load had lifted from her shoulders.

"He seems to be, at least he feels better but the ugly knot is still there. He couldn't wait to get to the fort today."

"Oh? Is something special happening at the fort?" Not that she cared, but she wanted to know what made Daniel so eager to go there.

"Not that I know of, but he was excited to try a new idea with the Indians." Mrs. Worthington took a sip of her juice and Judith took the opportunity to speak.

"Daniel made some sketches yesterday and thought the Indians might like to copy them."

"Really? I wonder if they will." Was he sketching when she saw him yesterday? She didn't remember seeing his sketchbook.

"I'm sure we'll find out when he gets back."

Cora couldn't take her eyes off the gorgeous brooch Mrs. Worthington wore on a chain around her neck. The pink stone in the center reflected the light from the window.

"Your brooch is lovely," she said. "The scrollwork is so unique."

Mrs. Worthington touched the brooch. "Thank you, it's one of my favorites. My husband bought it for me when we were in Europe. The stone is pink tourmaline."

"It's so pretty." Cora tried to count the diamonds surrounding the stone, but lost count.

Judith eyed the bag beside Cora. "Are those my clothes?"

Cora glanced down. "Yes, I can show them to you when you're finished here."

"I am." Judith pushed away from the table. "Mother, are you? If not, we can go on up to the room and you can join us later."

Cora was amused to see Judith assert herself. Clearly, she was eager to see her "new" clothes. And for Judith, they would indeed be "new."

Mrs. Worthington folded her napkin and placed it beside her plate. "I have finished as well. Let's go see what Mrs. Miller has done to your clothes."

"Do you think Sterling went to the fort with Daniel?" Cora hoped she didn't sound too nosy.

"Oh, heavens no." Mrs. Worthington waved like shooing a fly away. "That's the last place he'd go. I doubt he's even awake yet."

"Sterling likes to stay up late." Judith offered an excuse.

Her mother emitted a slight cough. "Judith's right. Sterling's days and nights aren't the same as most people."

Certainly not like those with children. Or jobs. Yet, Daniel was out early and didn't have either one. He must perceive his work with the Indians equivalent to a job.

When they reached the hotel room, Cora opened the bag and spread the clothes out on the bead. She spotted Judith's new hat on the dresser and laid it in the midst, noting how each piece coordinated.

Judith's smile was worth Cora's efforts. The young woman touched every detail that had been added, a look of awe and satisfaction on her face. "They're so pretty." She looked up at Cora. "Thank you."

Cora beamed, pride in her work and grateful for her customer's satisfaction. "You are quite welcome, Judith. I truly enjoyed the project."

"Your talent is admirable. You are every bit as much an artist as my son."

Cora was flattered. She appreciated the compliment but wondered if Daniel would agree their work fit in the same category. "I'm so happy you are pleased."

"Have you finished your new dress yet?" Mrs. Worthington held up one of Judith's bodices, examining it.

"Not quite. I finished Emily's dress first. I still have more work to do on mine."

"I'm sure it will be lovely, if this work is any indication." Mrs. Worthington fanned herself. "It's getting warm in here. Would you care to join us out on the balcony?"

"Thank you, but no. I must get back to the shop in case my other customers drop by."

"Certainly." Mrs. Worthington stepped to the open door of the balcony. "But you're not finished with us yet."

"Oh? Of course, you need to pay me for Judith's bodices. I almost forgot." Thank goodness Mrs. Worthington mentioned it so she didn't have to ask.

A look of surprise crossed Mrs. Worthington's face. "Yes,

that's true." She crossed the room to her reticule and pulled out some money, then handed it to Cora. "But that's not what I meant."

"Do you have more for me to do?"

"Yes. I'd like another hat for myself and Judith while we're in town. I certainly wish your shop was in Boston."

Cora swelled with happiness. The door to her success had just opened wider.

Chapter Twenty

Cora was in her shop experimenting with various hat designs for Mrs. Worthington and Judith when the bell on the door rang behind her. Startled, she turned around to find Sterling entering.

"Sterling! I didn't expect to see you."

Sterling grinned, sauntering in and touching one of the hats on display. "I like to surprise people."

"Well you did. What brings you in here today?" Cora set down the hat she was creating on the glass countertop.

"Do I need a reason to see a lovely lady?" He approached the counter and leaned across it.

Heat scorched Cora's face as she searched for a response. "Is there someone you'd like me to make a hat for?"

"Hmm. Perhaps. Why don't you make one for a pretty little blonde lady, about this tall?" He held his hand up to the top of her head.

It was uncomfortably warm in the shop, and Cora grabbed her fan and tried to keep the perspiration off her face. "I'm afraid it's not profitable for me to make hats for myself."

"What if I paid you for it?"

"You'd pay me to make a hat for myself?" Cora fanned more rapidly. "Why on earth would you do that?"

"So I could see you wear it, of course." Sterling's eyes gleamed almost unnaturally.

He leaned in closer and Cora instinctively stepped back.

"Sterling, that's foolishness."

He straightened and chuckled. "Actually, what I really came in here for was to ask if you'd join me for dinner, allow me to make up for the unfortunate events of our outing last Saturday."

"Tonight?"

"Is that too short a notice?" Sterling glanced down at the countertop, back up at her. "I hoped that perhaps we could enjoy an evening with just the two of us, have dinner then take an evening stroll on the seawall."

Her breath caught. "You mean, without Emily? I wouldn't leave her alone."

"Of course not. Perhaps there's someone who might look after her for a while?"

The prospect of an evening alone with Sterling was inviting, but who could stay with Emily?

"No, no one. I don't have family here."

"Oh, but you do. What about your cousin over on the island?" He fiddled with a feather on one of the hats. "I saw you with her family yesterday in the park."

"You did?" He had noticed her? She thought he was completely unaware that she was nearby.

"I certainly did. You and Emily seemed to be having a delightful time."

"We were. But Katie doesn't come to town often."

"Perhaps Mrs. Worthington or Judith wouldn't mind."

Cora drew herself up. "I would never ask them to do such a thing. That would be very presumptuous of me."

The bell rang behind Sterling and a woman entered, someone Cora didn't recognize.

"Excuse me, Sterling. I need to help this customer." She squeezed past him to approach the lady.

"Well, think about it. Maybe not this evening, but another night."

Cora didn't answer as she drew close to the woman, turning her back on Sterling. "Yes, ma'am. Can I help you find something?"

"I hope you can. A friend of mine told me you made her hat. I admired it so much, I wanted to see your shop."

From the corner of her eye, Cora saw Sterling approach the door. "Excuse me, ladies. I'll leave you to your business." He paused with his hand on the doorknob. "I hope you can work something out, Cora. I'll be waiting to hear from you." As the door closed behind him, Cora blew out a breath.

Cora turned to the woman again. "I'm sorry for the interruption. I'm Cora Miller, and I didn't get your name." Cora extended her hand.

"Margaret Lowell. Pamela Worthington's family and mine have been friends for many years. I had planned to go to the other millinery shop instead before Pamela told me about yours."

Alarm coursed through Cora. Other millinery shop? She'd hardly call a corner of Farley's store a real millinery shop. Surely, she wouldn't buy any of those hideous hats.

Cora swallowed hard and forced a smile. "Well, I'm so glad you came to my shop. My hats are unique, especially created to suit each of my customer's specific tastes."

"Well, Pamela was pleased with your work."

Cora silently thanked Mrs. Worthington. She scanned the room for an idea, then spotted the black felt hat she'd been working on and retrieved it to show to Mrs. Lowell. "Here's a hat I'm making for Mrs. Worthington. Would something similar be to your liking—of course with your own preferences in trims?"

Mrs. Lowell examined the hat. "What sort of decoration would you put on it?"

Cora motioned to the drawer of accessories on the counter. "I have a few jeweled hat pins, feathers, ribbons and these roses made from satin." Cora pointed to a finished hat decorated with two white roses.

Mrs. Lowell walked over to the counter and picked up various accessories, studying them. "Hmm. I see." She faced Cora. "We're leaving next week, so I know you don't have much notice, but do you think it's possible to make me a hat like this before we go?"

"I'd love to, but the amount of time depends on whether I already have the right materials. "Do you know what you'd like? Why don't you browse a while and see?"

"Thank you. I will." Mrs. Lowell examined each display while Cora waited, hands clasped. "I see you made the acquaintance of Sterling Cunningham."

Cora shouldn't have been surprised that the woman knew Sterling if she knew the Worthingtons that well but wondered why she made the comment.

"Yes, I've only known him a short time since he's visiting as you are." Cora moved to a hat and adjusted the ribbon. "I assume you know him fairly well? Since he's a friend of the Worthingtons also?"

"I don't know him personally. But we've often been to some of the same social events in Boston. Some of my friends thought he'd be a good suitor for their daughters."

Cora could picture mothers in Boston trying to match their daughters with Sterling. "Oh? I can see why—he's attractive and amiable."

"Oh, there's no doubt about it." She inclined her head to Cora. "Not to mention the fact that he is very affluent. He inherited a fortune from his grandparents."

Cora wiped her sweaty palms on her skirt. This was the same man who had just invited her to dinner. Alone. "What a surprise that he's never married."

The woman clicked her tongue. "He's been associated with several young ladies, some whom I'm sure expected a proposal. But he can't seem to settle down. He hasn't any relatives to encourage him in that regard either. No doubt Pamela has tried to convince him, but without success." Mrs. Lowell lowered her voice. "Some say he's spent his fortune already in gambling and carousing. But I wouldn't know about that."

"I see." Cora didn't want Mrs. Lowell to think she was very interested in Sterling. Searching for a way to change the conversation, she selected a hat and held it in front of the woman. "So, is this hat similar to what you'd like to have?"

"That's perfect, but can you add a few of those roses to it?"

"Yes, I can. Is there anything else you'd like—a ribbon or a hat pin perhaps?"

Mrs. Howell picked up a hat pin from the drawer. "I like this one."

Cora nodded. "Excellent choice. That's a real ruby, not like these glass stones."

"I'm aware of the difference, Mrs. Miller. I have quite a nice jewelry collection. In fact, rubies are my favorite." She pointed to her earrings that were suspended ovals with diamond-encircled rubies.

"Yes, I see. Those are lovely." Cora brushed aside the slight and arranged the items for the hat on the counter. "All right then. I'll get right to work on this."

"I'll be back at the end of the week for it."

As Mrs. Lowell left, Cora exhaled, thankful for another customer, and thankful for Mrs. Worthington's recommendation. What if other tourists went to Farley's instead and didn't know about her shop? Word-of-mouth endorsements were so important to her business.

Cora set to work so she could get the hat ready before Mrs. Lowell left town, laying aside Mrs. Worthington's hat design for the time being. But as she worked, the conversation about Sterling resonated through her mind.

Obviously, many women found Sterling handsome and entertaining. Who wouldn't want to win his affection? Mrs. Lowell's words made Cora feel like she was just another woman striving for his attention. How foolish of her to think his attention for her was unique, yet she hadn't had such attention from a man for so long, she was thrilled to receive such once again, especially now that she had reached the age when flirtation was rare. She knew from the moment she met him that he wouldn't be staying in town, so she had known he wouldn't be part of her future. Still, she'd harbored a glimmer of hope that his attention could develop into more than a casual acquaintance. Common sense told her she was foolish to hope such a thing. But why not enjoy his company while she could? She didn't believe he had no money, not from the way he dressed and seemed to have whatever he wanted.

If only she could find someone to watch Emily for a short while, she could get to know him better and find out the truth about his character. Suddenly she remembered a conversation she'd had with the lady who ran the boarding house. Mrs. Gardner loved Emily and had offered to watch her before. It was short notice, but perhaps she wouldn't mind. After all, she lived there as well, so it shouldn't be much trouble. Her heart raced as she watched the clock. She needed to ask her as soon as possible.

She should work on Mrs. Lowell's hat, but there wasn't enough time, and first, she had to get Emily from school. As she put her accessories away, she noticed an empty space in the drawer. One of the jeweled pins was missing. Had Mrs. Lowell picked it up and laid it somewhere? She glanced around to see, even searched the floor in case it had been dropped, but the pin was nowhere in sight. Where did it go? She'd apparently had too much on her mind and couldn't remember what she'd done with it. Surely, it would come to her. But first, she had to go meet Emily. She hurriedly locked the shop, then walked briskly toward the school. As she rounded the corner toward the red brick schoolhouse, she bumped into Daniel Worthington.

"Oh! I'm sorry," she said, moving to the side and out of his way.

"Cora. The fault is all mine. I'm afraid I wasn't paying attention to where I was going. I was looking for the haberdashery that's supposed to be around here somewhere. It appears I need a new hat."

He was wearing the Panama hat she'd seen him in on Sunday, but the style didn't quite fit him.

Cora collected herself and pointed down the street. "It's just down there on the left. Do you see the sign—Farley's Haberdashery?" Seems like that name kept coming up today.

"Ah yes, thank you." He paused as if he wanted to say something.

She peered up at him. "How is your head?"

He took off his hat and showed her. "I'm afraid I'm still a 'knot-head,' but I do feel much better today. I rested most of yesterday."

"Your mother told me when I saw her and Judith at church." Cora hesitated. "Did I see you yesterday afternoon on the town square?"

"Yes, I confess. I was tired of languishing in the hotel room and needed to stretch my legs. Wasn't very sociable though. The bright sunshine and noise were particularly bothersome." He smiled and put his hat back on. "But that's passed now."

"I'm happy to hear that you're better. You had us worried." Cora recalled the fear she'd had when he fell overboard.

He raised an eyebrow. "A bit of excitement for your day, heh? I'm afraid I must also apologize for my rude behavior."

She put her hand out to touch his arm. "Please don't worry about that. You were quite out of sorts, through no fault of your own. I understand. I'm just sorry I couldn't have done more to help."

"That's very nice of you. I hope I can make up for my rudeness."

"You are. In fact, you seem to be feeling more cheerful than usual today." Remembering Emily, Cora resumed her walk to the school, and Daniel changed directions to accompany her.

"I am, in fact, very cheerful. My time at the fort today was quite productive."

The fort again. Next, he'd talk about Indians.

"That's nice."

Daniel launched into telling her what had happened with the Indians that day. She had never seen him so animated, and much as she didn't want to hear about the Indians, she listened. When he told her about Lone Bear and the big water and big fish, she giggled, surprising herself.

"So he can speak English?"

"Apparently he knows a little. I must say I was bowled over when I heard him use English words."

They arrived at the school in time for the children to let out. When Emily spotted Cora and Daniel, she ran over.

"Mr. Daniel! Are you all better now?"

Daniel took his hat off and leaned over so Emily could see his head.

She pointed to his injury. "You have a bobo. Does it hurt?"

"Not much. It's getting better." He put his hat back on and straightened. "Well, I suppose I need to find that haberdashery." He bowed to them. "Ladies, it was a pleasure to see you."

Cora smiled as she watched him walk away. What a curious man. Most the time he was serious, brooding even. But today, he was quite the opposite. And all because of Indians.

Chapter Twenty-One

Standing in front of the mirror, she studied her reflection, congratulating herself on how well the dress had turned out. The lavender color was even prettier than she'd envisioned for the dress.

"Momma, you look beautiful!" Emily bounced on the edge of her bed, dressed in her nightgown, ready for Mrs. Gardner to tuck her in bed later.

Cora turned, glancing over her shoulder at the ruffled bustle that matched the pleats she'd added to the lower skirt. The top of her bodice was trimmed with wide lace that graced her shoulders and met in a V neckline in the front and the back. A ribbon of violet was tied at the elbow of each sleeve that ended in tiny pleats trimmed with lace.

Cora admired the accent silk roses she'd made, also in violet, that were placed at each V. She'd used the same roses only smaller, "rosettes," she called them, on the small hat that matched her dress. Half of her hair was braided as usual and twisted into a bun where the hat perched. But for this evening, she'd let the rest of her hair hang down her back, loosely twisted in a mock braid.

A knock on the door signaled Mrs. Gardner's arrival. Emily hopped down from the bed and ran to the door. When she opened it, she said, "Mrs. Gardner! Look how pretty my momma is!"

Mrs. Gardner surveyed Cora from head to toe. "She is very pretty indeed, Emily." The woman entered the room and walked around Cora. "You are a fine seamstress as well as a hatmaker, Mrs. Miller."

"Thank you. I'm pleased with the way the dress came out. I haven't made one for quite some time."

"She's making one for me too!" Emily pranced about. "We're going to match!"

"Why, I can't wait to see the two of you in your new dresses."

"I'm almost finished with Emily's. It should be ready by Sunday."

Would Sterling be as impressed? Cora had anticipated this evening so much, her hands were wet with perspiration. She'd pictured herself strolling through town on the arms of a dashing man like Sterling. Who might they encounter on their outing? Perhaps some of the affluent townspeople or even women from the benevolence society. What would they think, seeing her so well-attired with a wealthy man?

She dabbed some lavender water behind her ears and sprinkled some on her handkerchief before placing it in her tiny evening reticule. After pulling on lace evening gloves, Cora grabbed her lace shawl, then faced her daughter and Mrs. Gardner.

"Mr. Cunningham should be arriving soon. I think I'll go out on the veranda to wait for him."

She leaned over to hug Emily and gave her a kiss on the cheek.

"You be a good girl. Mrs. Gardner is going to read to you. Don't wait up for me." Turning to Mrs. Gardner, she said, "Thank you so much. I'm sorry for the short notice."

Mrs. Gardner waved her off. "It's not a bother. Emily and I are going to have a good time, aren't we?"

Emily nodded. "Yes, ma'am."

As Cora stepped onto the veranda of the boarding house, Sterling was coming through the gate.

Her heart beat faster at the sight of the man who would be her evening escort. He looked refreshed, his wavy dark hair combed back and sporting a top hat. His tailored gray jacket, trimmed with darker gray lapels, was fitted, but open to reveal his brocade vest and gold watch chain. The white shirt beneath had the broad collars that were fashionable and a black string tie at the neck. He was clean-shaven except for his trimmed goatee and perfect mustache. She had seldom seen a more strikingly handsome man.

His brilliant smile appeared as he spotted her on the veranda. Crossing the yard in great strides, he removed his hat and bowed low when he reached her. "Good evening, my dear lady."

He stood, took her hand and kissed the back of it. "You are a vision." Lifting his gaze to her, his eyes shone in such a way that heat raced through her. When he let go of her hand, she withdrew her fan and made use of it. "Shall we?" He extended his elbow and she clutched it with her hand as they exited the gate.

"I've made reservations at the Palmetto Restaurant." Sterling smiled down at her. "I've heard it's the best restaurant in town."

Yes, it was, at least according to what others said about it. The restaurant was also the most expensive in town which was why she'd never dined there. But tonight she'd join the diners who could afford to go there. Obviously, Sterling was one of them. A little thrill rippled in her stomach.

The waning sunset had dappled the white walls of the homes they passed in pastels of pink and rose. A cool breeze wafted from the bay resulting in comfortable temperate weather, perfect for a promenade through town. The atmosphere was almost magical as they entered the restaurant and were seated near a fountain in the courtyard. A Spanish musician strolled among the tables, singing and playing romantic tunes.

Sterling removed his hat and ran his fingers through his thick hair. The waiter approached, and Sterling ordered a bottle of wine. When the server finished recanting the restaurant's specialties, Sterling said, "We shall have one of each!"

"Are you that hungry?" Cora placed her napkin in her lap. "How can the two of us eat so much?"

"I doubt that we can, but we will get to taste their repertoire."

In the back of her mind, Cora heard her parents' admonishment not to be wasteful. What a different perspective the wealthy had who could discard whatever was unwanted or unneeded. She'd always been more frugal, saving every scrap of fabric so she could use it to accessorize other dresses or hats. In fact the very rosettes on her hat were products of scraps.

When the waiter returned with the wine, he opened it for Sterling to taste, and upon Sterling's approval, poured a glass for each of them. Cora seldom drank wine, so she doubted she'd drink the whole glass. Sterling lifted his glass. "Here's to our lovely evening together." Cora raised her glass and tapped his before taking a sip. Sterling downed his glass in one swallow, then poured himself another.

"Where will you go when you leave St. Augustine?" Cora set down her glass, barely touched.

"Hmm. I'm not certain at this time, but more than likely Europe. I haven't been to Italy for some time, so I might go there."

"So you've been there before?" Did she sound so unrefined not having ever gone to Europe?

"Oh yes. Many times." Sterling drank half a glass of wine. "You haven't seen Europe?"

Was she the only person who hadn't? She shook her head. "No, I'm afraid not."

"Then you should! Nothing like it here in the States."

Going to Europe was probably not going to happen for her. She just barely made enough to keep a roof over she and Emily's heads. "I'd love to. I just don't know when I'll be able to go."

Sterling began to talk about all the places he'd visited in Europe. When the waiter arrived at their table with a platter of roasted oysters, Sterling stopped briefly to sample one. Then he talked about the many places he'd traveled—England, Scotland, Ireland, France, Greece, Italy, even Egypt—and his favorite features of each country. He spoke of exotic delicacies, spectacular sights, and unusual customs.

The waiter then brought out bowls of fish chowder, platters of smoked mullet, fried fish, and roasted pork, dishes of paella and ceviche, and arroz con pollo. The huge amount of food stunned Cora, but she tried to take a bite of each item just to be polite. Sterling helped himself to everything, ordering another bottle of wine in the process. Why the man wasn't portly was a mystery. Instead, he was tall and thin. Perhaps he only ate one meal a day.

Cora enjoyed hearing Sterling's animated stories and pictured the scenes he described. She barely said a word. After all, her life had been pretty boring compared to his. She hadn't been anywhere exciting and didn't have much to tell. Sterling didn't seem to notice the conversation was one-sided, but rather appeared to relish sharing his life exploits with her. He certainly enjoyed an enviable life of leisure and pleasure.

When he paused to take another swallow of wine, she found a

chance to speak. "Thank you for sharing your adventures with me. You've traveled quite a bit."

He nodded, spearing a bite of pork. "Yes, and I plan to travel even more. There are so many places I have yet to see."

"It must be nice to have such freedom. Have you never had to work?"

Sterling laughed. "My grandfather tried to teach me his business when I was younger, but I just never had the aptitude for it." He ate the pork, then chased it with more wine, then wiped his mouth and grinned. "Good thing he did, though, as he left me with a sizable inheritance."

The waiter approached and asked if Sterling needed anything.

Sterling waved his hand toward the food. "We're finished with this. You may remove it. However, please bring another bottle of wine."

"Yes, sir." The waiter stacked the dishes, many still full of food. "May I bring you our signature dessert, sour-orange pie?"

"Sounds delicious. Yes, bring two pieces."

"Yes, sir. And some coffee too?"

"Not for me. I'll stick to wine." As if remembering Cora was still there, he looked across the table at her. "Unless my dear lady would like some."

Cora smiled at the waiter. "I would, thank you." She hadn't finished her first glass of wine, but feared she'd fall asleep if she did, since she was beginning to tire.

Soon after the waiter returned with the pie and coffee, and Sterling dug in with his fork. "Um. Very good. I've not tasted a dessert such as this."

Cora tried the pie which melted in her mouth. "Oranges are so plentiful in this area they're used in a variety of ways."

Sterling finished his pie, then pushed the plate aside. Leaning across the table, he reached for her hand and covered it with his own. "Cora, I have the most fantastic idea." His eyes gleamed as his gaze penetrated. "You should come with me."

"C...come with you? Where?"

"Anywhere you want to go. We can travel together. It would be great fun."

Cora swallowed her shock and her heart pounded. Was this a proposal of marriage?

Sterling waved his hand in the air. "Just think of all the places we could visit—the pyramids of Egypt, the Louvre, the Mediterranean—why Cora, we could go around the world!"

She didn't know what to say. She wasn't even sure what he was asking. If this were a marriage proposal, shouldn't he profess his love first? And what about Emily? Would she travel with them?

Cora slid her hand out from his and sat back, staring at Sterling as she envisioned the life he described. The prospect sent a thrill rippling through her as she saw herself riding elephants or seeing the ancient ruins of Rome. What a carefree life that would be. She wouldn't have to work or worry about paying bills anymore. How would Emily enjoy that type of lifestyle?

"Sterling, you surprise me. I'm flattered you would want my company on your travels."

"My dear lady, why wouldn't I? We would have such a splendid time."

The waiter returned to see if they needed anything else, and Sterling tapped his wine glass. Cora needed to stand, though, to move after so much food. "Sterling, would you be open to going for a walk? I am absolutely stuffed and simply must get some exercise."

A look of surprise crossed Sterling's face, then comprehension. "Yes, we must take our evening stroll on the seawall!" He stood, taking a wad of money from his pocket and flipped through it, then handed a pile of it to the waiter. "There. That should cover our expenses."

"Thank you, sir," the waiter said with a bow.

Cora wondered just how much their dinner had cost and how much Sterling had paid. The latter appeared to have been substantial.

They left the corner restaurant and walked two blocks toward the bay. Other couples were already enjoying the evening promenade on the seawall. Sterling held her hand as she stepped up, then he joined her. As they passed other folks, Sterling tipped his hat and Cora smiled. She still ruminated on Sterling's proposal, not certain what he has asked. Perhaps he was asking to court her, but wasn't he already? Unfortunately, there were no parents to ask permission of, much less advise her. If only she could talk to Katie.

Cora's head swam with confusion as she tried to sort things out.

She drove those thoughts aside and inhaled the fresh air, letting herself float along on Sterling's arm. What a handsome couple they made as they strolled arm-in-arm. Cora reveled in the realization that she was where she had wanted to be—one of "them," one of the privileged. Surely, she was one of the best dressed as well. As she scrutinized others on the seawall, she was assured that no one else had a dress so fine nor a hat so perfectly suited.

Walking to the point where the seawall came to an end, the fort loomed ahead, dark and foreboding in the night. A shudder shook her as the image of the Indians came to her mind, laying on the hard floors. Had the blankets she'd handed out made any difference to their comfort? Why did she have to think about the Indians now?

Sterling tripped, and Cora steadied him. She glanced at him. "Are you all right?"

He grinned and spread his arms out wide. "Perfectly fine. Ready to walk a tightrope." He moved to the edge of the seawall and tried to walk with one foot in front of the other, teetering on the wall.

"Sterling, please don't." She reached out to him. "Please," just as he wobbled on the edge and fell over into the water.

Chapter Twenty-Two

Cora scrutinized the hat in her hand, then set it on a stand and stepped back. Mrs. Lowell's hat didn't take as long to create as she'd thought, only two days. The hat was black straw with red ribbon around the crown, then the same ribbon was folded into bows and ruffles stacked high on the top, as the woman had requested. She was especially pleased with the silk roses that adorned the brim. Experimenting with fabric scraps, folding and sewing them, she had created replicas of real roses with rows of petals. Five roses of varying sizes in shades of red, pink and burgundy were the result with the ruby hatpin resting in the center of the large red rose in the center of the cluster.

The roses had taken some time to perfect, but Cora loved the finished product. After showing Mrs. Lowell the samples she had in the shop, Cora decided to make these roses her signature specialty, especially if customers liked them as much as she did. While she waited for Mrs. Lowell to stop by the shop to check on the hat's progress, she'd fashion more roses in various colors to add to her inventory. Cora hoped she'd be pleased with her hat.

She was just finishing a pink rose when Mrs. Lowell arrived.

"Good morning, Mrs. Miller. How is my hat coming along?"

"Good morning, Mrs. Lowell." She withdrew the hat from the shelf behind her and held it out. "It's finished. How do you like it?"

Mrs. Lowell's eyes widened as she reached for the hat, touching it as if it might break. "Oh my. How marvelous." She looked at the mirror on the wall. "May I try it?"

Cora beamed. "Of course. I can't wait to see it on you."

The woman placed the hat on her head and Cora came around the counter to adjust the angle above the woman's high chignon. Mrs. Lowell faced forward, then turned left, then right, eyeing her reflection.

"I absolutely adore this hat, Mrs. Miller." She continued to take varied glances at the mirror. "You have surpassed my expectations!"

"I'm so pleased you like it. The hat is very becoming on you."

Mrs. Lowell carefully touched one of the roses. "These are beautiful, unique. You made these yourself?"

Cora clasped her hands while she watched the woman admire her hat. "Yes, ma'am. They're one of my specialties."

Mrs. Lowell touched Cora on the arm. "Mrs. Miller, you do have a flair for design. You are quite an artist."

"Thank you. I do enjoy what I do."

"What a blessing, that what you do blesses others so much. God has given you a special gift, Mrs. Miller." Mrs. Lowell withdrew some money from her reticule and handed it to Cora. "I believe this should be adequate for your work."

"Thank you very much." She resisted the urge to count the money and placed it in her skirt's side pocket, but was hopeful she had enough to pay Mr. Beasley the rest of her rent. "Shall I put it in a hatbox for you?"

"Yes, please. I'm tempted to wear it back to the hotel, but I believe I should save it for a special occasion."

As Cora took the hat from her, she remembered the missing pin. Maybe Mrs. Lowell would recall it. "Mrs. Lowell, when you were in here the other day, do you remember seeing a hatpin with emeralds on it?"

"No, I don't recall an emerald one. Why?"

"I've misplaced it and am trying to determine when I last saw it."

"I'm sorry, I can't help you. I've misplaced my ruby earrings as well. I've been frantic searching for them."

"Oh dear, I'm so sorry. You wore them in here last time, and I noticed how beautiful they were." As Cora handed her the hat box, the door opened and in walked Mrs. Worthington and Judith.

"Hello, ladies. I believe you know Mrs. Lowell?"

The women exchanged pleasantries.

"I see Mrs. Lowell took my advice." She looked at Mrs. Lowell. "Is Mrs. Miller going to make a hat for you?"

"She already has, a superb hat." She opened the hatbox and held it so they could see the contents.

"Why it is lovely!" Mrs. Worthington said.

Judith pointed to the roses. "Ooh, I like these. I've never seen them before."

"I just began making them. I must say I'm pleased with the way they turned out."

"They're wonderful. I want a hat with some of those on it too."

Mrs. Worthington nodded. "I'm sure Mrs. Miller can make you one." She raised her gaze from the hat to look at Cora. "Can't you, Mrs. Miller?"

"Yes, of course."

When Mrs. Lowell took her leave, Cora and Judith began talking about designs for another hat. Mrs. Worthington sat in one of the chairs and observed the two. "You see, Mrs. Miller. I told you I would tell others about your shop. When Margaret gets back to Boston, you'll be the talk of the town."

"Me?" Cora blushed. "I hardly think the rest of Boston wants to hear about a milliner in St. Augustine."

"Oh, but they do. The women will be after their husbands for a trip to this town just to have you make them a hat."

"Please, you flatter me."

"As I should. Never underestimate your ability, Mrs. Miller. Too many women do."

"I won't. I'm thankful I enjoy what I do."

After she and Judith had completed plans for Judith's next hat, Cora turned to Mrs. Worthington. "Would you like to order your new hat?"

"I'm thinking about it. Let me have some more time to figure out what I want." She pushed up from the chair. "You know, there is something I'd like you to do for me though."

"Yes, ma'am? I'll do whatever you wish."

"I'd like to go over to Anastasia Island. I know I don't need permission, but I'd like to see your cousin Mrs. Harn and have her show us around. Can you arrange that?"

"Yes, I'm sure I can. When would you like to go?"

"This Saturday. I'll tell Daniel to arrange for transportation for us if it's all right with Mrs. Harn."

"All right. I'll contact her."

"And I hope you and your daughter can come with us."

"Emily loves to go over there, so we'll be happy to accompany you."

"Then I'll await word from you."

"I'll send a message right away."

When Mrs. Worthington and Judith left, Cora straightened up the shop, so she could close early. She took a piece of stationery and jotted down a quick note to Katie, put it in an envelope and sealed it. After locking up the store, she hurried downtown to the boat basin and hailed one of the fishermen sitting in a boat working on his net.

"Would you please take this note over to Mrs. Harn on Anastasia? I need to get a message to her today. Perhaps you can wait on her response?" She grabbed a couple of coins from her bag. "This is for your trouble."

"Yes, ma'am. Where will I find you when I get back?"

"Mrs. Gardner's Boarding House. They will make sure I get it."

Cora and Emily were having supper when Mrs. Gardner's house servant brought an envelope for Cora.

"Who sent you a letter, Momma?"

"I believe it's a note from Aunt Katie. Cora opened the missive addressed to her in Katie's handwriting, her heart thumping with anticipation. She finished reading it and put it in her lap.

"Emily, would you like to go over to Anastasia Saturday?"

"Yes, Momma. You know I would!"

"Maybe you could stay there overnight now that they're moved into the new house."

"Momma, that would be grand!" Emily clapped her hands together.

"I'll pack your Sunday dress so you can wear it when Katie brings you to church with her family on Sunday."

"I can't wait to wear my new dress!"

Cora knew Emily wanted to wear her dress when Cora wore hers, so they'd match. Hopefully, Emily could keep it clean between the island and town on the boat ride across.

Now all Cora had to do was tell Mrs. Worthington. Would Sterling be accompanying them to the island? Maybe she would have an opportunity to talk with him to find out his intentions.

~

On Saturday morning, Cora got Emily and herself dressed for their outing. As they approached the hotel, Sterling hailed them from the front porch. "Good morning! If it isn't the two prettiest ladies in St. Augustine!"

Cora blushed and Emily scurried up the steps to meet him.

"Good morning, Mr. Sterling! Are you going with us today?"

"Well, of course. I'm looking forward to a tour of the lighthouses."

Emily raced over to the Worthingtons who were coming out the front door, leaving Cora and Sterling alone for a few minutes.

Sterling took her gloved hand and kissed the back of it. "You know, it's not just the lighthouses I want to see."

Cora looked away from his scorching gaze. "There are other things on the island to see."

He continued to hold her hand. "Cora, you know it's you I want to see. I'm delighted to be with you on these family excursions."

Was he waiting for her to give him an answer about his proposition to travel together? She couldn't answer until she understood the question.

~

Daniel sat in the bow of the boat, keeping some separation from Sterling as they headed toward Anastasia Island, thankful the distance across the bay was short and the sky was clear. Numerous boats were scattered across the water, some with sails like they'd hired for the last trip. Many tourists liked to go to the North Beach beyond the fort, while others simply were out to enjoy being on the water with no particular destination in mind.

Sea gulls squawked as they soared over the fishing boats, hoping for a spare morsel. Both tourists and serious fishermen like the Minorcans, some in traditional black dugout canoes, were trying to catch fish from the salty blue water. Lone Bear's request was still on Daniel's mind as he watched the fishermen use nets or cane poles to make their catch. If only Lone Bear could join them.

He had broached the subject with Lieutenant Pratt but was met with complete refusal.

"Mr. Worthington," the lieutenant had said. "There is a vast difference between allowing the Indians on top of the fort and allowing them to go on a fishing excursion. We are here to educate them, not entertain them."

But Daniel wasn't about to give up. There must be a way he could engineer such an undertaking. He needed to do something for Lone Bear, something that made him feel better. The old Indian's wracking cough had not gone away, and he seemed to be shrinking from not eating much. One thing Daniel admired him for was his stoic attitude. Although the man did not feel well, he seemed to enjoy seeing the other younger natives explore new skills, even appearing amused at times. And the younger men showed him great respect as well, as if he were a grandfather to them all.

Perhaps the lighthouse keeper could advise Daniel as to how to achieve his plan. Daniel looked forward to speaking with him. As the boat grounded in the shallow water, the boatman jumped out and pulled the vessel onto the beach. Captain and Mrs. Harn greeted them, along with their family of girls. After introductions were made, Captain Harn took the lead to show them around. Daniel walked alongside the lighthouse keeper in order to speak with him privately as Sterling followed behind, his silly banter keeping the women occupied. The children ran ahead, knowing the way.

Daniel did his best to ignore Sterling, hoping the day wouldn't turn out the disaster of the last daytrip. He tried to block the man's conversation from his ears. Why did the man have to speak so loudly? Must he always be the center of attention? Surely, he hadn't already imbibed this early in the day. Still, Daniel would keep a wary eye in case Sterling became too wild and put someone else in danger. He just couldn't understand why Cora didn't see through Sterling's façade. Nor did he understand why he cared.

Captain Harn escorted them over to the old lighthouse property first. He explained that the United States had converted an existing old Spanish tower into a lighthouse some fifty years ago, adding to its height so that it reached sixty feet.

"I want to show you this building first, so you can appreciate the need for the new lighthouse."

The old lighthouse appeared to be leaning slightly and was located behind the two-story keeper's house, both buildings made of coquina. The climb up wasn't too steep, even for Mother, but the view from the top was shocking. Looking down, the water appeared to be almost at the tower's base.

"Why did they build the lighthouse so close to the water?" Judith asked, peering over the edge.

"They didn't. The water is coming closer to the tower. It's a barrier island and they have a habit of shifting. The water has moved significantly closer in the past few years and will no doubt undermine this tower soon. The government decided to build a new lighthouse half a mile back, but higher, so it can be seen farther out to sea."

"And a new house for you as well." Cora said.

"Yes, as you know, Katie is very proud of our new home. We're mostly moved in now."

"I know she must be thrilled to be in the new house."

"Yes. Katie was anxious to get into it."

Sterling leaned way out over the balcony. "I think I could dive into the water from here."

Judith gasped. "Sterling! Don't you dare!"

He laughed aloud as he turned back around, receiving a frown from Captain Harn, who motioned toward the stairs. "I believe we've seen enough of this one now. Pretty soon, this tower will be closed off so no one will get hurt." He directed his comment to Sterling. "Ladies, go first, please."

As the women headed down stairs, Daniel saw Sterling slip a flask from his coat pocket and sneak a swig before putting it back. He was getting an early start today. When they exited the lighthouse, Mrs. Harn called over to her children who were playing with some puppies.

"Bring Ida to me. We're going over to the new house."

The children scampered over, the oldest carrying the youngest before handing her over to her mother. Then they ran toward the new lighthouse across the way. Daniel wondered if he'd ever have a family full of children like these. The island seemed like an ideal home for them, certainly one he'd have enjoyed as a child, one where a child could run with abandon and not be confined to walls in the city as he had been.

As they walked the distance to the new lighthouse, Daniel wished he'd had his sketchbook to capture the scenes around him. Perhaps he'd come over alone some day and do that. Or if he could bring the Indians…

"Captain Harn. I have a matter to discuss with you."

"Yes?"

"Yes, I've been working with the Indians at the fort, encouraging them to draw and communicate with me through their art. But I feel they need some exercise. One Indian expressed a desire to go fishing."

"Katie told me about your efforts at the fort. Very admirable of you, and quite brave, I must say."

"I don't see any reason to fear them. They're constantly guarded, so they'd be shot if they tried to harm me. No, they're pretty resigned to their positions at present. I'm trying to earn their trust and show them some human dignity, which many people think is a strange idea."

Captain Harn nodded. "We are all created in God's image."

"I'm glad to hear that you feel that way." Daniel viewed the dense foliage on either side of the sandy path. Saw palmettos clustered in thickets which no one could walk through. "Captain, could you use some help here on the island clearing some of this undergrowth?"

"I certainly could. This stuff requires hours of chopping through to remove." Harn looked up at some scrub pines between them and the lighthouse. "I'd also like to remove some of those trees before they get too tall." He stopped walking and faced Daniel. "Are you proposing some work for the Indians?"

"Yes. I believe Lieutenant Pratt would agree to some prison labor, with guards, of course. And in return for their labor, we could allow them to go fishing. You know these men have never seen the ocean before."

"Well see what you can do. I'm willing to give these men a chance."

But would Lieutenant Pratt?

Chapter Twenty-Three

The excitement of sharing her friends with Katie's family on the island invigorated Cora. Add to that the children's enthusiasm, and she couldn't keep the smile off her face.

The spring weather was perfect, warm but cooled by a constant breeze blowing from the ocean. Everyone in their party was in a festive mood, well almost everyone. Daniel and William were engrossed in a serious conversation, but she couldn't hear what it was about. If she had to conjecture though, she'd say "Indians." Was there any other topic Daniel talked about? But as they reached the new brick keepers' house, she noticed his spirits had lifted. What had William told him that had such an effect?

"Please come in and I'll show you our new home." Katie gestured for the women to follow her as she carried Ida up the steps to the broad veranda. Inside, Katie showed them each of the rooms, a decided improvement over their former home. Even though they would share half the two-story house with the assistant keeper's family, the home was still more spacious than the old one.

"Smells like fresh wood and paint," Mrs. Worthington said. "It smells new."

"Which is quite refreshing after the musty smell of our other home." Katie had already hung freshly-made curtains over the windows, giving the home an inviting feel.

"I can't wait to sleep here!" Emily said.

"Let's go see our room," said Molly, taking Emily's hand and running upstairs where the bedrooms were located.

"You're staying here tonight?" Judith said to Cora.

"I'm not, but Emily wanted to."

"So you'll be alone this evening?" Mrs. Worthington said. "Why don't you join us for dinner then?"

"Thank you, I might take you up on that, if we're not too tired when we return."

Cora surveyed the new home, fighting jealousy for not having one herself. Katie deserved a new place for her large family though. Cora chastised herself for not appreciating her own place to live, which was just big enough for her and Emily. The boarding house was comfortable, and she didn't even have to prepare the meals, since a cook provided them for the residents. Besides, so far, Cora was able to pay for their lodging with her meager earnings. Perhaps she shouldn't even wish for a home of her own.

The men waited on the veranda, uninterested in touring the inside of the house. As Cora spotted them through the screen door, Sterling saw her and grinned. Her heart skipped, and she glanced away.

"Ladies, shall we go to the lighthouse now?" Sterling called through the door. "I can't wait to go to the top of the world."

"Coming," Katie said, then moved to the bottom of the stairs and called up. "Girls, come on downstairs. You'll have plenty of time in there later."

The girls came giggling down the stairs and ran out the front door.

Katie turned to Mrs. Worthington and Judith and lifted her hands in exasperation. "I apologize, ladies. The girls don't get company very often and they're overly excited to have Emily here."

"No apology necessary." Mrs. Worthington offered a smile. "I believe my own children were young once."

Judith glanced at her mother with a wry smile.

Katie opened the door and motioned for the ladies to exit where they joined the men outside.

The black and white lighthouse, striped like a barber's pole, was about a hundred steps behind the house. As they gathered at the base, they looked up toward the top.

"My goodness, this is high." Mrs. Worthington shielded her eyes.

"It's 162 feet, to be exact," William said. "The tallest lighthouse in Florida."

"And there's 219 steps!" Ruby, the Harns' oldest daughter, affirmed with a shake of her head.

"I don't think I'll attempt to climb it," Mrs. Worthington said. "May I sit down here?"

"Of course, you can," Katie said. "I'll stay here with you. If we moved away from the tower, we'll see the others when they come out on the gallery."

"Are you worried about your daughters up that high?" Mrs. Worthington said.

"No, they've run up it so many times, it's no problem for them. And they know the rules when they reach the top. They're not allowed to climb or lean over the gallery when they're up there."

Cora gazed up at the dizzying height, then steeled her nerves. "If you don't mind, I'd like to accompany Emily," Cora said. "I'd prefer to go with her."

"I quite understand." Mrs. Worthington nodded. "You young people go on up and I'll wave to you when you get to the top."

"We can sit on that bench in the shade and look," Katie said to Mrs. Worthington.

"Thank you," the older woman said.

"Shall we conquer the summit?" Sterling said, stepping forward.

At the base of the lighthouse a small building was attached through which one entered before reaching the stairs to the lighthouse. Entering the vestibule, William pointed out the rooms on either side, one for his office and the opposite one for oil storage. The girls had already disappeared through the door to the lighthouse by the time Cora reached it, the sound of their steps and laughter echoing throughout the brick and granite structure.

"Emily, wait for me." Cora looked up into the open vestibule surrounded by the staircase leading to the top.

"You may have to run, if you want to catch up to her," William said smiling. "Those girls can scurry up the steps quicker than a frog's tongue catching a fly."

"I'll go after her," Sterling said. "I can climb faster than you with that long skirt."

"Thank you." Cora's heart swelled at Sterling's chivalry as he ran up the metal staircase after the girls.

"After you ladies." Daniel gestured toward the stairs. William brought up the rear as they proceeded up the steps in single file. They stopped at each landing to catch their breath. Cora wished her skirts could be shorter—calf-length like Emily's for such a task. A third of the way up was a small open window. Emily and Judith stood beside it, inhaling a gasp of fresh air from outside before she climbed any more steps.

"How much farther?" Judith fanned herself with the small fan attached to her wrist.

Daniel looked up the center of the stairs. "Still a way to go, sister. Are you considering forgoing the mission?"

"Yes, I think so. You and Cora go ahead though. I'll rest here, then go back down and wait for you with Mother."

William faced Daniel and Cora. "Are you ready to continue?"

They nodded, then resumed their climb. Cora refused to look down as she continued up, thankful for the handrail she grasped to pull herself up. She no longer heard the children and fought the worry about Emily. Thank goodness, Sterling had gone up after them. When they reached the next little window, they were two-thirds of the way up, according to William.

"You're farther up than down now," the lighthouse keeper said. "Not too much more to go."

"Thank God," said Daniel, whose upper lip was dotted with perspiration, as was his hairline. "I didn't expect the climb to be such a challenge. And you climb these stairs several times a day?"

"Yes, sir. You do get used to it after so many times up and down."

Cora took a deep breath at the window and made the mistake of looking down. Fear threatened to overwhelm her, but anxiety about Emily propelled Cora up the rest of the steps.

Finally reaching the top step, Cora gulped in the breeze coming through the open door to the gallery. She froze at the view from the door, unable to step through the opening. Daniel must've sensed her trepidation because he took her hand and pulled her forward. "You'll be fine. There's a railing all the way around."

She glanced up at him and saw his assurance. "But where are the girls?"

William stepped outside. "They're 'round the other side."

Taking Daniel's hand, she allowed him to pull her through the opening. The panorama before her was spectacular. As she looked from east to west, she took in the view of the entire island from above the trees and stretching all the way to the level blue sea. The wind blew briskly as she moved around the gallery, drowning out all other noises. But when she reached the other side, she saw all the girls and Sterling pointing to town landmarks across the bay where toy-size boats floated.

"Momma! You're here!" Emily glanced her way for a moment then back out at the view.

Yes, she was. The vista was exhilarating, but the height made her lightheaded.

"Look!" One of the girls pointed. "That man caught a huge fish!"

"Where? I can't see!" Emily stood on her tiptoes to get a better view.

"Here. I'll help you." Sterling swooped Emily up in his arms and held her above the railing.

Cora's breath caught as her daughter dangled over the earth. Suddenly, Sterling stumbled and lost his balance. The scream left her throat before she could move, but Daniel leaped forward and grabbed Emily out of Sterling's hands as Sterling fought to regain his footing. Cora watched in horror expecting Sterling to fall over the railing and down to the ground below. However, he fell backwards against the tower instead, a move that steadied him.

Daniel handed Emily over to Cora who was shaking. Emily was trembling as well and began to cry against her mother. "Momma, I'm scared. I want to go back down."

Cora held her daughter tightly while frightening scenes of what could have happened taunted her. She glanced up at Daniel and mouthed "thank you." He nodded at her, then glared at Sterling who seemed to be stunned.

"I'll go down with you." Daniel put his arm around Cora who still held Emily and guided them back to the door. They entered and headed toward the steps, where Cora put Emily down.

"Hold tightly to the railing, Emily." Cora did the same as she followed closely behind her daughter all the way down the stairs. Daniel stayed just behind them, while the other girls trailed behind. Cora's heart pounded as she tried to calm down.

"Emily, are you okay?" one of the girls said.

Emily muttered a timid, "Yes," without looking back.

When they reached the bottom of the stairs, Emily ran across the yard to Katie. "I almost fell from up there, Aunt Katie!" She pointed to the top of the lighthouse.

Katie's eyebrow raised. "You did?" Katie glanced over at Cora as she approached.

Cora didn't know what to say in front of Judith and Mrs. Worthington, so she remained silent, hoping to fill Katie in with the details later.

"Mr. Sterling almost dropped me."

The women exchanged glances, and Cora needed to offer some kind of explanation without impugning Sterling. "He was holding Emily and he stumbled."

"Oh my." Katie stroked Emily's hair. "Were you scared?"

Emily nodded her head. "Umm hmm. I don't never want to go to up there again!"

"Well, you don't have to, Emily. You can stay right down here."

The girls ran over to Emily, surrounding her and asking her questions.

Cora looked over her shoulder at Daniel who waited at the door to the lighthouse, no doubt, for Sterling. When Sterling did appear, Daniel had what appeared to be a serious conversation with him. Cora expected Sterling to be embarrassed, but he showed no such emotion, appearing unfazed by the events just moments ago. Instead, he straightened his vest, then turned away from Daniel and strode across the yard toward them.

"Judith, Mrs. Worthington, you ladies missed seeing an exceptional vista. I believe you can see for a hundred miles up there."

Emily shrank back from Sterling, but Sterling didn't seem to notice.

"Cora, did you make it to the top?"

Cora tilted her head. Did he not know she had been up there? Was there no offer of apology? He seemed unaware of what had happened. Now she wasn't sure she should leave Emily. She didn't give him an answer. Instead, she called Emily aside and bent over to speak to her privately. "Emily, do you still want to stay here, or do you want to come home with me?"

Emily shook her head. "No, I want to stay here, Momma."

"All right then. If you're sure."

"Yes, ma'am. I am."

Katie's brow puckered. "Cora, you can stay here tonight if you'd like."

"Thank you, but I'm not prepared to stay. Don't worry. I have plenty to keep me busy."

She glanced over to see what Sterling was doing, but he had wandered toward the front of the keeper's house. Cora had some questions for him but didn't want to ask him here or now.

Mrs. Worthington spoke. "Cora is having dinner with us tonight. Daniel can escort her home."

Cora smiled at the woman, thankful for her protective attitude. She would miss having Emily with her tonight. With a start, she realized they'd never been separated before. But Emily would have an enjoyable time with her cousins.

~

The atmosphere on the boat was subdued as they traveled back to town. Sterling napped while Cora and the Worthingtons talked about their trip to Anastasia especially the lighthouses. But no one mentioned the incident with Sterling, even though Cora thought it must surely be on everyone's mind. Although Judith and Mrs. Worthington hadn't seen what happened, Cora felt sure that Daniel had told them about it. The whole scene kept repeating itself through Cora's mind, yet she still couldn't understand what had happened. Had she overreacted?

When they arrived back in town, Sterling came back to life.

"Cora, may I walk you home?"

Cora hesitated before answering. She glanced at Daniel, whose jaw was clenched. Much as she wanted to discuss matters with Sterling, she didn't feel that either of them was up to it.

"I'm sorry, Sterling, but I have some errands to run before I get home. But perhaps you'll be at dinner tonight?"

Sterling frowned. "Dinner? Where and with whom?"

"At the hotel. Mrs. Worthington invited me."

Sterling grinned. "Excellent! I'll see you at dinner then."

Before she headed home, she looked back at Daniel who stood with his arms crossed and forehead creased. Did he not want

Sterling to join them?

Sterling didn't offer to come for her, so she assumed no one would. She returned to the boarding house alone and to an empty room. Goodness, it was quiet without Emily there. Cora freshened up and changed into a clean skirt and blouse. As she was about to leave the boarding house, Daniel appeared downstairs to collect her.

"Hello, Daniel. I didn't expect you."

"I'm sorry. I should have told you I would come for you." He offered a polite smile as he opened the gate for her.

"Thank you. It's so strange to not have Emily with me."

"You've haven't been apart before?"

"Never, other than the time she's at school and I'm at the shop."

"Lieutenant Pratt is trying to reunite the families of the Indian prisoners. Most of them have wives and children back at Fort Sill or the fort in Texas."

He was talking about Indians again. But this time, she was interested in what he was saying. "Do you think he'll succeed?"

"I hope so. The families have no home to return to, and they just want to be together, even if it's here at the fort."

"I never realized they had families—other than the two women and children I saw the first day."

They walked past a yard where a tall date palm curved upward as it leaned toward the sun.

"I hope the lieutenant succeeds," she said. She could only imagine how lonely it must be for the families to be separated, especially in a strange place. She remembered how much she had missed Jacob when he was gone away during the war and how relieved she had been when he returned.

He glanced at her with a raised eyebrow but didn't speak.

Judith and Mrs. Worthington were waiting for them in the dining room, but Sterling was nowhere to be seen.

"Good evening, Mrs. Miller," Mrs. Worthington said. "Have you recovered from your trip today?"

Did she mean recover as in rested or was she referring to the incident with Sterling? Cora glanced around. "Isn't Sterling joining us?"

"Last time I saw him, he was headed to the billiards hall down

170

the block, so I doubt he'll be here for dinner." Daniel took his napkin and snapped it before placing it in his lap.

Hadn't Sterling told her he would see her at dinner?

"That's a lovely cameo you're wearing, Mrs. Miller. That's an aquamarine, isn't it? Very unusual piece."

"Thank you. It was a gift from my late husband." Cora ran her finger over the raised edges of the cameo.

"A sentimental piece, I'm sure," Mrs. Worthington said. "I can't find my favorite brooch. I've looked all over our room for it."

"The ruby and diamond one you wore the other day?" Cora remembered the beautiful jewelry. "I do hope you find it."

"Yes, I do too. It's a special piece for me too."

Cora sensed Daniel's stare. Why was he looking at her? What was he thinking? She drew in a breath and faced him. "You and Captain Harn were engrossed in conversation. Are you interested in becoming a lighthouse keeper?"

Daniel's eyes registered surprise. "Dear God, no. However, I do admire Captain Harn's devotion to his position." Daniel took a sip of tea, then set down his glass. "We were discussing the Indian prisoners."

Why was she not surprised?

Daniel continued. "I'm coordinating with him to have the prisoners do some work on the island for him."

Cora sat back. "On the island?"

"Yes, for an outing, but also to provide them with work to do."

"And what did he say about that?"

"He's in favor of it. I plan to ask Lieutenant Pratt first thing in the morning."

Did she denote an air of excitement? "But, what about the safety of the captain's family? Isn't he concerned?"

Daniel frowned. "No. There will be guards, so any threat of violence will be quickly subdued. I think the Indians will be too busy enjoying some freedom to consider doing anyone harm."

"You really trust them, don't you?"

"I believe they trust me, so the feeling is mutual."

Mrs. Worthington and Judith had quietly observed the conversation between Cora and Daniel.

"Daniel is a bit of an idealist," Mrs. Worthington said.

Daniel squinted at his mother, his jaw set. "Someone has to be,

Mother."

His mother smiled, and their meals arrived as conversation returned to the day at the island and the sights they'd seen. When the subject of Katie's girls came up, Cora winced, remembering that Emily was with them and not with her.

"Mrs. Miller?" Judith began.

"Judith, please call me Cora. You too, Mrs. Worthington. Please."

"All right, Cora. I will."

"We went in the haberdashery the other day and saw the women's hats," Judith said, pushing some food around on her plate.

Cora's breath caught. Would they take their business to Farley's?

Judith leaned in toward Cora, her voice lowered. "The quality isn't as good as yours, and the designs are not well-done. Rather tacky, I'd say. Don't you agree, Mother?"

Mrs. Worthington nodded. "Yes, Judith's correct. The hats weren't nearly as nice as yours, Cora. However, the hats are priced very inexpensively, for people who prefer cheaper hats. "Personally, I'd rather have quality."

Cora breathed again. "Thank you."

"I suppose it's only natural for the wife of the man who owns the haberdashery to offer women's hats."

"Perhaps so." Cora wanted to take a look at the other hats herself but didn't see how that was possible.

Mrs. Worthington leaned over and placed her hand on Cora's. "You don't have anything to worry about. We'll tell all our friends to go to your shop instead."

"Thank you, that's very kind."

They finished their meal and rose to take their leave. Daniel pulled out Cora's chair for her. "I'll escort you home."

Cora started to protest, but actually preferred to have company, now that it was growing dark outside. "Thank you, that would be nice."

She bid the other women good night, and then took Daniel's arm as they stepped out on the street. It occurred to her that others might consider the two of them to be courting. Did Daniel wonder about that?

"Daniel, may I ask you something?"

"Certainly. What is it?"

"Sterling told me you and he have known each other a long time."

"That's true."

"I thought at first that you were friends, but you don't seem to care for him. Is there a reason?"

Daniel worked his jaw as if trying to get the right words out. "Sterling can be annoying, and I suppose I've tired of his behavior."

Why did she feel he wasn't telling her everything on his mind?

"He's extremely cheerful and entertaining—most of the time." The lighthouse incident came to mind.

"Perhaps too much so. I believe there are occasions when he needs to be more serious and consider the consequences of his actions. But I've been around him a long time, and as they say, "familiarity breeds contempt.""

Would she feel the same way if she knew him a long time?

Their conversation shifted to Daniel's time studying with the artists in Paris, a subject he eagerly discussed, and his mood lifted.

When they reached the boarding house, Cora thanked him for walking her home. He smiled and said good night, then walked away.

Cora's room was strangely quiet and empty. Without Emily to put to bed, Cora had extra time on her hands and decided to work on Judith's new hat. She had brought her supplies home so she could. As she emptied the items onto the bed, she arranged them the way they would appear on the hat. The hat! She'd forgotten the hat she was to put them on. What could she do without the hat?

She looked out the window at the pitch black sky. Where was the moon? If she could just find her way in the dark, she'd go to the shop and get the hat. After all, it was only a few blocks, and she knew the way. It wouldn't take long, especially if she walked very quickly. Yes, she could do it.

No one was outside the boarding house when she left her room and walked downstairs. She saw one or two people down the street opposite the direction she needed to go, but the street appeared empty toward the shop. Cora slipped out the gate, then hurried along, her ears and eyes alert to anyone or anything unusual. From one of the homes, she heard guitar music and a male voice singing a Spanish ballad.

As she rounded the corner to her shop, she noticed a figure ahead and slowed her steps. She squinted, trying to see what he was doing. With a start, she realized his hand was on the doorknob to her shop and he appeared to be trying to unlock it. A small creature skittered across the sidewalk in front of her and she shrieked. The person at her shop door stopped and glanced her way, then ran away. Cora's heart raced. Who was he and what was he doing?

Should she go into the shop and see if anything was missing? She should, but her feet were frozen in place. What if whoever that was came back while she was in the shop? Cora shuddered. No, she wouldn't chance that. Right now, she wanted to get back to the boarding house as quickly as possible. She turned and went back the way she'd come, practically running until she reached the gate.

Judith's hat would have to wait. She kept seeing the man in her mind, trying to focus more clearly. Who was trying to get into her shop? It had been too dark to see his face, and his clothes were dark as well. But as he ran away, he passed a lighted window that revealed his shape, tall and slender, very much like someone else she knew. Sterling?

Chapter Twenty-Four

Daniel was at the fort early Sunday morning, eager to speak with Lieutenant Pratt. He wasn't certain Pratt would come to the fort on a Sunday, but the guard on duty told him Pratt would be there after early mass. Daniel asked if he could see the Indians but had to wait until they finished breakfast, so he paced the ground in front of the lieutenant's office, pondering the best way to present his argument.

"Mr. Worthington. You're here sooner than I expected." ·

Daniel turned to greet Lieutenant Pratt who ushered Daniel into his office.

"Have a seat. You must have a pressing matter to discuss, coming to the fort today."

Daniel removed his hat, placing it in his lap as he sat down. "Yes, sir. I'll get right to the reason I'm here." He steadied his gaze on Lieutenant Pratt whose hands were clasped on the desk in front of him. "As you recall, I suggested we take the Indians fishing."

"I remember. And do you remember my answer?"

"Yes, sir, however, you were opposed to an activity that was purely entertainment. I've spoken to Captain Harn, the lighthouse keeper on Anastasia, and he has some work he could use some help with. I asked if he would allow the Indians to help him and he agreed."

Pratt leaned back in his chair. "What kind of work?"

"He needs some of the land around the lighthouse cleared— palmetto, brush, scrub pines and such. So, I thought that when the Indians get finished with their work, they could be allowed some respite, or reward for their labor, by fishing."

Pratt rubbed his chin. "Hmm. Sounds like you've been working hard on this plan, Worthington."

Daniel studied his hat, turning it with his hands, then looked up. "Yes, sir. I have given the idea quite a lot of thought."

"Will you accompany them?"

"Yes, sir. I'll bring my sketchbook and draw them doing the work. Perhaps you can show it to your superiors."

"Perhaps. But to tell you the truth, I've been thinking of giving them some more leisure outside the fort, guarded of course."

"Sir, I believe it will be good for morale."

"That would come in handy at this time." Pratt looked past Daniel into the parade ground. "We cut their hair this weekend. They've been adjusting to their new look."

Daniel swallowed the lump in his throat. "You did? And they didn't refuse?"

"No, not completely. They were a bit skeptical at first though."

His gut clenched. How did the Indians feel about losing their long hair? Now, more than before, he wanted to give them something to look forward to.

"They'll be fine. We've explained to them that only women wear hair long and braided as theirs used to be. Today, we'll be issuing uniforms to the boys and showing them how to march."

"The boys, sir? What about the older ones?"

Pratt chuckled. "I call them all boys. Most of them are pretty young, like many of our soldiers here."

"And Lone Bear? Did he have a haircut too? Will he have to march?"

"Not yet. He still isn't well."

"But I'd still like to take him with us to Anastasia, even if he can't do the work. Would you agree to that?"

"I don't see why not. I think the outing might do him good."

"Then, shall I make the arrangements, or will you?"

Pratt puffed out his chest. "I will take care of them. I know people in town who will be more than happy to provide a boat and whatever else we need."

"Of course, sir. What day do you expect to go?"

"I don't see why we can't go tomorrow. Let me check on some things and I'll let you know as soon as I can." Pratt stood, and

Daniel followed suit.

"Will it be possible for me to meet with them now?" The two men walked toward the doorway. "And should I mention the trip to Anastasia?"

"Yes, you may see them now. They're in the classroom. Oh, and you may tell them that I would like to take them to the island tomorrow for some work and perhaps more." Pratt winked. "Let them be surprised."

"Yes, sir. I understand." Daniel realized Pratt wanted credit for something the Indians would enjoy, and that was fine with him as long as Pratt followed through on his word.

The men shook hands, and Daniel headed to the room in the fort that had been converted to a classroom. As he entered, the Indians were seated on benches and glanced at him. His astonishment of their new appearance riveted him in place. Trying to hide his shock, he searched the group for a familiar face. They all had the high cheekbones and square chins, and they all wore white shirts, making them even more indistinguishable. Soon they'd receive their uniforms, further concealing their individuality. Thank God, they still had their art to identify their personalities.

When one of them lifted his hand, Daniel recognized him as Making Medicine. Daniel raised his hand in greeting and the Indian acknowledged him. Mr. Fox had not yet arrived, but Daniel wanted to ask how they felt about having their hair cut. He walked over to Making Medicine and motioned to the Indian's hair. Making Medicine nodded, then pointed to Daniel's hair, then to all the other Indians. Was he saying they all looked alike now that they had short hair?

"Yes. Short hair," Daniel said. He spread his arms out to the side. "All have short hair."

Making Medicine pointed to Daniel's hat. Daniel removed it and showed it to the Indian. Making Medicine took the hat and placed it on his own head, looking around the room for the others to see. Some of them laughed and pointed at him, then Making Medicine laughed too, and Daniel joined in.

Daniel motioned to the Indian. "You will have hat too." The Indians wouldn't be getting the same hat as his though. They'd be receiving military caps with their uniforms, one more step to make them blend in with whites.

Mr. Fox arrived, and taking in the scene, said, "Your new haircuts are very good." He then repeated the sentence in the native tongues he knew. Daniel was always thankful when Fox arrived because the Indians seemed to like him. They must've trusted him more because he knew their language, creating a bond between them. Daniel pulled him aside and told him about the plans he'd discussed with Lieutenant Pratt.

"You don't say. Well, I look forward to such an outing. The men will really enjoy it."

Daniel noticed that Fox called the Indians "men" whereas Pratt called them "boys." Perhaps it was that attitude toward them that fostered respect. One trains boys, one respects men. However, at least the two men treated them as fellow humans and not animals as some people in the country saw them.

"Let's take them up to the terreplein and show them the island, then tell them what they're going to do." Daniel wished he could tell them himself. "Tell them to bring their sketchbooks with them, and I'll ask them to draw the island."

"Sounds good." Fox conveyed Daniel's words to the Indians, and they all stood and filed out behind Daniel and Fox with soldiers bringing up the rear. Making Medicine went over to where Lone Bear sat, his body quaking with each cough, and helped him up. He was the only native that still had his long hair. Making Medicine stayed close to him, holding him steady as he slowly made his way up the stairs with the others. When they all reached the top of the fort, Daniel and Mr. Fox took positions on the side facing Anastasia Island.

Daniel pointed to the island. "Lieutenant Pratt is taking you over there to that island. It is called Anastasia Island. You will work over there, then he has planned something for you that you will enjoy." Turning to the translator, he said, "Will you please translate for me, Mr. Fox? I wish I could mention fishing, but Lieutenant Pratt wants to be the one to reveal that surprise."

Fox communicated the message to the Indians. They turned to each other and chattered with eyes widened as they gestured toward the island. Daniel discerned their excitement, thankful he could share it.

Lone Bear pointed to the island and then poked his own chest.

"Me catch big fish."

How did he know they were going fishing? Could he read Daniel's mind? Daniel just smiled, so he wouldn't give away Pratt's surprise. He lifted his sketchbook and began sketching the scene in front of them and motioned for them to follow suit. His students showed more enthusiasm than usual after hearing the news about their outing.

A soldier approached and told Daniel his time with the prisoners was over for the day, that it was time for their midday meal. Daniel bid Mr. Fox goodbye, agreeing to meet each other in the morning for the excursion. He scanned the group of Indians, their hands busy at work on their sketches, and he was pleased with their efforts. As he reached the bottom of the stairs, Lieutenant Pratt met him.

"Good news. I have procured a vessel to take the prisoners over. A man in town, a Mr. Pacetti, has a boat he uses to take tourists out fishing, and it's large enough for at least twenty-five Indians with five guards. We will meet him at the dock below the fort at seven o'clock tomorrow morning. He'll take everyone over to the island and deposit them there so they can work. At noon, he'll come back and take them fishing. If they catch something, which I'm sure they will, they can make a fire and cook it themselves." Pratt rubbed his hands together and rocked on his heels. "Excellent plan, don't you agree, Mr. Worthington?"

"Yes, sir. It certainly is." *And you're welcome for using my idea.* So, you will choose which Indians go? May I request that Making Medicine accompany Lone Bear? The younger man has been a great help to his elder."

"So I've noticed. Yes, they will go together. Unfortunately, I cannot send all the Indians at once, but if this trip is successful, we'll take others another time. In fact, if the lighthouse keeper doesn't object, I've thought they might be able to camp out overnight sometime. How does that sound?"

Daniel raised his eyebrows. "It sounds...very adventurous." Pratt must not be concerned about the prisoners trying to escape from the island. Where would they go? Daniel doubted any of them could swim. "Then I'll meet you at the fort's dock in the morning."

Pratt tipped his hat as did Daniel, and the two parted.

As Daniel crossed the parade ground, he imagined the next day's events, hoping it would all go as planned. He was thankful Captain Harn had agreed to the arrangement. Would the Indians be allowed near the lighthouse? What would Mrs. Harn think about having the prisoners so near her family?

Tomorrow's visit would certainly be different than his last trip to the island. What a contrast between tomorrow's fellow travelers and his previous ones. How strange that he had less concern about what the Indians would do than he did about what Sterling would do? One thing for certain: he wouldn't be rescuing a child from falling from the lighthouse.

~

Cora waited at the front door of the church for Katie to arrive with Emily. Pretty soon, she saw the whole family headed toward the church, Emily holding hands with Ruby, swinging them as they walked. When Emily saw Cora, she broke into a run, throwing her arms around Cora's skirt when she reached her. "Momma! I missed you!"

"I missed you too. Did you have a good time?"

"Yes! It was great fun! Thank you, Momma, for letting me stay."

"I'm happy you had fun." She raised a finger to her lips. "Let's go inside now."

They entered the church and filled the back pew just as Daniel Worthington rushed in and sat next to his mother and sister.

"Hmm. Wonder where he's been?" Katie nudged Cora.

Cora shrugged, then hugged Emily against her on the pew. It felt wonderful to have her near again.

After the service, the family filed out behind the Worthingtons. They approached the group to exchange pleasantries. Daniel's smug smile intrigued her. What was the source of his amusement?

"I'm glad to see you here today," he said, addressing Captain Harn. "I just came from the fort before church."

"Yes? And what was the decision?"

"Lieutenant Pratt is setting up the outing for tomorrow."

Cora's eyebrows lifted as she looked at Katie. "Outing?"

Katie nodded. "Apparently the Indian prisoners will have an outing on Anastasia tomorrow."

So Daniel managed to convince the lieutenant.

"And you don't mind? Katie, are you afraid?"

"No, Cora, I'm not. I trust the good Lord that if I treat them well, they won't want to harm us or run away,"

Cora eyed Daniel. "What about the old Indian? Is he feeling well enough to go?"

"I wish I could say he's doing better, but he still has the cough. Tomorrow's outing should do him good."

"But what will they do on the island?"

"They're going to help clear out some of the property." Daniel leaned down to Cora, lowering his voice. "And afterwards, they will be able to fish."

"Truly? I'd like to see that."

"Would you like to? Perhaps we can arrange for you to go too. Not with the prisoners, of course, but you and I could go on a separate boat."

Mrs. Anderson stepped up to the group. "Good morning."

"Good morning," chorused the others.

"Mrs. Miller, may I have a word please?"

"Yes, of course." Cora followed Mrs. Anderson out of hearing range.

"Mrs. Miller, I have a favor to ask of you. Have you, by any chance, seen the brooch I wore into your shop the other day?"

Alarm raced through Cora.

"No, ma'am, I haven't. Is it missing?"

"I'm afraid so. I don't know when I lost it, but the last time I saw it was when we discussed it in your shop."

Was the woman accusing her? "Well, I'll search all over the shop, but I'm pretty certain it isn't there. I remember what a beautiful brooch it was—I hope you find it."

"I do too. It's irreplaceable." She nodded toward the others. "I'll leave you to your companions. Good day, Mrs. Miller."

Cora remembered the man outside her shop the night before. Was he a thief? Could he have stolen Mrs. Anderson's brooch? And Mrs. Worthington's? She hadn't been to the shop yet to see if anything was missing. Perhaps she could do so after lunch.

When she rejoined the others, Daniel said, "If you decide you'd like to accompany us tomorrow, let me know, and I'll make the arrangements."

Katie squeezed her arm. "Oh Cora, please come."

Cora glanced over at Emily who was with the other girls. "All right. I'll drop Emily off at school first." Facing Daniel, she said, "Yes, I'll go with you."

"I think you'll be happy that you did. I'll meet you at the boat basin around nine tomorrow morning." Daniel, Judith and his mother took their leave and walked toward the hotel.

After Cora told Katie and her family goodbye, she and Emily went back to the boarding house for lunch. Emily talked nonstop about her visit with the girls.

"Momma, what did you do? Were you all by yourself?"

"Mrs. Worthington invited me to have dinner with them at the hotel, then Mr. Daniel walked me home." She didn't dare tell Emily she went out by herself at night, not to mention her frightening experience.

"Were you scared sleeping by yourself?"

Cora chuckled and hugged her daughter. "I didn't like it, but I wasn't too scared." They went outside to the veranda where other boarders sat in rocking chairs, a couple of the men smoking cigars.

"Emily, why don't we go down to the shop? I forgot to bring home a few things to use on Miss Judith's hat."

"Are you going to work on Sunday, Momma? Won't God be mad?" Emily looked up with round questioning eyes.

"I don't think He'll be angry, Emily. I'm not going to open the shop for business. Besides, God gave me the gift to create the hats, so He is pleased when I use that gift."

Cora took Emily's hand and they strolled down the street. "Emily, let's go a different way."

Emily peered up from under her hat brim. "A different way?"

"Yes, we'll just take a little longer stroll and enjoy the day." Cora assumed the haberdashery would be closed like most other businesses on Sunday, and she wanted to look in the windows without her competition's notice.

They walked the extra block to Charlotte Street passing others out for an afternoon stroll. Ahead, the sign reading *Farley's* featuring a picture of a top hat was affixed to a building. Cora slowed her steps, glancing around in hopes that no one would see her. The business was large, as it sold men's clothing items as well as women's hats. Two large storefront windows faced the street, and Cora gazed at the items displayed. Sure enough, a small section of the window was devoted to women's hats and bonnets. Cora wanted to chuckle at the poorly designed headpieces, evidence of garish creativity.

"Momma, look at those hats!" Emily pointed in the window. Cora wanted to shush Emily, but it was too late. "They're not as pretty as yours."

Cora gripped Emily's hand to hurry her past the window, but as she looked ahead, she saw Jane Farley and Mr. Farley headed their way. Heat rose to her face, but she tried to act poised.

"Mrs. Miller, so you're admiring our collection of hats?" Mr. Farley said, his portly pride evident as he stuck out his chest. "My wife is a woman of many talents, isn't she?"

Cora offered her best smile, although it was difficult. "Yes, I had no idea you had such talent, Mrs. Farley."

Jane Farley's smug grin matched her husband's bravado. "My customers are very pleased with my hats."

Emily piped up. "My momma's hats are—"

"Look, Emily!" Cora pointed to a seagull flying over. "Did you see what that bird had in its mouth?"

Emily gazed up at the sky. "Where?"

"Excuse us, please," Cora said. "We need to meet someone."

"Who, Momma?"

Mrs. Farley smirked. "One of your gentleman friends, no doubt."

Cora's mouth dropped open before the remark sank in. She sucked in an angry response to protect her daughter's hearing.

"Truly, Momma? Mr. Sterling or Mr. Daniel?"

As her blood boiled, Cora faked a laugh. "Mrs. Farley was just teasing. We're not meeting either of those gentlemen." She pulled Cora along as she passed the Farleys. "Good day."

Cora walked briskly to the end of the block, practically dragging Emily. As they turned onto Treasury Street, Emily whined. "Momma. Please slow down, you're hurting my arm."

Cora halted and collected herself. "I'm sorry, Emily. I didn't mean to."

Emily stuck out her lips in a pout. "Why did we have to go so fast?"

"I—I just didn't want to stand around talking. I needed to get to my shop."

Emily's face lifted, then her eyes focused ahead. "Look, there's Mr. Sterling. So we *were* going to meet him."

Cora followed Emily's gaze. Sure enough, Sterling was walking toward them, his bright grin spreading across his face. "But, I didn't expect to see him. Truly." She hoped Mrs. Farley didn't see them meet Sterling. They'd think her a liar.

Sterling strolled up with outstretched arms as if he were going to embrace them. "How are you lovely ladies today?"

"Fine, thank you, Sterling."

"And you, Emily?" Sterling bowed toward the girl who regarded him with apprehension.

"I'm fine, too. I stayed with my cousins on the island last night."

Cora noted that Emily was more subdued than usual. Was she afraid of Sterling now?

Sterling's eyebrow lifted. "You did? And left your mother all alone?" He studied Cora's face.

"She wasn't all by herself. Mr. Daniel was with her."

Sterling crossed his arms, peering at Cora. "He did, huh?"

Cora's face heated, and she shook her head. "I had dinner with the Worthingtons, and Daniel accompanied me home."

"Had I known, I would have gladly kept you company." He winked at her, causing a stir in her middle. She didn't miss the fact, however, that he should have known, if he had paid attention to yesterday's conversation.

"We're going to Momma's shop." Emily grew solemn. "Don't worry, though, God's not mad at her."

Sterling twisted his mouth. "I'm glad to hear that."

Cora exhaled. "I have to pick up some things, and Emily was worried that God would be angry with me for working on the Sabbath."

"I see. Can't have that." He extended his arm in the direction of the millinery shop. "May I escort you?"

Cora nodded, recalling the shadowy figure she'd seen the night before and comparing it to the man in front of her. Why did she think it had been Sterling? She must be mistaken. Why on earth would Sterling be trying to get into her shop?

When they reached the store, Cora unlocked the door and gently pushed it open. Emily rushed inside and spread her arms out, spinning in a circle. "These hats are much more beautiful than those ugly hats in that other store!"

"Another store?" Sterling's brow creased. "I didn't know there was another millinery shop in town."

"It's not exactly a shop, it's part of Mr. Farley's store. His wife runs it."

Cora scanned the contents of the store and didn't see anything amiss. Everything seemed to be in place. She hadn't left any money in the store since the last time some had gone missing, just in case it had been stolen. Going to her accessory chest, she pulled open each drawer before opening the one with the jeweled pins, afraid that something else would be missing.

As she examined the contents, she gasped.

"Something wrong, Cora?" Sterling leaned on the counter.

Resting in the drawer beside the pins with the fake jewels were a pair of earrings that didn't belong there. Not only were they very real, they didn't belong to her. In fact, the ruby earrings belonged to Mrs. Lowell. How had they ended up in Cora's possession?

"Nothing, Sterling, nothing at all."

How would she explain the situation to him without telling him about the incident last night? Why did she think she couldn't trust him?

Chapter Twenty-Five

Early the next morning, the Indians marched down the hill to the fort's dock where a large sailing vessel waited. Two of the guards boarded, then the Indians stepped into the boat one at a time until the other guards, Mr. Fox and Lieutenant Pratt joined them. Daniel waved them off as the boat pushed away.

"I'll meet you over there," Daniel called out as the wind caught the sails. The eager look on the Indians' faces warmed his heart. Even Lone Bear had an air of anticipation. The old Indian lifted his hand to Daniel in acknowledgement as the boat moved away.

Daniel spun on his heels and hurried down the street to the boat basin where he was to meet Cora. He had been somewhat surprised to receive her note, yet grateful for her response. They would take one of the small boats over to the island and he'd deposit her with her cousin before rejoining the men. He spotted her in her white blouse and blue skirt long before he reached the basin. Golden curls peeked out from under a straw bonnet that topped the rest of her hair, and she carried a basket on her arm.

Her smile dazzled as he approached. "Good morning, Daniel."

"Good morning to you, Cora." He peered down at the basket. "What have you there?"

"Oranges. I thought they would be refreshing for the men."

"Marvelous idea. I don't know if they've ever tried one."

Daniel held his sketchbook as he and Cora climbed into the waiting boat and soon they too were headed toward the island. The trip across was pleasant and the wind was in their favor. How peaceful the crossing was with just the two of them, the boatman notwithstanding, instead of the number in their last outings. Cora seemed more relaxed than she'd been on their previous outings, as if the experience gave her pure joy.

He gestured to a spot on the beach away from the boat used to convey the Indians to and from the larger vessel that was anchored in deeper water. As they beached the boat, Captain Harn came up to greet them.

"Good morning, Mr. Worthington, Cora." He helped them pull the boat up onshore. "Cora, Katie's expecting you at the house. I'll walk you down, then come back and get the work going."

"I can show them what you want done until you return." Daniel straightened and brushed the sand off his hands.

"Of course. You and I discussed that." He reached for Cora to help her out of the boat. "I'll be back soon."

Daniel strode over to where Lieutenant Pratt and Mr. Fox watched the Indians unload their supplies from the larger boat. "Are you ready for me to show you what Captain Harn would like for them to do?"

Pratt nodded. "We brought a few tents to put up so they can rest and get some shade if need be. They can put those up while you show me." He turned to Mr. Fox. "Fox, tell them what they're going to do and show them where to put the tents."

"Yes, sir."

"Good idea." Daniel waited for Pratt to follow, then walked to the path between the old lighthouse and the new one. "All along this trail are a lot of saw palmetto, very thick. I hope the men have gloves because the stuff can cut their hands."

"We have a few pairs. The Indians need to be shown how to best cut the stuff without getting cut themselves. Some will use the machetes and others will pick up what they cut."

"Good. They can use any decent wood to build a fire later."

"My thoughts exactly."

When Daniel and the lieutenant returned, the tents were almost up. Lone Bear sat in the entrance of one tent, gazing out toward the water. Daniel walked over to the old Indian who seemed to be shriveling up more each day. The old man looked up at him and the trace of a smile crossed his face. He sniffed the air. "Good wind."

Daniel squatted beside him and inhaled the sea breeze. "Yes, it is good. Fresh. Clean air."

Lone Bear nodded and attempted to suck in a deep breath, but it ended up initiating a coughing attack. If only he could spend more time out here getting good air, his health would improve. Today's outcome would determine whether Daniel's idea worked (or Lieutenant Pratt's). Daniel prayed it would.

~

"Cora! I'm so glad you came today." Katie squeezed another lemon into the bowl.

"I am too." Cora picked up an orange and cut a hole in one end, the placed it in another bowl. "I was surprised when he told us about it at dinner Saturday night."

"It was nice of them to invite you to dinner so you wouldn't be alone."

"Yes, it was." Cora picked up another orange. "Daniel was so excited about this excursion for the Indians. He really cares about therm."

Katie tilted her head. "He's seems to be quite compassionate."

"I must admit I haven't shared his compassion. Even though I went to the fort to do my part with the benevolence society, I was more concerned about my own comfort instead of the purpose of my visit—to provide others with comfort."

"Hmm. So you don't have any fear of the Indians anymore?"

"Not as much. Some of them are quite harmless."

Katie squeezed the last lemon then took her colander and placed it over another, larger bowl and began pouring the lemon juice and pulp into the colander. "How so?"

Cora shook her head and she cut another orange. "Daniel has told me about them. There's a very old Indian who hasn't been very well. His name is Lone Bear, and there's a younger Indian named Making Medicine that seems to be looking after Lone Bear as best he can."

"How interesting. Did those Indians come here today?"

"I don't know. Daniel wanted them to, but Lieutenant Pratt was the person responsible for choosing which Indians would come."

"Well, when we get this lemonade ready and you get finished with those oranges, we'll take it over and ask Daniel to introduce us."

Cora paused in her task and studied her cousin. "You want to meet them?"

"Why yes, of course. Don't you?"

Up to now, Cora thought she had been close enough to the Indians. But she'd still wanted to keep a respectable distance.

"Honestly, the idea hadn't even occurred to me. I'm not even sure how to communicate with them. Daniel uses art, but how would I? They don't speak English."

Katie pushed the pulp until the juice came through the strainer free of pulp and seeds. She stopped to face Cora. "Isn't there an interpreter with them?"

"Yes, there is. A Mr. George Fox. From what Daniel says, he's well acquainted with them."

Katie poured several cupfuls of sugar in with the lemon juice, then added water and stirred. "Then there's no problem, is there?"

"No, I don't suppose there is." Why did Katie make things seem so simple and uncomplicated?

Cora helped Katie pour the contents of the bowl into two large pitchers. "This should be nice and refreshing for them after such hot work. Thank goodness our well water is cool, so the lemonade is as well."

Ruby and Mollie, the oldest two daughters, entered the room.

"Momma, we want to help," Ruby said.

"You know what your father said," Katie said. "He wants all of you girls to stay in the house while the Indians are here." Katie faced Cora. "William didn't take the children to school today, so he'd be here to receive the prisoners."

"But Momma," Mollie said. "We're not scared of them."

"Perhaps not, but you must follow Papa's instructions."

"Yes, ma'am." The girls echoed, their faces crestfallen.

"What you can do to help is get some tin cups out of the cupboard."

The girls obeyed their mother, and Katie put the cups in a tote sack to hang over her arm.

"Is someone coming to meet us?" Katie said to Cora when the girls left the room and headed back up the stairs.

"Yes, I believe Daniel is."

"You seem to be getting on quite well with him."

"We have become friends, I believe. He's an honorable man."

"And what of the other man, Mr. Cunningham?"

"I didn't have a chance to tell you about our evening together last week. It began beautifully, even romantic. Everything was perfect —the restaurant, the food. And being with Sterling was enjoyable as well. He talked quite a bit about his travels."

"I'm sure that was interesting. He's gone many places, I assume?"

Cora walked to the front window to look out. "Yes, he has."

"And? What happened next?" Katie joined Cora at the window. "Please, tell me."

Cora looked at Katie and sighed. "He asked me to go with him, to travel together."

Katie's eyes widened? "He proposed?"

"Not exactly. He never said anything about marriage, just traveling together. Should I assume that means as a married couple?"

"What else could it mean? Surely, he knows you're a virtuous woman. Would you marry him?"

"I don't know. His life seems so exciting, so inviting, but I don't know how we feel about each other. I suppose he cares for me, but he hasn't said so. And honestly, ever since the incident at the lighthouse, I've questioned my attraction for him. I was so frightened and concerned about Emily's safety."

"Cora, should you judge him over an accident? You said he stumbled. I'm sure he wouldn't intentionally harm Emily."

"You're right. I'm sure he didn't mean to frighten her. Or me."

"People get married for many reasons—companionship, for one. Not all marry for love like William and I did. Did you love Jacob?"

"Of course I did. At least I thought so when we were courting. I knew I wanted to marry him."

"And you don't have such feelings for Sterling?"

"He's attractive and entertaining, but I really haven't had time to know him very well, so l can't determine my feelings about him. Besides, there's Emily. I need to consider what's best for her too. I'm not sure traveling around the world would be the best life for her. And after being without her Saturday night, I know I don't want to be without her."

Katie laid her hand on Cora's arm. "Pray about it, cousin. Seek

God's will for your future."

"I will." Cora pursed her lips. Should she tell Katie about the missing jewelry and the man she saw? She hesitated to give Katie another reason to be concerned about her, yet who else could she discuss such things with? "Katie, I …"

"Oh, there's Mr. Worthington," Katie said, motioning through the window where Daniel was approaching the steps. "He must be coming to get us." She blew out a breath. "Let's go serve the Indians!" She tied on her sunbonnet, and Cora also secured her casual straw hat to go out in to the sun.

A knock sounded on the door. Katie moved to open it, then paused. "Was there something else you needed to tell me, Cora?"

Cora shook her head. "It can wait."

Katie opened the door where Daniel stood waiting, his face glistening under the heat of the midday sun. He removed his Panama hat and fanned himself with it.

"Greetings, ladies. Are you ready to meet our visitors?"

Katie grinned. "I am indeed. Would you mind carrying one of the pitchers, please?" She walked to the table and picked up a pitcher, handing it to Daniel, then she lifted the other one.

Cora carried the tote of oranges, and they went out to the porch and down the steps.

"How do the men like it here?" Katie asked as they trod the sandy path. "Can you tell?"

"They appear to be fascinated but pleased with being outside the walls of the fort."

"I'm sure they are."

Cora noticed the way the path had been cleared on either side. "They've been busy."

"They've worked hard, and I'm sure they'll appreciate some refreshment."

Daniel led the women to the area near the beach where a couple of tents had been set up. The Indians sat cross-legged in the shadiest area and glanced over at them when they approached. Mr. Fox and Lieutenant Pratt were leaning on a tree, but they moved forward to greet them.

"Welcome, ladies," said Lieutenant Pratt, removing his cap. He turned to Katie. "Mrs. Harn, I presume? I'm Lieutenant Pratt and this is our interpreter, Mr. George Fox."

"It's very nice to meet you gentlemen," Katie said. "Your efforts to help these men are commendable." She retrieved a metal cup from the tote sack. "Would you men like some lemonade before we offer it to the others?"

"Sounds most appealing, thank you." Lieutenant Pratt reached for the cup as Daniel assisted Katie with the heavy pitcher as she poured it. The lieutenant took a long drink, then exhaled. "Excellent, thank you very much. The boys will enjoy this."

Katie poured some for Mr. Fox, then she and Daniel moved to the Indians, pouring cups of lemonade as they moved down the line, reusing the cups. The Indians eyed the beverage suspiciously before tasting it, then nodded and gulped the drink down, handing the cup back to Katie for the next person. Cora followed with the oranges, handing them out to each man. At first self-conscious, she soon realized the men were not as interested in her as in what she handed out. She also realized they didn't know what to do with the oranges, so she demonstrated. Mr. Fox stepped up and helped show the Indians how to get the juice inside while communicating in their own language.

"What are they saying?" she asked the interpreter as each man received an orange.

"They're saying it's good, tastes sweet like honey but drinks like water."

Cora smiled, pleased that the Indians enjoyed the fruit. Most of the men had been served when Cora noticed the old Indian near a tent opening. The same Indian who had brought him a blanket was showing him an orange and demonstrating how to drink the juice. She remembered the older man was called Lone Bear and was glad to see he had been allowed on the outing.

Daniel appeared at her side. "That's Lone Bear and Making Medicine beside him. Would you like to meet them?"

Cora gave him a glance, then said, "Yes, yes I would. They look so different now with short hair. It looks like the older man is the only one that didn't get a haircut."

"That's correct. For some reason, Lieutenant Pratt didn't force him to conform to the same standards as the others, thank God. At least he allowed the old man some of his dignity."

Cora noted the bitterness in Daniel's tone. Apparently, he didn't always agree with the lieutenant.

She and Daniel approached the two men who peered up at them. Daniel pointed to the old man. "Lone Bear." Then he pointed to the other man. "Making Medicine."

Cora pointed to herself. "Cora."

Lone Bear repeated, "Cora." He motioned to Daniel, then to her. "Wife?"

Daniel's cheeks pinked and Cora knew hers had as well. Daniel shook his head. "No, not wife. Friend."

Lone Bear studied Cora, then shook his head. "Wife."

Cora glanced over her shoulder and caught Mr. Fox's attention, and he walked over to them. "Can I help?"

Daniel turned to him. "Lone Bear thinks we're married. He doesn't seem to understand that we're friends."

Mr. Fox spoke to Lone Bear who responded in his native tongue, coughing the words out.

"He thinks you should marry her. I'm not sure what his reasoning is."

Cora wished for a fan to cool herself. "There isn't a word for friend in his language?"

"That depends." Mr. Fox pointed to Cora, then Daniel and said a Cheyenne word. Lone Bear responded with a different word. "In the Cheyenne language, a woman can have a woman friend, or a man can have a man friend, but there's no word for members of the opposite sex to be friends."

"How odd." Daniel cleared his throat. "Excuse me, I need to ask Lieutenant Pratt about something." He strode off to where the lieutenant was speaking with Katie. When Daniel arrived, Katie collected the pitchers and cups and left to carry them back to the house.

Cora wasn't sure what to do with herself as she stood before Lone Bear. Thankfully, Mr. Fox stayed nearby. The old Indian spoke something, and when Cora looked at him, he motioned to her hair.

"He said your hair is like sunshine," Mr. Fox said.

Cora smiled, observing the crinkles in the tanned, leathery skin as Lone Bear smiled in return. His black eyes danced with kindness, emitting a warmth she'd known when she was a little girl sitting at her grandfather's feet, a feeling she'd long forgotten and didn't realized she'd missed.

Daniel returned with Lieutenant Pratt. "Now for the big adventure," he said, leaning down to her ear.

"Mr. Fox, please tell the boys that they are finished with their work for today. They've done a good job and now we will reward them with a special privilege."

Mr. Fox communicated the message which the Indians regarded with suspicion as they glanced at each other. The lieutenant grinned and appeared to be pleased with his announcement.

"Please ask them to line up. They're going fishing!"

Excitement registered on the men's faces, especially on Lone Bear's. Making Medicine helped him to his feet and get in the line.

"Will Lone Bear get to go?" Cora asked Daniel.

"Absolutely. He's one of the main reasons we're here today."

"Why does Lieutenant Pratt refer to them as 'boys'?"

Daniel twisted his lips. "I don't know. I suppose he feels rather parental, as if he's raising them."

"Perhaps it's a term of endearment."

Daniel huffed. "In a strange way, I suppose."

William and Katie joined them as Cora and Daniel followed the guard at the rear of the line, and they walked down to the beach where the boat waited. The prisoners boarded the large vessel with the soldiers, then Daniel, Cora, and the others climbed into the smaller boat to watch. The boat sailed to the opposite beach, a favorite fishing place that was a deep channel between the island and the harbor.

"Mr. Pacetti says this is the best place to catch big fish," William said. "He takes tourists here quite often."

When they reached the beach, the Indians were taken by rowboat where they watched and waited. Lone Bear sat on the beach, observing the event. A large post was set deep into the sand with a heavy line attached to it. At the end of the line was a chain and at the end of the chain, some smaller fish were attached to a large hook. Mr. Pacetti climbed into the rowboat with the line, chain and bait coiled on top, and as he rowed into the deep water, he fed the line out until he dropped the hook overboard.

It wasn't long before something snagged the bait and started swimming away with it. "Grab the line!" Lieutenant Pratt said, and Mr. Fox interpreted. The line went taut as it reached the end of its length. "Pull!" What ensued was a tug of war between the Indians and a very large fish. The Indians tugged and pulled while the fish tested their strength. Loud whoops rang out as the Indians fought the fish, some stumbling and falling on the sand in the process, then laughing, getting back into the fray. After some time, the fish surrendered, and the Indians dragged it onto the shore.

"A shark," William said. "A big one too. Must be several hundred pounds."

Cora kept her eye on Lone Bear, who motioned to Making Medicine to help him up. When on his feet, he walked over to the fish where the Indians stood around, pointing and jabbering about their catch. Lone Bear squatted and touched the shark, saying something she couldn't hear.

Mr. Fox called out to the Indians and they removed the hook from their catch, then rebaited the hook. The process was repeated two more times, each time resulting in a larger shark.

"They are certainly enjoying themselves," Cora said.

Daniel's smile radiated delight as he watched the Indians. "I've never seen them so happy."

The Indians danced around the day's catch, whooping and hollering, while Lone Bear looked on, a grin on his face as well.

"Lone Bear seems to be elated as well," Cora nodded toward the old Indian. "I'm so glad he was allowed to come too."

Daniel glanced at her with a questioning gaze. "I am, too."

The fishing finished for the day, the Indians were returned to the larger vessel and the fish was hauled aboard. They returned to Anastasia, where everyone was unloaded, as well as the fish. Lieutenant Pratt ordered two large campfires to be started. One of the fish was cleaned and cut into steak-size portions, then the Indians speared them with sticks and held the meat over the fire.

Cora sat with Daniel, Katie, William, Mr. Fox and Lieutenant Pratt on some tree stumps near the fires, observing the Indians as they cooked their catch. The aroma of the cooked fish aroused her taste buds.

Making Medicine carried a piece of fish to them and held it out to Daniel. He glanced at the lieutenant who nodded his approval.

"Thank you," Daniel said to the Indian, as he accepted the fish. He turned to Cora. "Would you like to try it?"

With her fingers?

"Sorry I don't have the proper utensils." Daniel broke off a small piece of the fish and held it up to Cora's mouth.

She gazed into his eyes, trusting him as she opened her mouth. The tender morsel melted in her mouth. "It's delicious."

He broke off a piece for himself and ate it. "It is." He held out the fish for the others to try, and they each took some.

"Excellent," the lieutenant said.

"There's plenty to eat, that's for certain." Katie motioned to the slabs of fish waiting to be cooked.

"We'll take the rest back to the fort and get some ice from the icehouse to keep it fresh. Should provide a few meals." Lieutenant Pratt turned to William and Katie. "And of course, leave some for your family as well."

"Thank you," William said. "I believe your outing was a success."

Lieutenant Pratt beamed. "I agree." He pulled out his handkerchief and wiped his hands. "In fact, I'm sure we'll do it again. Next time, we bring the Indians who weren't able to come this time."

"When these men return and tell the others all that happened today, no doubt your morale will be boosted," William said.

"That's what I'm counting on. "Lieutenant Pratt stood. "Well, let's get these boys back."

Cora looked around for Lone Bear and spotted him enjoying a piece of shark. "Daniel, I want to go see Lone Bear before we leave."

Daniel looked surprised. "You do?" His face broke into a smile. "I'll go with you."

Cora and Daniel moved over to where the old Indian sat. Daniel pointed to the fish in Lone bear's hand. "You like?"

Lone Bear nodded. "Good."

Daniel spread his arms out wide. "Big fish."

"Water buffalo," Lone Bear replied.

Daniel chuckled and repeated. "Water buffalo. Good name."

Cora squatted down beside Lone Bear and laid her hand on his arm. "Can you tell him I'm glad he went fishing?"

"I'll try. I've learned a few of their words." Daniel made hand signals and spoke some Cheyenne words.

Lone Bear smiled, then coughed. Pointing up, he said "Mahe-o-o. Good."

Cora glanced at Daniel. "What does Mahe-o-o mean?"

"God." Daniel took Lone Bear's hand and shook it. "Yes. God is good."

Chapter Twenty-Six

Cora hurriedly told Daniel goodbye as soon as they returned to town, telling him she had to get Emily from school. She still had enough time to go by her shop first. She rushed into the store and went straight to the drawer with the accessories. Mrs. Lowell's ruby and diamond earrings sparkled beside the other items, taunting her with their presence. Her pulse raced as she tried to decide what to do. She should just take them to Mrs. Lowell and tell her she found them in the store. That was the truth, even if someone else put them there.

She picked up the earrings, holding them while she considered what to do. Where was Mrs. Lowell staying? She hadn't asked and didn't remember hearing. She'd just have to go to the three hotels in town and ask for her. Surely Mrs. Lowell wasn't staying in one of the boarding houses, although some tourists did. But what if she already left town? Cora was so frazzled she couldn't think clearly.

The bell on her door jingled as it open and Cora looked up to see Jane Farley coming in.

"Mrs. Farley … how are you today?"

Mrs. Farley offered a smug smile. "I'm well, thank you."

"What can I do for you?"

"I just wanted to drop by and ask you about the next benevolence meeting." Mrs. Farley's eyes roamed the store, then settle on Cora's hand. "What lovely earrings!"

Cora flinched. She forgot she was still holding them. "Oh, thank you." She dropped them in her reticule. "I need to return them to a customer who left them here."

"I see. One of our well-heeled tourists, no doubt." Mrs. Farley touched one of the roses on a display hat. "Hmm."

Cora cringed seeing Mrs. Farley handle her merchandise. She needed to get Mrs. Farley out of the store. The last thing she wanted was the woman trying to copy her designs. "I'm sorry to rush, but I need to go meet my daughter at the Peabody School. Can we discuss the benevolence meeting another time?"

"Why of course." Mrs. Farley sauntered toward the door. "Please don't let me keep you."

As soon as the woman left the store, Cora grabbed her reticule, went out and locked the door behind her. She hurried down the street, her stomach in knots over Mrs. Farley's visit. Why did she have to see Mrs. Lowell's earrings? Cora had no reason to feel guilty, so why was she worried? It wasn't her fault that the earrings ended up in her shop. Was it? Who would play such a nefarious trick on her?

Cora reached the schoolyard in time to see Emily come out the building. She skipped over to Cora. "Hello Momma! Did you see the Indians today? Were they scary?"

"Yes. I mean no." Cora frowned at her daughter's comments but shouldn't have been surprised. After all, Cora was the one who gave her daughter those thoughts. "I have an idea. Let's go to the drug store counter and get us each a vanilla phosphate!"

"Ooh, Momma, I *love* those!" Emily's eyes danced with delight.

"All right, but first I need to go to the St. Augustine Hotel."

"Are we going to see the Worthington ladies or Mr. Sterling? Or even Mr. Daniel?"

"Neither. I'm looking for Mrs. Lowell, the lady I made a hat for last week, and I don't know which hotel she's staying in, so I'm going to check at each hotel and see if I can find her."

At the St. Augustine, a Mr. and Mrs. Lowell were not on the guest register. Cora sighed.

"Momma, what's the matter?" Emily peered up at her, concern on her little face.

"Nothing. I just hoped to find her here. Don't worry, though. We'll check at the Florida House."

"But I thought we were going to the drug store!" Emily stuck out her lips and pouted.

"We will. I promise, but this is very important." Cora tried to hide her anxiety from her daughter. She couldn't let Emily become upset too. "I have something of hers I need to return before she leaves town. Can you wait just a little longer? If she's not at the Florida House, she might be at the Magnolia Hotel."

Mrs. Lowell wasn't at the Florida House either. Cora's stomach tightened even more than before as they went another two blocks to the Magnolia.

"No, ma'am. She's not here." The clerk shook his head as he looked at the register. "I see she and her husband checked out yesterday."

Cora sighed, and her feet turned to lead as she led Emily out of the hotel.

"What are you going to do, Momma? Are you going to her house to return her things?"

Cora gazed at her guileless daughter. "No, honey. She lives too far away. I'll have to think of another way to get them to her." Seeing Emily's crestfallen face, Cora added, "Now let's go get our sodas!"

Emily brightened and began skipping alongside Cora.

The pharmacist greeted them at the soda fountain counter. "Hello, ladies. What can I get for you?"

"Two vanilla phosphates, please."

"Coming right up!" The man took two glasses from the shelf on the wall, and put a couple of spoonfuls of vanilla in the bottom of each glass. Next, he added a spoonful of phosphate, then filled the rest of the glasses with soda water. He stirred the drinks, dropped a little bit of chipped ice in each, then handed them to Cora. "That'll be a nickel."

Cora took the coin out of her reticule and handed it to the man. "Thank you." She picked up the two glasses and carried them to a small wrought iron table with two chairs beside the window. As they sipped their beverages, Emily said, "Amanda's mother won't let her have sodas. She says sodas are bad."

Cora frowned and set down her glass. "Bad? How so?"

"She said it makes you drunk like liquor and ladies shouldn't drink it. Children either."

"I disagree. There's no liquor in it." Cora remembered

Amanda's mother was Hazel Evans, a member of the benevolence society. Would she be judged as a bad mother by allowing her child to drink a phosphate? "But please don't argue with Amanda about it."

"Well, I'm glad you let me drink it. It's so good!"

Cora smiled at her daughter, happy to see her daughter's joy.

"Emily, today I got to know the Indians a little better."

Emily's eyes widened. "*You talked* to them?"

"A little, with the help of Mr. Daniel and a man who speaks their language, Mr. Fox."

"You're not scared of them anymore?"

"No, I don't believe I am. They have no reason to harm me." How could Cora explain her changed perspective to Emily? "I think they just want to live peacefully like we do."

"But I heard they killed people out west."

"I don't know what these people did. But I know they were fighting for their lives out there, and now they're not. They don't want to fight anymore." Cora sipped her drink, then put it down. "I don't want to fight either. Do you?"

"No, ma'am." Emily slurped the rest of her drink. "Can I go talk to them too?"

Cora paused. Did she trust the Indians enough for her daughter to go near them? Lone Bear's smile appeared in her mind. Maybe she did.

~

As Cora hurried away, Daniel wondered why she had become so agitated. The closer they got to town, the more anxious she'd become. Perhaps it was concern over meeting her daughter after school. She was certainly a devoted mother. But he was sorry that they hadn't had more time to talk about the day. Cora and Lone Bear had liked each other. More than that, Daniel believed there had been an understanding between them. In fact, for a moment, it seemed the three of them were united in spirit. The experience had lifted him as the memory of it still did.

Had Cora felt the same?

Daniel opened his sketchbook and looked at the sketches he'd done today. The Indians boarding the boat, clearing the brush, drinking lemonade. He chuckled at the drawing of them hauling the huge fish onto shore, their muscles taut as they fought the "water buffalo." In another sketch, the men dragged a shark across the sand back to the campsite. Still another sketch showed Lone Bear sitting cross-legged in the tent opening as he probably had so many times in the past when he saw before his own tent in a life he wouldn't know again.

Yet, he'd said God was good. Of all people who could be angry or sorrowful, Lone Bear showed none of those emotions. Instead, he had faith and the peace the Bible called that "passeth understanding." When had Lone Bear found that faith? Before he got to the fort or afterwards? Those were questions Daniel hoped to ask him some day.

Daniel glanced over at the hotel. He should let Mother know he had returned. She'd be interested in the outcome of the day's excursion. He crossed the lobby and heard Sterling's voice from the card room down the hall. Was Sterling winning or losing today? One could never tell by his behavior. Daniel shook his head. Why didn't Sterling spend his time doing something worthwhile?

Daniel climbed the steps to Mother's room and knocked. Judith opened the door, a worried look on her face.

"What is it, Judith? Is Mother well?"

Judith twisted her lips. "She's very agitated."

"Oh, Daniel. There you are!" Mother called out from the room's sitting area. "I am quite distraught."

Daniel crossed the room to his mother. "Whatever for, Mother? What happened?"

"It's my brooch, the pink tourmaline your father bought me in Europe. It's missing."

"Missing? Have you searched all over?"

"We've looked and looked. Over and under the furniture—everywhere, and it's gone!"

"When did you last see it?" Daniel glanced around, hoping to find the jewelry in plain sight.

"The last time I remember wearing it was the day Cora Miller came over and brought the items she made for Judith. I haven't seen it since then."

"Do you think Cora might remember where you put it?"

Mother waved her hand. "We could ask, but I hardly think she'd know more about where it is than I do."

"I'll ask her next time I see her." If only to have an excuse to go see her.

Mother sighed. "Fine. Now sit down and tell me about what happened today."

Daniel sat on a chair besides the settee while Judith joined Mother on the settee. He had much to share with them.

~

The next morning, Cora returned to her shop to put the finishing touches on Judith's hat. Mrs. Lowell's earrings were still in her reticule, as she was too afraid to leave them anywhere else. While adjusting a rose on the hat, it occurred to her that the Worthingtons might be able to take the earrings with them and give them to Mrs. Lowell when they returned to Boston. They were friends, after all, and it shouldn't be a problem. Cora wouldn't be able to explain how they arrived in her possession. The truth sounded too ludicrous, so just saying she found them should be sufficient.

Cora went to her accessory drawer for one last detail to add to the hat. When she opened it, her heart fell. Laying among the other odds and ends was Mrs. Anderson's sapphire brooch. Cora's hand flew to her chest as she tried to breathe. She couldn't be seeing this. It couldn't be Mrs. Anderson's brooch. But there was no doubt about that piece of jewelry, so unique and distinctive. Why was this happening? How was the jewelry ending up in her possession? How could she explain finding it?

She picked up the piece and dropped it in her reticule where it would be safe. No one would be able to steal it from her handbag. Somehow, she'd have to return the jewelry to Mrs. Anderson.

Someone tapped on the store window and she jumped. As she looked up, Daniel entered the store. His friendly smile was a welcome sight, forcing her to smile back.

"Good morning, Cora."

"Good morning, Daniel." She motioned to the hat she was working on. "I'm almost finished with Judith's hat."

"She'll be pleased to get it, I'm sure. I believe she's developed a penchant for your hats, Cora."

Cora blushed, averting her eyes to the hat. "I'm happy she's been satisfied with them."

"Shall I tell her to pick it up tomorrow?"

"Yes, it'll be ready." Cora eyed him. "Is that why you came by?"

"No, actually. I wanted to talk to you about yesterday." He drew closer, his spicy orange scent attesting to his use of Florida Water. "Lone Bear genuinely liked you. I believe you noticed."

Cora looked for her fan. "Yes, he's such a gentle man. I find it hard to believe he could harm someone."

"He wouldn't now, that's for certain. Not that he'd want to." Daniel reached out to touch the hat and brushed her hand in the process, sending a ripple of warmth up her arm. "I think he's a changed man. Although when he changed, I don't know."

"Are you referring to his reference to God? I wondered about that too. I know the ministers have been to the fort on occasion."

"That's true, but the other teachers have shared about God too. So I don't know if He accepted our God as the one true god here or before he arrived."

"So that gives us something in common—our faith," Cora said, lifting her gaze to Daniel's chiseled face.

Daniel returned her gaze, the depth of his eyes drawing her in. "Yes, and our humanity."

The bell on the door jangled as someone opened it. Cora stepped back from Daniel and glanced to see who it was, her face heating from being seen so close to Daniel.

Mrs. Abbott entered and nodded to both of them. "Mrs. Miller, I just came by to remind you of the benevolence society meeting tomorrow. I do hope you can make it."

"Why yes, I'll be happy to be there. Same time at the church?"

"Yes, nine o'clock." Mrs. Abbott turned to leave, then stopped. "Oh, Mrs. Miller, I should warn you about something."

"What is it?"

"It appears there's a thief in town. I don't know what all he's taken, but several of us are missing jewelry. You might want to make sure your store is securely locked, and your valuables are hidden."

Cora gulped. "Oh dear. Are you missing something too?"

"Yes, my ivory cameo. I'm sure you've seen me wear it."

"Yes, I believe I remember it."

Daniel cleared his throat. "A thief you say? My mother is missing some jewelry as well."

"She is?" Cora's pulse quickened. "Not her pink tourmaline?"

He nodded. "Yes, and she's just frantic about it."

Cora felt ill. "Oh my."

Mrs. Abbott grabbed the door knob. "We've told the guard to be alert for anyone suspicious. Just be careful."

"I will." Cora leaned against the counter for strength as Mrs. Abbott left.

"Cora, are you all right? You're pale as a ghost." He reached out and grasped her arm. "Are you afraid the thief may steal from your store?"

"Maybe he already has. I'm missing a valuable hat pin. I thought I had misplaced it." She wouldn't tell him what she'd found.

"Where did you keep it? Here?"

She nodded. "Yes, in my accessory drawer." She motioned to it. "The drawer's not locked, but the door always is. How would someone get in without breaking the glass?"

"Have you ever heard of someone picking a lock? We've had burglars who do that in Boston. Obviously, there's someone here with the same seedy skill."

"You must be correct. What should I do?"

"If I were you, I'd take all your valuable pieces home with you. I doubt someone would come into the boarding house to steal."

"That's a good idea. I don't have that many pieces, but I don't want to lose any of them."

Cora walked behind the counter to retrieve her accessory drawer, almost afraid to open it again, lest some magical force had added another item that didn't belong, that belonged to someone else.

"I suppose I should go then." He offered a smile. "It's time for my art class at the fort." He headed for the door. "Are you sure you'll be all right?"

"Of course. No one's going to break in here during broad open daylight."

"No, scoundrels do their devious deeds in the dark." As he opened the door, he paused. "Would you consider accompanying me for the art class sometime?"

Cora's heart warmed. "I would like that."

Daniel grinned and gave a wave before walking out.

Chapter Twenty-Seven

Cora slid into the pew at church in the back of the room, feeling like a wild animal trapped in a cage. These were the very women she'd sought so hard to please, to become one of their circle. Instead, she'd never felt more like an outsider than she did now. Not only was she not local, now she felt like a criminal, even though she hadn't done anything to deserve that title. But what would she do now? Who would vouch for her?

Before she came to the meeting, she'd gone by her shop, to make sure Judith's hat was ready for her to pick up. She'd also looked in her accessories drawer. Even though she'd taken her own valuables out as well as those that belonged to Mrs. Anderson and Mrs. Lowell, her curiosity had forced her to look. And there, sitting proudly by itself where Cora's other valuables had been was Miss Abbott's cameo as well as Mrs. Worthington's brooch. There was also a pair of men's diamond cufflinks. Where did they come from?

She almost swooned at the sight. Although finding someone else's jewelry in her possession was not a surprise anymore, it was the number of items that appeared this time. For some reason, the thief had a wicked sense of humor, a sadistic type of Robin Hood who stole from the rich and gave to her. But she didn't want their jewels. She wanted their acceptance. And when they found out she had their jewels, she'd never be accepted. She'd added the new discoveries to her reticule along with the others. At least they wouldn't be stolen again.

If only she could tell someone the truth about what had happened. Katie was her only confidant, but there was no way to talk to her right now. Judith and Mrs. Worthington were coming to the shop today to pick up Judith's hat. She wanted to return Mrs. Worthington's brooch and explain but was afraid they wouldn't believe her. The truth was too unreasonable for anyone to accept.

Mrs. Anderson and Miss Abbott each took turns denoting the needs of the people the society served. Cora kept silent, trying to be unnoticed in the rear as her mind reeled from today's discovery.

"Mrs. Miller, would you like to tell us about the Indian prisoners' trip to Anastasia this week?"

Cora jumped at the sound of her name and gave her attention to Miss Abbott, the speaker. "Excuse me, what did you say?"

"I said I understand you went to Anastasia with the Indian prisoners on Monday. Is that true?"

"Well, yes, and no. I did go over there at the same time. You know my cousin is married to the lighthouse keeper and her family resides there. I did not actually travel *with* the Indians. However, I did observe them. My cousin and I served them lemonade when they finished their work."

Murmurs went through the group while heads turned to look at her as if she were some carnival performer. "Mrs. Miller, that was very commendable of you."

Jane Farley spoke up. "Do you think it's safe to have these prisoners roaming free? I know we need to make them comfortable, but should we fraternize with them?"

Anger burned in Cora. What had Jane Farley done to help them? Hadn't she only helped herself? To Cora's business? She clenched her fists and bit her tongue to keep from responding.

"Jane, they are still guarded by soldiers. I'm sure we are safe."

"Hmmph. We read in the newspaper what they did to the poor settlers out west. Safe indeed. I think we should tell Lieutenant Pratt we don't want them outside of the fort."

Cora could barely contain herself. She wished she had the right words to say. What would Daniel say? "Lieutenant Pratt is trying to show these men how civilized people act in a humanitarian way. He is implementing the Golden Rule, 'Do unto others as you would have them do unto you.' Is that not the way we should all act?"

"Well said," Miss Abbott said. "Thank you, Mrs. Miller."

Jane Farley glared at Cora, the dead bird on her dreadful hat bobbing as she spun back around to face the front.

"Is there any other business we need to discuss?" Miss Abbott scanned the group.

Mrs. Farley lifted her hand. "I believe we need to make everyone aware of the theft that's happening right here in our city."

The women turned to each other and started chatting.

"How many here have something missing?" Miss Abbott asked.

Miss Abbott, Mrs. Anderson, Cora, and Mrs. Farley raised their hands. "Was it jewelry or something else?" Mrs. Anderson said.

"Jewelry" was the common answer.

Cora raised her hand. "I heard that a couple of the tourists have also lost some jewelry."

"Is that so?" Miss Abbott said. "Oh dear, we mustn't let the tourists be scared off from visiting our dear town."

"Are these customers of yours, Mrs. Miller?" Mrs. Farley asked with a smirk.

Cora's face heated. "Yes, as a matter of fact they are."

"How interesting." Mrs. Farley scanned the room. "Miss Abbott and Mrs. Anderson are customers of yours too, are they not?"

"I have not had the pleasure of making a hat for Mrs. Anderson yet, but she has visited my store. I haven't made a hat for *you*, either, Mrs. Farley." Even though the woman needed a decent one.

Mrs. Farley narrowed her eyes. "Of course you haven't. However, I *have* been in your store."

"Mrs. Farley, what is the meaning of this interrogation?" Miss Abbott crossed her arms.

"I just thought it was quite a coincidence that the people who have had contact with Mrs. Miller are missing jewelry. Perhaps her store should be searched."

Cora stood, hands on hips. "And how do you suggest I took this jewelry? Do you think I sneak around in the dark, leaving my child alone in her bed?"

"Well, now that you speak of it, you were seen in the company of a gentleman one evening without your daughter. Did you leave her alone, so you could cavort with the male tourists?"

"I beg your pardon! I would not leave my child alone. I do not appreciate your insinuations."

"My daughter told me she gives her child soda. Everyone knows the beverage is sinful and shouldn't be consumed by women or children," Hazel Evans, Amanda's mother, said.

More murmurs ran through the group.

"Ladies! Settle down!" Miss Abbott raised her arms. "This meeting has gotten out of hand. Mrs. Miller, I apologize for the accusations that have been laid on you."

Cora could stand it no longer. Her voice quivering, she had to speak up. "I'm afraid I am not comfortable with this group anymore. I respected you for what you did for others. I came here new to this town, looking for refined women to associate with. However, this experience is not what I expected and certainly not representative of the society I want to be associated with. Please excuse me. I am needed elsewhere."

And with that, she scooted out of the pew and stepped into the aisle. As she did so, the handle of her reticule snagged on the end of the pew, wrenching itself loose from her arm. When the handbag hit the floor, the contents scattered. There, in full view of everyone, was the missing jewelry.

Chapter Twenty-Eight

"There it is! I told you she took it!" Mrs. Farley pointed. "Arrest her!"

A symphony of gasps filled the church as the women moved closer to see the jewelry.

"Why, that's my brooch," Mrs. Anderson said, hand outstretched to the elongated sapphire pin.

"Those are the cufflinks stolen from our men's furnishing store!" Mrs. Farley accused.

So that's where they came from.

Miss Abbott approached, leaned over and picked up her cameo. "This is mine." She fixed her gaze on Cora who leaned against the end of a pew for support.

"How did you acquire these pieces, Mrs. Miller?"

Cora sagged as if the wind had been punched out of her. "They appeared in my accessory drawer in my store. I have no idea how they got there."

"They *appeared*?" Mrs. Farley stood over the jewelry and leaned into Cora's face. "Are you a magician, Mrs. Miller, who can make things disappear from one person and appear in her store?"

"No, of course not. I promise. I'm telling the truth. In fact, one night I ran down to my store to get something and saw a man at the door to my shop. When he saw me, he ran off."

"Mrs. Miller, why would someone steal from others and put the items in your store? How would that profit a thief?"

Cora slowly shook her head. "I don't know. I know it doesn't make sense. I was going to give every piece back to its rightful owner."

"So why didn't you?"

"I haven't had a chance to yet. In fact, three of those pieces showed up this morning."

"Ladies, I think Mrs. Miller has quite an imagination. That, or she's demented." Mrs. Farley's face was only inches from Cora's. "Do you really think we believe that ridiculous story?"

Cora leaned back, away from the woman's breath. "I know it sounds ridiculous. But it's the truth." She lowered her head and slumped into the nearest pew. "I knew you wouldn't believe me."

Miss Abbott approached. "Mrs. Miller, I truly wish I could believe you, but perhaps Mrs. Farley is right. Maybe we should call the doctor instead of the sheriff."

Voices buzzed around her head, none of them making sense. Somewhere in the haze, Cora thought about Emily. Who would take care of her?

When the sheriff arrived, Miss Abbott told him what had happened. The other women had gone, leaving her alone, save Miss Abbott. The man listened, his bushy eyebrows raised. Miss Abbott handed him the unclaimed jewels that belonged to Mrs. Worthington and Mrs. Lowell. Now she'd never be able to return them.

"Mrs. Miller, what do you have to say to these charges?"

Cora sighed, tired of repeating herself. "I told them. These items appeared in my shop. I don't know how or why."

"And you didn't put them there?"

She shook her head. "No."

"If you didn't, then who did?"

"I saw a man one night when I was going back to the store for something. He had his hand on my door. When he saw me, he ran away."

"Could you identify this man?"

Cora recalled the silhouette she'd seen. The only person who matched it was Sterling. But why would he do something so peculiar? "No, it was dark. I just saw the outline of his body. I think he was tall, but I'm not sure."

"That's not much to go on." The sheriff looked at Miss Abbott.

"Do you know Mrs. Miller very well? Has she been ill?"

Miss Abbott shook her head. "She hasn't lived here long, but she's seemed perfectly fine to me. She accompanied me to the fort to give blankets to the Indians. I thought she was a nice Christian woman. In fact, she attends church here."

"Does she have any relatives?"

"She's a widow and stays at Mrs. Gardner's Boarding House. Her cousin is the lighthouse keeper's wife. Oh, and she has a daughter who is in school right now. Someone should see about her?"

"Yes. I'll go see Mrs. Gardner. We may need to search Mrs. Miller's room too."

Cora was dumbstruck while they talked about her as if she weren't there, as if she were someone else entirely.

The sheriff grasped Cora's arm. "Please come with me, Mrs. Miller."

She obeyed, then paused. "Emily?"

"Her daughter," Miss Abbot said.

"We'll see to her," the sheriff said.

~

Daniel passed by Cora's shop and noticed it was empty. He checked his watch and noted the time, too early for the shop to be closed. In fact, Mother and Judith were going there today. Had they been already? It was still before noon, so perhaps they hadn't yet, even though Mother had said she wanted to go by this morning. Where was Cora?

Surely, the benevolence society meeting was over by now. Did someone come take her to an early lunch? Sterling? He gritted his teeth, wishing Sterling would stay away from Cora. Of course, he wasn't jealous; he just didn't want Sterling to waste her time, since she had responsibilities to take care of, unlike Sterling. No, it was too early for Sterling yet. Obviously, Mother and Judith had taken her out to lunch.

Perhaps he'd join them if he could figure out where they went. He strode to the hotel and looked in the dining room. They weren't there. Disappointed, he stood in the lobby trying to figure out where else they might have gone.

"Daniel." He turned around to see Mother and Judith entering the hotel.

"Did I miss you for lunch? I was just looking for you."

"We haven't had lunch yet. We went to Mrs. Miller's to get Judith's hat, but she wasn't there, so we stopped at one of the curiosity shops to browse souvenirs. I thought you said she was expecting us."

"She was, but she did have a meeting earlier. She told me it'd be over by ten o'clock, though."

"Well, it's eleven now. It must've been a long meeting."

Daniel motioned toward the dining room. "Shall we have lunch, then?"

The women headed into the room and were seated. Daniel checked at the front desk for any messages before joining them. While they perused the menus, the sheriff approached the table.

"Excuse me for interrupting you. Is your last name Worthington?"

Daniel stood. "Yes, sheriff. What can I do for you?"

The sheriff opened a handkerchief and held it for them to see the contents. "Do you recognize these?"

Mother's brooch lay next to a pair of ruby earrings.

"That's my brooch!" She reached for the item. "Where did you find it?"

"It was in the possession of a Mrs. Miller, a local hatmaker. Do you know how she came by it?"

Mother shook her head. "No, I don't. I've been missing it."

Daniel tensed. "Did you say Mrs. Miller had it? Was it in her shop?"

The sheriff shook his head. "No, it was in her handbag apparently. She dropped it at a meeting this morning and it fell out, along with some other pieces of jewelry, I might add."

Mother's eyes widened, and Judith gaped. "Oh my. Why did she have them?" Mother asked, incredulous. "Are you saying she *stole* them?"

"I don't know for certain how she got them. Her story is rather unbelievable."

"What did she say?" Daniel asked.

"She says someone put them in her shop. Sounds pretty strange, doesn't it?"

"My word," Mother said. "I just don't believe Cora would steal. Do you, Daniel?"

Daniel shook his head. "No, I don't." Not the Cora he knew. "Sheriff, where is she now?"

"Had to lock her up. She's in jail right now until I figure out what to do with her."

"Jail? Oh, that poor woman. What about her daughter?" Mother said.

"I notified the lady who runs her boarding house. She said she'd take care of the little girl until we can get her over to her relatives on the island."

"Daniel, you must do something." Mother pleaded.

"I intend to. Please excuse me, Mother, Judith." Daniel addressed the sheriff. Will you please take me to her?"

~

Silent tears streamed down Cora's face as she sat on the dilapidated bed in the jail cell. How had things turned out so wrong? She'd worked so hard to establish herself in town. And now, she was ruined. All her efforts to build a business for herself and Emily had been futile. She'd never be able to take care of the two of them now and would have to accept Katie's charity to live with them. What would she say to Emily? What would the Worthingtons think of her now?

Someone had done this to her. Someone had put her in this predicament. Who hated her so much to do such a thing? Why did Sterling keep crossing her mind? She couldn't get that shadowy figure out of her mind. Daniel said there were people who picked locks in Boston, but she'd never heard of that happening here. Cora stood and began pacing the floor in the tiny cell.

Sterling had lived in Boston. Did he know how to pick locks? Mrs. Lowell said he'd lost all his fortune, but he didn't live as if he were penniless. Was he stealing to pay his debts? But if he were stealing, why was she ending up with the jewelry? Was he using her shop to hide it before he could take it out of town and sell it? Maybe that was it. But did he not think she would see it? She needed to talk to him and find out if it was indeed he who she saw. Was that his reason for asking her to travel with him?

Slowly, her sorrow changed to anger. She was not to blame, but someone was. And whoever it was belonged here in this jail, not her. But how was she to convince the police that someone else was guilty instead? No one believed her story.

The hinges on the outer door squealed as it opened. "She's in here," the sheriff said.

Cora glanced over and saw Daniel walking toward her, his hat in his hand and a somber expression shadowing his face. Suddenly, she felt guilty. Not for crimes, but for being here in this disgusting, smelly place. He walked up to the bars on her cell.

"Cora. I heard what happened."

"You heard what? That I'm a thief? Because I'm not, Daniel. I promise."

"The sheriff said you had the jewels in your possession. He said you told him someone else put them in your shop. Is that what you told him?"

She grabbed hold of the bars. "Yes, Daniel. That is the truth! I started to tell you when you were in the store yesterday, but I didn't think you'd believe me. And your mother's brooch showed up in my accessories this morning. How would I steal them from her?"

He glanced away, as if his eyes would reveal his true feelings, his disbelief.

"I don't know, Cora. I don't believe you're that kind of person."

"I'm not, Daniel. Please believe me."

"Do you have any idea who would steal and put the jewels in your shop?"

Cora looked down at her feet, then back up to his face. "I've been thinking about that, going over and over in my mind. Daniel, do you remember the night you walked me home after the trip to the lighthouse, the night Emily wasn't with me?"

"Yes, I remember."

"Well, after you left, I had planned to work on Judith's hat in my room at the boarding house. I had brought the decorations home with me the day before, but I forgot the hat. So I decided to make a quick trip to the shop and get the hat, then go back to the boarding house."

"You went out by yourself after dark?"

She nodded. "I know. That was not a wise thing to do, but I figured it wasn't far and I'd hurry. But when I turned the corner to the shop, I saw a man fooling with the door knob. When he saw me, he ran off."

"Do you remember what he looked like?"

"It was dark, so I didn't see him well. I just remember his general shape." She searched his face, wondering how he would accept her speculation.

"Was there anything remarkable about that?"

"He reminded me of someone. He reminded me of . . . Sterling."

Daniel's eyebrow rose. "Sterling? Do you suspect him?"

"I don't know what to think. I heard that he had spent all his inheritance, so I thought he might have resorted to theft. And he seemed very interested in jewels. When the jewelry ended up in my shop, I didn't understand why. I thought at first it was a practical joke, but when more items showed up, I knew it wasn't a joke."

"Cora, why would Sterling do that? I know he does some pretty outlandish things, but why steal and then put the stolen goods in your shop?"

"I've been thinking about that. Daniel, Sterling asked me to travel with him. What if he wanted me to keep the jewels until he left and would take them with us to sell out of the country. Do you think he would do that?"

Daniel rubbed his chin. "I don't know if Sterling is capable of being that underhanded. Sometimes I don't think very highly of his behavior, but I've never expected him to stoop this low."

"I want to talk to him, Daniel. I need to find out what his motive was in asking me to travel with him."

"I do too. Let me get you out of here and we'll go talk to him. Together."

Chapter Twenty-Nine

She was innocent. Daniel knew she was. Cora Miller was not the kind of person who would steal. He had gotten to know her well enough to realize she worked hard for her income and she possessed integrity.

Seeing her in such a wretched situation tightened his chest to the point of aching.

If he had to compare Cora's character to Sterling's, Cora would come out superior. But how unprincipled was Sterling willing to be in order to get what he wanted?

Daniel paid the bail for Cora and waited for the sheriff to release her. When the sheriff brought her out, Daniel placed his hand on the small of her back and escorted her out the door. After she stepped outside, Cora lifted her head and inhaled fresh air. She glanced around as if worried that someone might see her leaving the jail. He didn't blame her. No respectable person would want to be in jail, and Cora Miller was a respectable person.

"Let's go find Sterling," Daniel said.

"Where is Emily? I must see her."

"Mrs. Gardner picked her up from school. She's being taken care of. I don't think we should wait to clear your name, though."

"You're right. I doubt some of the women at the society will ever believe my innocence, though."

They went down Marine Street beside the bay and stopped in front of the saloon. "Wait here," Daniel said before stepping inside."

He came back out shaking his head.

"Do you really believe he'd be drinking this early in the day?" Cora asked.

"Apparently, you don't know Sterling very well. It's never too early to drink, in his opinion."

"Oh. I didn't know that." Cora recalled Sterling's odd behavior at times. Perhaps he had been drinking and she wasn't aware of it.

They tried the two billiards halls in town and didn't find him there either. "Do you think he's at the hotel?" Cora asked.

"No, he's not one to stay in his room all day—just until noon."

"So where do you think he could be?"

Daniel frowned and rubbed his chin, then his eyes sparked with an idea. "I bet he's playing cards."

"That could be anywhere—even a boarding house."

"True, but I think I heard him mention playing with some men at the Magnolia."

Cora and Daniel walked to the hotel and inquired about the game room. They were directed down the hall, and Daniel asked Cora to wait for him. "This is no place for a woman."

A few minutes passed, and Daniel returned with Sterling. "I had a winning hand, Daniel! You just robbed me of my chance to win the pot!" Seeing Cora, he said, "Cora, what brings you here?"

Cora kept a straight face, not knowing how to respond to him. Was he responsible for her predicament?

"Let's go somewhere private," Daniel said. "Cora, do you have the keys to your shop?"

"Yes, my reticule was returned."

Sterling glanced between the two of them. "What's this all about? Why all the mystery?"

"You'll find out."

When they reached Cora's shop, she unlocked it and they went in.

"Daniel, you're wasting my time. I do not need a hat." Sterling's tone became more serious.

"Sterling, do you know where Cora keeps her valuables?"

"What? Why on earth would I care about that?"

"Just answer, Sterling. This is important."

"I've seen her put some things in that drawer over there, but I don't know if that's where she keeps *all* her valuables. Why are you asking me that?"

"Have you ever taken anything from that drawer?"

Sterling backed away, hand up. "Of course not!"

"Have you ever put anything in that drawer?" Cora asked.

Sterling frowned. "I've had nothing to do with that drawer!"

"Sterling, are you in any financial trouble?" Daniel asked. "Do you owe any gambling debts?"

"No, I lose some, but then I win some too. What are you getting at?"

Cora had to ask him. "Sterling, do you remember asking me to travel with you?"

Sterling looked confused. "I might have, I don't recall for certain."

Cora's mouth dropped open. "You don't remember the night we went out to dinner asking me to travel with you?" How could he not remember?

Sterling shook his head. "Not really. Did we have champagne? Champagne sometimes makes me forgetful."

Cora recalled all the wine he had drank. Was he so drunk he didn't remember the evening?

"Maybe that's why you fell off the seawall," she ventured. A vein in Daniel's neck twitched.

Sterling chuckled. "Ah yes, I'm sure that was it."

Daniel glanced at Cora. "Is there anything else you want to ask him?"

"Yes, Sterling, have you ever come here during the evening when I wasn't open for business?"

"Now why would I do that?" He winked at her. "Why would I come here except to see you?"

Cora looked at Daniel. "I don't think it was him."

Daniel shook his head. "No, I don't think so either."

"Would you two please tell me what is going on?"

"Some items that were stolen were found in Cora's shop," Daniel said. "We're trying to find out how they got here."

Sterling drew back, his hand over his heart. "And you think *I* had something to do with that? Why would I? Why would anyone do such a bizarre thing?"

Why indeed? Cora's perception had been wrong. And so had been her perception of Sterling.

~

Daniel walked with Cora back to the boarding house, the two of them silent as they pondered the conversation with Sterling. He was even more confused than before. Sterling was obviously not guilty. He had been oblivious to the clandestine activity. Cora wasn't guilty either. He knew as well as he knew himself that she was incapable of such deeds. But who was?

He deposited her inside the fence. "Don't go anywhere tonight."

She looked surprised. "Why would I go anywhere? Do you still doubt me, Daniel?"

"Oh no. I just want to make sure you're safe."

"I'll be fine. I may be a shunned woman, but I'm safe here."

Daniel grabbed her hand as she was turning away. "I will never shun you. Nor will my family. We still believe you, even if other people in this town don't."

She gazed at him with tears in her eyes. "Thank you, Daniel. That means more than I can say."

His arms yearned to take hold of her and comfort her, but it wasn't his place. It wasn't Sterling's either. She'd seemed disillusioned by Sterling's remarks and the fact that he didn't remember what he'd told her during their dinner. She didn't realize the effects of strong drink, especially on someone who consumed as much as Sterling. He doubted Sterling remembered much about what he did every day, with drinking all day long. Daniel had tried to make him exercise more restraint, but Sterling wouldn't listen, and Daniel wondered whether Sterling could stop drinking if he wanted to.

Cora deserved someone she could count on, someone who would take care of her so she wouldn't have to worry about keeping her business. And now that there was a black mark on her reputation, her business was sure to suffer. If only he could do something about it. Mother and Judith couldn't keep her busy enough.

"Well, good night, Cora. I'll check on you tomorrow." He started to walk away.

"Daniel?" Cora said. He turned to face her. "I'd like to go with you to the fort tomorrow. Would that be possible?"

"Yes, of course. But aren't you concerned about what's going on here in town?"

"No, actually, I'd like to see Lone Bear. I'd prefer to be around someone who actually likes me, someone who is authentic."

"That he is. He certainly is."

~

"Daniel, I still need to get Judith's hat to her. Do you think she would want to come to the shop today?"

"I don't see why not." He had met her at the boarding house early in the morning so he could accompany her and Emily to school. "Or after we finish at the fort, we could go by the shop and pick it up, then take it to her at the hotel."

"Whatever you think is best. Judith and your mother might be embarrassed to be seen in my company."

"No, they wouldn't. They believe you."

Other people, though, weren't so willing to accept Cora's story. Several women they saw on the way either turned their heads away from her or lowered their heads to avoid eye contact. She indeed was a woman shunned by the very people she'd hoped to impress, if not befriend. Cora straightened and lifted her chin. She would not be humiliated by these people. Thank God, Daniel was by her side. His presence gave her strength to face the snubs.

When they entered the fort, Cora was shocked to see the Indians on the parade ground, dressed in uniforms and being instructed in marching drills.

"Daniel, are they training to be soldiers?"

Daniel frowned at the scene. "They're being trained to look like soldiers and act like soldiers, but I doubt they will ever actually be given any authority. Lieutenant Pratt insists on uniformity among his men, or as he calls them, his 'boys.'" Daniel scanned the rows of Indian 'soldiers.' "He's made a few of them leaders to keep the others in line. Making Medicine is one of them."

"And he still allows their art lessons, I hope?"

"Yes, thank God. A couple of them have talent that is really standing out—Zotom and Making Medicine."

"Seems like Making Medicine is a leader in many ways." Cora found the Indian at the head of one of the rows. "Do the other Indians respect him?"

Daniel nodded. "I believe they do. He sets a good example.

You might be interested to know that he too, has expressed faith in God. I don't know who believed first—he or Lone Bear—but they have been good influences on each other. Making Medicine encourages Lone Bear in his welfare, while Lone Bear encourages Making Medicine in his drawing."

Cora scanned the throng. "Where is Lone Bear? Is he not required to participate?"

"No, the Lieutenant has some semblance of mercy."

The men were dismissed, and Daniel and Cora followed them to an area set up as a classroom with several tables and benches. Lone Bear was in the room already, stretched out on a cot alongside the wall. Cora's heart went out to the frail old man. "He doesn't look well." Lone Bear's body shook with each cough. She wanted to go to him but waited for Daniel's directions to the class.

"No, he doesn't. I'd hoped the outing would improve his health, but it did so only temporarily. And unfortunately, we haven't been able to procure the herbs Making Medicine requested. I guess they're only available out west where the Indians used to live."

"But it improved his spirit, didn't it?"

"Yes, I believe so."

The Indians took their places at the tables while Making Medicine passed out their sketchbooks to them.

"You should see the pictures they drew about their day on the island." Daniel greeted each of the men and introduced Cora as best he could. Mr. Fox was not going to join them today, and Cora was impressed with Daniel's level of comfort with the men. Opening his own sketchbook to a scene from the island, he held it up and pointed to it, then to their books. They nodded in understanding and opened their books as well. Daniel motioned to Cora to walk among the tables and look at he pictures.

She smiled at each of them as they proudly displayed their artwork. There was a wide range of ability, just as there would be with any group of students, but each was eager to show her what they'd drawn. Cora communicated with her hands and nodded, saying "Good," or "Well done." When she reached the end of a row closest to Lone Bear, she noticed he had pushed himself up.

He was gazing as if in a trance. She approached him. "Good morning, Lone Bear."

His eyes came into focus and he looked at her, then offered a feeble smile. Cora squatted down beside the cot, so they were eye to eye. "How are you feeling?" she said, hoping he understood.

"Ese-he He-e." He said, probably in Cheyenne but she had no idea what he meant. Lone Bear extended his arm and touched Cora's hair. "Ese-he H-e."

Making Medicine appeared at his side. Lone Bear pointed to Cora and repeated, "Ese-he He-e."

Cora tilted her head as she looked at the younger Indian. "What is he saying?"

"He say 'Sun Woman.'"

She smiled and took the old Indian's gnarled, leathery hand. "I'm praying for you."

He nodded, practically rocking on the cot. "Pray," he said. "God hear." Then a bout of coughing ensued.

Cora gripped his hand and closed her eyes. "Lord, please heal Lone Bear of his cough."

Making Medicine said, "I pray too." He uttered some Cheyenne words.

Lone Bear turned to the other Indian and responded in the same language. Then he pointed to Making Medicine's sketchbook. The younger Indian handed it to his elder who flipped the pages until he found the ones he was looking for. He pointed to Cora, then to the drawing, then to himself. Cora studied the sketch which showed Indians on the island. There were several sketches Lone Bear showed her, pointing to himself, then Making Medicine, then to Cora.

She chuckled at the drawing that appeared to be of her giving oranges to the men. The lighthouse with its barber-pole stripes was in the drawing as well. In another picture, the Indians were pulling a shark on shore. In still another, they were dragging one to the fire. Cora exclaimed and identified each picture, while Lone Bear did the same in his language. She and Lone Bear laughed and smiled as they talked about the drawings, although each of them spoke in their own language, with only a few words from Lone Bear's English vocabulary.

It was like visiting an old friend, and Cora didn't realize how much time had passed. Other than Lone Bear's increasing cough, Cora enjoyed their bilingual communication. When Daniel approached, Cora was almost surprised to see him. "Is it time to leave already?"

Daniel grinned. "I see you're having a pleasant conversation with Lone Bear."

"Oh yes, we've very much enjoyed each other's company."

Lone Bear reached up and grabbed Daniel's hand. "Ese-he He-e. Good."

Daniel glanced at Cora. "He's saying 'sun woman good.'"

Cora grinned. "That's me."

Lone Bear turned to Making Medicine and spoke in Cheyenne. The younger Indian shook his head, speaking as if arguing.

Cora glanced from one to the other. What were they saying?

Making Medicine looked at her and said, "He say he go soon. See God. See our fathers."

She covered her mouth with her hands to hide her gasp. Tears filled her eyes. Did Lone Bear know he was dying?

Lone Bear looked at her and patted his heart. "Good." He poked Making Medicine in the chest and repeated, "Good," punctuating his words with coughs.

"He's saying his heart is good and so is Making Medicine's." Daniel placed his hand on Cora's shoulder. "The doctor says he has consumption and there's not much else he can do. We can be thankful he knows God."

Lone Bear then reached for Cora's hand. "Friends."

"Yes," Cora said. "Good friends."

"I'm afraid we have to go now." Daniel said to Cora, then turned back to Lone Bear. "Come back tomorrow."

Lone Bear nodded, then lay back down on the cot, suddenly looking very tired.

Cora wanted to kiss the old man on the cheek as she did Emily's. Instead, she patted him on the shoulder. "Rest, friend."

Lone Bear muttered, "Friend."

As they left the fort, a wave of sadness swept over Cora.

She turned to Daniel. "You know, I find it ironic that the people I thought were my friends aren't, and yet someone I never would have considered a friend is now a true friend. Don't you find that odd?"

"Not really, Cora. Because God is always surprising me. I didn't even want to come on this trip, but I was pressured into doing it. Yet now, I believe God wanted me here to help the Indians. Perhaps he wanted you here at the same time to show you the humanity of these people."

But why did God want her to be accused of doing something she hadn't done?

Chapter Thirty

As they walked back to town, Daniel's heart was full. Seeing the way Cora interacted with the Indians, especially Lone Bear, gave him such satisfaction. Knowing she had appreciation and true concern for the prisoners was fulfilling but knowing the two of them shared this interest pleased him more than he expected.

Cora Miller had become a good friend, like Lone Bear had said. But she was more than a friend now, and having her by his side was akin to having a partner, a beautiful, wonderful, partner. His pulse raced at the thought and he realized his feelings went beyond friendship. He was in love with this woman and he wanted to protect her, help her out of her predicament, whatever it took.

"Daniel, I was thinking it would be best if we stop by my shop and get Judith's hat and take it to her at the hotel instead of her having to come get it. Perhaps that would be less embarrassing for her if she encountered any of the women who think me guilty."

"If you prefer to handle it that way, it's fine with me."

They turned down Treasury Street and passed the intersection of Charlotte Street where the Farley's business was. Cora kept her eyes straight ahead but couldn't help glancing down the street toward the competitor's store, as did he. A man was entering the store at the time.

Cora looked up at him. "Daniel, did you see that man go into Farley's?"

"Yes, I saw him. Do you know him?"

"No, I don't, but there's something familiar about him."

Cora frowned in thought as they walked on to her shop. As she was unlocking the door, she paused.

"Daniel, that man was built just like Sterling—tall, slender, rather long hair. Maybe it wasn't Sterling I saw. Maybe it was that man. I wonder who he is?"

"Wait here," Daniel said. "I'll make a quick visit to the Farley establishment and see what I can find out."

"You'll be discreet?"

"Absolutely. I'll be back soon with information."

Cora went inside her shop and Daniel hurried back down the street, turning the corner toward the Farley establishment. He assumed a nonchalant appearance and strolled in, perusing the store as he entered.

"May I help you?" A rather large gentleman approached him. "Thaddeus Farley, at your service."

"Thank you, I've been admiring your wares through the window and thought I should come in and examine them more closely."

Mr. Farley swept his arm across the store. "Help yourself. I carry the finest quality you'll find for miles around."

"Thank you." Daniel ambled through the store, glancing around to find the man he and Cora had seen. There he was in the back of the store, standing by a display case.

Mr. Farley followed him, pointing out various items and bragging about them.

When the front door opened, and another man came in, Mr. Farley said, "Excuse me, I need to help that gentleman. If you see anything you like, ask my son Henry." Mr. Farley motioned the man by the case. "He can answer any questions you have."

Daniel looked over at Henry, a tall, slender lad with dark long hair. He looked up at the mention of his name, then back down again at the case. A woman's shrill voice came from the opposite side of the store. "We can't have the likes of Cora Miller in our city. She's in jail where she belongs."

Daniel glanced toward the voice, his temper flaring, and saw one woman speaking to another in a corner of the store surrounded by women's hats. He bit his tongue to keep from defending Cora's character. So this was Cora's competition. No doubt her hats were as inferior as her integrity. She was happy to get rid of Cora as she'd gain from not having a rival. In fact, who else in town stood the most to gain?

He turned to leave, and Mr. Farley spoke up. "Please come back soon. We're getting some new things in on the next steamboat."

Daniel nodded, trying not to look too anxious to get out of the store. He strode quickly to Cora's and burst in the door, startling her.

"Did you find out who he is?"

"I did, and I know now who stole the jewelry and placed it in your store."

~

Daniel accompanied Cora back to the hotel and took her upstairs to meet Mother and Judith. They both greeted Cora with hugs, giving him an appreciation for his family and making him thankful they knew Cora's character was above reproach.

He left them raving over Judith's new hat. He had business to handle. At the jail, he gave the sheriff his conclusion about the thefts. Thankfully, the sheriff was not too surprised. Seemed young Farley had previous run-ins with the authorities. The sheriff immediately left to arrest the man and was confident a confession would be forthcoming. The challenge would be proving who put him up to the thefts—his mother, more than likely, and maybe his father, who wanted to put Cora out of business.

When Daniel returned to the hotel, he raced up the stairs, eager to share the information about the arrest. The women were ecstatic over Cora's name being cleared. Cora beamed, her eyes wet with tears.

"We knew you were innocent." Mrs. Worthington said. "I never believed for a moment that you could do such a thing."

"Even though your brooch was in my possession." Cora shook her head. "I'm so thankful that you trust me."

"We know you're a woman of strong character, Cora."

Daniel knew it too and appreciated her more now than ever.

He extended a hand to her. "Cora, would you please accompany me for a walk on the seawall?"

Her eyes widened. "You, Daniel?" Then she glanced at Mrs. Worthington who nodded. "Yes, of course, I'd be happy to take a stroll with you."

Daniel winked at his mother before escorting Cora out the room and down the stairs.

"You surprise me, Daniel Worthington."

He smiled and helped her up the steps to the seawall. As the salt breeze blew from the bay, he inhaled deeply, savoring the fresh air. They walked arm-in-arm a way in silence as he reflected on the recent events. When they reached a point directly across from the lighthouse, Daniel stopped. Cora peered up at him, her eyes searching his.

"Cora, I owe you an apology."

Her brow puckered. "Why?"

"I'm afraid I misjudged you."

She laughed. "You and the rest of the town."

Daniel smiled at her lovely face. "Oh, I didn't misjudge you about being a thief. I misjudged your concern for others. I hate to say it, but I thought you were selfish and only cared about material things. I know now I was wrong."

Cora shook her head. "No, you were right. I did care more about things. I thought I had to in order to be accepted. But I was wrong. And I have you to thank for that. You showed me the value of other people, no matter who they are."

"You have no idea how much it means to me that you understand my concerns."

"I really do, Daniel, and I want to help them any way I can. Will you show me how?"

"I'll try. I think we make good partners. What do you think?"

Cora blushed. "I suppose you could say that."

"Then perhaps you'd agree to making our partnership official?"

She tilted her head, a puzzled look on her face.

Daniel lowered himself to one knee and took her hand. "Cora Miller, I love you. Would you do me the honor of being my wife?"

Cora's mouth fell open and she clasped her free hand over her mouth. Then, she lowered it and smiled. "Why, Daniel Worthington. You have surprised me again. I would gladly accept the honor of being your wife."

He stood and pulled her into his arms. "I'm sorry I don't have a ring to give you right now, but I promise when we get to Boston, I'll have one made for you."

Cora beamed. "You know, that's one piece of jewelry I'll

definitely hold on to."

Daniel leaned down to kiss her, grasping her head to draw her lips to his. In the process, her hat fell off and blew into the water, drifting away in the current.

She gasped then laughed. "I suppose I can make another."

"Or perhaps you can take it to a new millinery shop opening soon in Boston."

Epilogue

Daniel and Cora, along with Judith, Mrs. Worthington, William and Katie, stood on one side of the grave while Lieutenant Pratt, Mr. Fox and Making Medicine stood in uniform on the other. An ocean breeze blew across the island, trying to dry Cora's tears as she said goodbye to her old, yet new friend. After the lieutenant said a few words, Daniel added his.

"Lone Bear suffered the loss of his family, his tribe, his home, and then his health. But He accepted his fate with dignity and gained the greatest reward when he accepted the forgiveness and acceptance of Our Savior, Jesus Christ. I am proud to say he was my friend."

As they left the gravesite, Daniel took Cora's hand, his thumb rubbing the ring Mother had given them to use until it was replaced by a new one. They walked over to Making Medicine and embraced him.

"We're looking forward to meeting your wife and son. The lieutenant told me they will be arriving in a few days," Daniel said.

Making Medicine nodded his head, his face solemn. "Thank you." The Indian gazed at the sky. "Lone Bear happy now."

Cora embraced him again. "We will miss him, but he won't miss us."

Daniel shook Lieutenant Pratt's hand. "Thank you for agreeing to hold the burial here on the island."

The lieutenant held onto his hand, clapping him on the shoulder with the other. "Daniel, you've been a great asset to our work with the Indians." He smiled at Cora. "I wish you and your new bride all the best."

Daniel shook Mr. Fox's hand as well. "Thank you for being their friend. They respect you, as do I."

"I've enjoyed working with you, Daniel. You've brought out the best in them."

The lieutenant, Mr. Fox and Making Medicine headed to the waiting boat while Cora and Daniel waved goodbye. Then they walked toward the lighthouse where they would join Daniel's mother and sister at Katie's house before returning to St. Augustine.

"I'm so glad Senator Pendleton has taken an interest in Making Medicine. The senator's intention to further his education makes it easier to leave here," Cora said, looking around the island.

"What excites me is his promise to encourage Making Medicine's art. The senator knows some patrons who would be willing to promote the drawings, which he is calling 'ledger art.'"

"It's hard to believe he or Lone Bear could have been guilty of the crimes they were accused of. They both seemed so gentle and incapable of such aggressive behavior."

"They changed, Cora. Thank God, we can all change." Daniel looked up at the lighthouse. "Even Sterling can change if he wants to."

"I'm sorry I didn't have a chance to tell him goodbye."

"He was in a hurry to go off on his next great adventure."

Cora stopped and gazed up at him. "I believe I've changed."

Daniel smiled down at her. "Yes, you have. You are now a Worthington." And then he pulled her into his arms and kissed her like no one ever had before.

The End

Discussion Questions

1. Which character did you identify with the most? Why? What did you like or dislike about them?

2. Cora wants to fit in with the wealthy people in St. Augustine so she can get more business for Miller's Fine Millinery. As an outsider, she must penetrate the wall of the town's established society. Have you ever tried to join a group to help make yourself look better? Have you ever felt like an outsider by a clique?

3. Daniel and Sterling both come from wealthy families. What is the difference in the way they behave toward others? Why do you think they behave differently?

4. Cora's daughter Emily looks and acts just like her, especially like Cora did as a child. Is that good or bad?

5. Ledger art was the name given to the art drawn by Plains Indians in the late 1800's. Lieutenant Pratt is recognized for encouraging this art form. Have you ever heard of it?

6. Lieutenant Pratt wanted to give the Indians a white man's education, thus civilizing them. He saw value in them when many others only saw them as savages. His motto was "kill the Indian, save the man." What do you think about his plan?

7. Sterling Cunningham lived a life of excess and leisure. Have you ever known anyone like him? What do you think is the benefit of such a lifestyle? What are the disadvantages?

8. Cora had a habit of judging others by appearances. Have you ever done that? Were you right or wrong? What does the Bible say about that?

9. Redemption can mean "saved from evil or sin," or "rescued" and "restored." Who do you think in the story was redeemed? Who was not? Are all people redeemable?

10. Cora was attracted to Sterling because he was fun and outgoing. Daniel, on the other hand, seemed boring. Have you ever been attracted to a Sterling instead of a Daniel?

11. Cora was accused of theft. The evidence clearly showed her guilty, yet she was innocent. How do you think Cora could have proven her innocence? Have you ever been accused of something you didn't do?

12. In 1875, women wore hats and gloves. Did you ever wear them? Do you think they should come back into fashion?

13. Daniel and Cora were both artists, yet in different ways. So were the Indians. Do you like to create anything? How do you feel when you've created something?

14. Lone Bear believed God is good, either though so much bad happened in his life. Do you wonder how he could say that? Have you ever known someone who experienced bad things but still said God is good?

About the Story

People often ask me where I get my ideas for books. The short answer is that I find them in history. When I decided to write the Coastal Lights Legacy series, I chose four lighthouses in Florida whose stories would coincide with other events that the books' characters would experience. *Redeeming Light* features the St. Augustine Lighthouse.

In May of 1875, a group of 72 Plains Indians of various tribes were brought to Fort Marion, now named Fort San Marcos (its original name) as prisoners. Lieutenant Richard Pratt was the officer in charge of these Indians and it was his goal to "civilize" and educate them. It was during this time that Ledger Art gained prominence, although it is unknown who coined the phrase. Although some of the characters in this book are fictitious, Lt. Pratt and George Fox were real people. So were Cheyenne leader Making Medicine, who later took the name of David Pendleton Oakenhater (O-ka-ha-tuh, his Indian name), and Zotom, a Kiowa Indian, who both became renown artists of ledger art as well as Episcopal ministers.

Shortly before the Indians arrived in St. Augustine, the new St. Augustine Lighthouse was activated, with William Harn appointed the keeper. Several months later, he and his wife and daughters moved into the new keeper's house. A sixth daughter was born two years later. The women were known for their hospitality to tourists, often serving lemonade on their front porch.

The city of St. Augustine, founded in 1565 by Spanish explorers, is the oldest continuously occupied European-established settlement in the continental United States. As such, the town has long been a tourist destination, especially for northerners who wanted to escape cold winters and enjoy a warm tropical climate. I was thrilled to find an account of such tourists in an article published by Harper's New Monthly Magazine published in 1874 entitled "The Ancient City," and written by Constance Woolson.

For history buffs like me, St. Augustine is a wonderful place to explore, and I am blessed to have a husband who enjoyed walking the historic city and discovering places that existed during the time of my book. I am also thankful that the people of St. Augustine have preserved so much of their city and their history so that visits to historic sites and museums are still possible.

I'd like to thank my editor, Cynthia Hickey, for her patience with me as I worked on this book. Also, I'd like to thank my prayer team and readers who support and encourage me. A big shout-out goes to my husband who "manned the fort" at home while I holed away in my office to work on the book. And a special Big Thank-You goes to Sarah Tipton, my editor, who amazes me with her ability to multitask as a homeschooler while editing my manuscript quickly and thoroughly.

And above all, I thank God, who planted these ideas in my mind. I hope I have adequately conveyed the message He wanted me to convey, that we can all be redeemed through Christ.

Don't miss the other books in the Coastal Lights Legacy

REBEL LIGHT

She ran away from the war only to find herself in the middle of it. Who will protect her now?

It's 1861, Florida has seceded from the Union, and residents of Pensacola evacuate inland to escape the impending war. But Kate McFarlane's impulsive act of rebellion changes her life and that of many others in ways she never expected.
As a result, Kate finds herself with an eccentric aunt in an unfamiliar place. Lieutenant Clay Harris, a handsome Confederate officer, offers a chance for romance, but his actions make Kate question his character. When a hurricane brings an injured shipwrecked sailor from the Union blockade to her aunt's house, Kate fights attraction to the man while hiding him from Clay. She's determined to warn her sea captain father about the blockade, but needs someone to help her. Who can she trust - her ally or her enemy?

"Rebel Light by Marilyn Turk is an absolutely delightful yet compelling read. If you like Civil War stories, romance, and heart-pounding action, you will love this book!" ---
Kathi Macias, award-winning writer of more than 50 books, including Red Ink, Golden Scrolls Novel of the Year.

REVEALING LIGHT

Sally Rose McFarlane follows her dream of being a teacher when she accepts a position as governess in post-Reconstruction, Florida. A misunderstanding of her previous experience in Ohio forces her to keep a secret to retain her job. When she learns about the recent Jim Crow laws, she realizes she also has to hide her biracial ancestry. When Bryce Hernandez, former Pinkerton agent, becomes a law partner to Sally Rose's employer, he and Sally Rose become involved with each other to stop a smuggling operation involving their employer's dishonest business partner. What will happen when the family Sally Rose works for learns the truth of her work experience and her parents? How will Bryce react when he finds out? And will anyone find her when she's captured by smugglers, or will it be too late? .

I enjoyed this book so much. It had suspense, romance, and historical information. It is written so well that it pulls you in and you feel like you are a part of the story. The characters were all developed and described so well I could visualize them and felt that I knew each of them. I was sorry for it to end because I wanted to know what happened next. - Amazon review

Made in the USA
Monee, IL
23 September 2021